For Jane

# Prologue

*How relentlessly man works to build, of his fears, a house for himself. No more seeing, as he makes each point of entry snug, secure from attack, than does the bee, forming wall after wall of wax for a honeycomb, or the hornet, fabricating little by little the paper for a nest, the grand design of that on which he labors. Never dreaming, until the last chink is closed against the winds of alarm (stuffed up, at never mind what cost to himself, with the last shreds of his personal resources), that what he has fashioned for himself is not a refuge, but a prison.*

James Everest stopped writing and, with a bitter smile that drew downward the corners of his mouth, read over the small, sharp-pointed script covering the top portion of the wide-lined paper.

Fiction, Jamie, it's fiction. It would be read on every continent, by people of every color, in languages native to countries whose borders he had never crossed; and no one would know that *this* book, alone of all his works, was about himself. That it was true. An allegory—oh, yes, the critics would say that again, and they'd be right; but true, nevertheless. Personal. And they would not guess—not the critics, not the readers, no one—what this book really was. A desperate last chance.

The very last chance.

Even his editor had failed him. Dwight—loyal, devoted, so much so that he had with all good intentions helped Jamie Everest, over a period of what was now an incredible twenty-some-odd years, cut himself off from the rest of humanity and immure himself in fabulous, luxurious, bought-and-paid-for isolation—even Dwight had let him down, failing utterly to interpret the cabalistic messages Jamie had so carefully framed and inserted in his letters.

*"Aren't you getting a little far out?"* Dwight had replied to one of these. *"Your obscurantism leads me to wonder whether you're not working too hard. Knock off for a bit."*

And to another, *"No, I* don't *think 'The Cask of Amontillado' updated would be a good subject for you. My God, Jamie, don't you ever watch television? I don't, but I'm sure this one has been done regularly several times a year by people like Alfred Hitchcock."*

And again, *"What's this with you and Poe? 'The Tell-Tale Heart'? You're not a horror writer, Jamie! I don't see why you want to do anything like that. You're a mystic, sure, but let's have no blood or ghosts—not your sort of thing."*

No use. And James Everest looked again at what he had written. Even yet he hadn't anything on paper but a metaphor. A prison of fears. It sounded merely trite. How to convey the horror of the actuality; the actuality of the horror. That was what the readers wouldn't know. That this was real.

The grisly, bright March day, more than a year ago now, came back to him; never would he forget any detail of it. The flight back from Abilene, with Reg Curtiss flying the plane. Helene beside him, in the comfortable little cabin, lively and talkative, pale from the six weeks without sunshine; eager to ride Tasha, her Arab mare. How lucky he was to have such a sister! Doubly lucky that she had been content to stay with him; though hadn't it been mostly because of Walter Carrington that she'd stayed? Whether anything would eventually have come of that—

Now that Walter was dead . . . Well, he and Helene would manage. He, too, missed his old friend; so many years that the tall Texan had looked out for him, managed everything so that it would go as Jamie wished.

The later memory, then, of that same day. Reg coming into the living room at the ranch, his spurs jingling as he came up the two steps from the hall, a smile in his bright brown eyes.

"Your sister says to wait lunch for her. She's just coming."

How the hell would *Reg* know his sister was coming, he remembered wondering. Reg was never upstairs in this part of the house. His quarters were in the single-story wing to the left of the courtyard. Helene must not have gone upstairs, then, as he had supposed—though she'd said she wanted to change, hadn't she?

He had heard her step then, in the hall. Out of the corner of his eye, as he watched through the window the plashing of the fountain in the courtyard, he saw her take Reg's arm, and the two of them crossed the room to where he stood.

He turned, then, and the blow fell. A thing he could hardly believe even now, after twelve and a half months of living with nightmare come true. A thing that would not have been possible had he not, himself, made it so.

No metaphor, his prison. Real. Very real.

# PART ONE

# 1

THE THOUGHTFUL-LOOKING MAN STANDING AT the hotel-room window stared downward at the street fourteen floors below. Now, at night, this could be a small town anywhere; except that only in Texas, he supposed, would anyone build a hotel in the shape of a skyscraper, when there was all that flat, empty land stretching away on all sides from this dot of civilization (Too valuable to build on?).

He ran his hand through smooth brown hair, and with a sigh turned from the night view, with its sparse pattern of lights, and sat down before the typewriter on the desk.

He was of middle build, being neither fat nor thin, when standing measured five feet ten, and he was thirty-two. His name was Jack Seavering. He was a contributing editor of the magazine *Perspective*—based in New York, where he had lived ever since he'd left his wife. And he was down here on an assignment.

Though the assignment was over. It was the other thing —was there a name you could put to it?—that was just beginning.

He cranked a sheet of paper into the Olivetti and started typing.

The rest of the fourth estate have gone—back to New York, or Dallas, or wherever they came from. Including Vern, who has my write-up of the Everest interview. He can turn it in to Tom Krug, for the magazine. And I'm sure the photographs he took will be as good as he hopes. But my article and the pictures are just routine stuff. They give no clue to what

13

happened—or didn't happen or may happen? That's why I've got to write down the rest of it, to refer to later if I need to; in case anything comes of this—what shall I call it, "Project Everest"? Or in case (am I kidding myself?) I am mysteriously run down in the street.

There is of course no portion of the globe in which books are read where the name of James Everest is unknown. Even in the Far East his books are read and admired, perhaps because of the strain of mysticism, more oriental than occidental, that runs through them. And thousands who cannot even read flock to the movies made from his stories.

For James Everest early became that rarity, a writer who was both a critical and a commercial success. He became also a legend in his own time—to use an expression long since grown hackneyed, but that fits marvelously well. Because to the world he is mostly legend. Not quite so obscure in his habits as B. Traven, but nearly so.

At nineteen he completed a novel that was more than "promising"—it read like promise fulfilled. Book after book followed—each better than the one before —and at twenty-five he was awarded a Pulitzer Prize.

During the next decade he produced books of an excellence so uniform that they were increasingly slighted by the critics, termed "repetitive," "turgid," "old hat"; only to be reappraised when *The Valley of the Shadow* won for him the Nobel Prize, and pronounced classics—an encomium long since bestowed by the reading public.

Yet during all this time James Everest had managed to remain personally anonymous. His picture—that of a thin man with a bony face and lucid, inquiring eyes—appeared on his book jackets, but never was there a word of biographical material. Questions addressed to his publisher about him were deftly parried. It was believed that "James Everest" was a pen name, and for years, up until the time of the Nobel award in the mid-nineteen-sixties, Everest's true identity was a subject for guessing games.

Jack Seavering paused in his typing—thinking of his own discovery of the early Everest works. He must have

14

been sixteen when he had first held in his hand an Everest novel, and with a quickening sense of excitement had opened it upon his own vision of the future. For it was with the reading of *The Kingdom Lost* that he himself had been smitten with the desire to write.

Oddly enough, it was that same book—Everest's first—that had brought him yesterday to Texas.

He went on, now, with the account he felt he must put down.

After the awarding of the Nobel Prize, there was at last a little information about Everest. Very little. He lived in seclusion, either at his West Texas ranch, or his penthouse apartment in New York, or in a hacienda in Mexico that he had used for years. His young wife had died not long after the publication of his first book, and he had not remarried. His real name—discarded, now, like an empty locust shell—had been James White; he never used it anymore.

After *The Valley of the Shadow* there continued a trickle of very controlled publicity. Occasionally some reporter or other was able to wangle permission for an interview. Or the script writer assigned to the job of readying an Everest novel for movie production would be allowed access to the writer for consultation —and would perhaps later publish an account of his experience. And somehow the custom became established of celebrating the anniversary of the publication of *The Kingdom Lost,* which has become a sort of Bible to each new generation of teen-agers, in much the same way as has the work of Kahlil Gibran; every year, on April 15th, one or two photographers and a couple of reporters make the journey to whichever of his homes Everest has shut himself away in, and are admitted, and the results appear in newspapers all over the world.

This year—the twenty-fifth anniversary of that first novel—is special. There is to be a new deluxe edition of *The Kingdom Lost,* with a preface by the author; in honor of which a larger group of newsmen than usual was to be allowed in, today, to see Everest.

And that was how I came to be driving along a Texas highway in a rented car, approaching James

Everest's Texas ranch; with half a lifetime of vague impressions about the man swirling about in my head, and more than a little hero-worship making me jittery as hell before we even got there. By the time you've left your twenties behind, you've precious few illusions left, probably no idols, anymore, that have not been shattered and tossed into the trashcan or patched up in purely makeshift fashion to serve as less than second-best. I didn't want to see James Everest's feet of clay.

I was glad Vernon Fix, *Perspective's* prize photographer, had been able to come along. He sprawled beside me in the passenger seat, looking more dead than alive. Vern is tall, scrawny, and loose-jointed almost to the point of seeming spastic. Yet his fingers are capable of the utmost precision, and there's nothing spastic about his work.

He's someone I've felt easy with from the first time we met—the day I started work for the magazine and he wandered into my office and confronted me with that gargoyle face of his. Being nearly thirty years my senior, he could have offered me advice. Instead he had asked, with a cheerful, puckish look, "Do you think this little outfit's going to be able to buck Time, Inc.?"

Well, we'd been trying ever since.

For both of us, this assignment was a first trip to the Southwest. The sere Texas hills, wide as the moors of England, rolled away from us to the horizon as the little caravan of cars made what seemed to be very slight progress over the larger-than-life landscape.

"You'd think, when it's so hilly," said Vern, "that some of the hills'd cut off some of the sky, but they don't. They just make it seem as if there's more sky."

"Well, there is. More sky. Hasn't every Texan you ever heard of claimed they've got more of everything? From what we've seen, I'd never deny it."

"Gladys always wanted us to take a trip to Texas. Not sure she'd have liked it. Monotonous." I'd never met his wife Gladys—she'd died before *Perspective* had even come into being. But by now I felt I knew her. Vern had always talked about her a lot, maybe because it kept him from feeling lonesome. And may-

16

be Gladys was another reason I've always been so comfortable with Vern—I wasn't constantly being reminded that just about everyone in the world but me seems to have someone to go home to.

The journey was turning out to be long and tedious. First there had been the flight from New York the day before, then the wait at Dallas, and a flight to the airport at Midland—smaller but very busy with its traffic of private planes, presumably belonging to millionaire ranchers and millionaire oilmen. There we had rented the car and driven to Western Spring, a small, undistinguished hamlet clustered around the base of a single skyscraper which turned out to be our hotel. We'd checked in, put in an evening with some of the other newsmen who had come for the occasion, got a night's sleep, and this morning the lot of us had been collected from the hotel lobby by an emissary from the Everest spread—a thin, red-haired, mustached cowboy type in boots, western getup, ten-gallon hat and all, who gave his name as Reg Curtiss.

We left in convoy and had been trailing after Reg for at least an hour along the highway which snaked forever and forever across the desolate hills.

And then at last we could see the gatehouse—or whatever they chose to call the structure sitting alone and forlorn far ahead of us.

When we reached it, our cavalcade drew to a halt and Vern snapped a picture. The halves to either side of the double metal gate looked like pieces of the old Alamo.

The next step was like going through customs. Queue up and present your papers. Two men who looked like practicing cowboys, even down to the chaps and spurs, questioned each of us, then unlocked the gates and opened them for us to pass through. Both men wore guns. Either could have walked onto the saloon set of any TV western and looked at home.

By the time we reached the house, a big, sprawling, Spanish sort of place of white stucco with a tile roof, my hackles were up. James Everest might be the world's greatest living author and, with pen in hand, the soul of sensitivity and understanding, able, with his artist's insight, to plumb to new depths the human heart, but only a complete bastard with an overgrown

17

ego would treat pilgrims to his shrine in this high-handed manner. He was just a bugger with pots of money, that was all. Next thing, they'd frisk us.

That was exactly what happened. Reg, our red-headed guide, did the honors before we passed through the front door into the house. I thought of jabbing him with my knee where it would count most.

And then I met him. James Everest. The legend. And my anger was forgotten.

He was one of those people with a magnetic presence. Even before he spoke, I knew we were in the company of greatness. The intelligence, the life, in his eyes, which were a luminous grey; the breadth, the shape, of his forehead, which curved somewhat unevenly, as though showing the outline of the brain beneath; the warmth and kindness of the mouth, which told me at once that if I had been inconvenienced in getting here or outraged at being frisked as though I were a potential criminal, these things could not be helped, there was a reason for them.

The man in person was someone only hinted at in his photographs. Younger, too, than I had expected. It was difficult to bear in mind that although he had for so long been a major star in the literary firmament, he was still only forty-four. A young forty-four.

"Welcome," he said.

He shook hands with each of the seven or eight of us as we shuffled into the big living room under Reg's guidance. "You do me honor indeed, coming so far."

"Our privilege," said someone.

But another reporter quipped, "You're about as easy to reach personally, Mr. Everest, as Howard Hughes, you know."

There was a ripple of not-exactly-mirthful laughter, and Vern, beside me, murmured, "You can say *that* again!"

"Yes, I know," our host acknowledged. "I'm sorry." He looked to one side, his eyes on a man who had just entered the room. A handsome, stocky character with broad cheekbones and brutal eyes, looking every inch a bodyguard. Wearing among other things a black silver-studded, fringed sleeveless jacket and a gun holstered on his hip.

"I don't believe," Everest said politely to his guests, "that you've met Dan Bayles." He introduced Bayles, and missed none of the newsmen's names as he reeled them off.

Our little bevy of reporters settled down to ask questions. To which Everest's answers were sometimes witty, and almost always evasive.

"Mr. Everest—you're not really telling us anything," said the man from *Time,* who had filled me in the night before on a couple of previous interviews with the eminent author.

Everest sighed. "There's not that much to tell. I stay cooped up with my pen and paper, year after year. That's all I do. All I've ever done. What I live in is the world of imagination. I wonder, sometimes, if the real world's still there." An odd quality in his voice caused me to frown, and I noticed that the *Time* reporter looked up sharply, as though alerted to something. "Tell me, is it? Or is what I read in your papers and your magazines merely maintaining, ever so skillfully, an illusion? Civilization has vanished, actually, in an atomic accident, but the secret is being kept?"

There was a rather uncomfortable laugh, or almost a laugh, which passed from listener to listener, a sort of token reaction, tinged with puzzlement.

"Come out and see," the correspondent for *The New York Times* challenged him. "Everything's still there—pollution, political scandals and all."

We had a tour of the house then.

In the dining room we were greeted by a striking-looking woman—dark-haired, in her mid-twenties, perhaps; not unattractive, but awkward and apparently nervous, and yes—hostile, I thought.

"How do you do. I'm James's sister." I could have guessed, I supposed, from the really marked resemblance. His sister, Helene.

"Miss Everest?" Vernon Fix asked. "Do you mind if I take a shot of you here in your dining room?"

She hesitated, looking across at Reg Curtiss as though in appeal. But then, "Oh . . . all right, I

19

guess," she said, and there was the brief and brilliant lightning of camera flash.

The tour included first the library, with its collection of beautiful old leather-bound volumes and two walls filled with newer books in their bright jackets, and then Everest's studio, where he did all his writing—a small room, white-walled, almost monastic in its furnishings.

A sheet of wide-lined paper, bearing a few words written in ink in a crabbed, sharp-pointed hand, stood all alone in the center of the grey blotter on the large scarred and blackened desk by the windows. Like the page of a letter carefully placed, just so, in the restored room of someone famous and long dead. I did not like the thought and wondered—had Everest really left it there, or had someone else placed it thus for the effect?

As our group filed out again into the hall, I came upon Vern, standing with hands clasped behind him, examining a row of mounted color photographs on the wall.

"Look at that!"

There were some desert scenes with mountains in the background, and a series of classic fisherman-and-fish portraits—the sportsman being Everest. But I barely had time to look at them all before Reg Curtiss, with his annoyance showing, came back for us.

"Thought we'd lost you." He stood to one side, arm extended in an invitation to precede him in the direction taken by the others.

No strangers permitted . . . Did he think we were planning to photograph some of Everest's work-in-progress? Or make off with pages of manuscript?

"Where were the marlin caught?" Vern asked, with reluctance tearing his gaze from the photos. Vern is the most avid fisherman I have ever met; which, he assures me, is only because I never met Gladys.

Curtiss shepherded us along. "In Mexico. Southern Baja."

"All those pictures taken there? The mountains, too?"

"Yes, same place. That's where Mr. Everest has his other house."

20

"Where, exactly? Looks like beautiful country."

"Cabo San Lucas. Isolated area, not too many people go there."

With the others we passed through an archway and into a service courtyard.

The stables, the last thing on the tour, were grand enough for human habitation, if only the manure were removed—with one box stall after another housing a string of fine-looking horses.

"You have many Arabs?" Vern inquired of a Mexican boy who was rubbing down a beautiful little mare.

"Just this one. This is Miss Everest's horse." Vern took some pictures of the horses—the Arab and the two which were Everest's favorites, Reg said, a sorrel and a black.

In the distance behind the horses' quarters we could see a small landing field, with its sock in the wind and a plane parked by the runway.

Reg Curtiss brought us back in time for a drink—served, from a bar in the living room, by a wizened little old man of indeterminate color.

Everest had not accompanied us on our inspection of the premises. On our return we saw him, through the glass, sitting in the shade of a small tree in the courtyard, a cloistered garden entirely enclosed by the stuccoed walls of the house, some sections of which were one story, some two. The bodyguard Bayles stood with arms folded by the door which opened from this room onto the inner garden. He gave no sign that he would prevent any of us from going out to join the author, but something in his stance seemed to act as a deterrent.

"Mr. Everest is easily tired when he talks to people," Bayles volunteered as I lingered near the door. "Especially the press."

"Ah," I said. But then I saw Everest crooking a finger at me. "He's beckoning me to come out; I suppose it's all right?"

"Of course." But he came with me, staying just behind as I crossed the central flagstone paving, drink in hand, to the far side of the courtyard. A fountain, with paving around it, occupied the center, and surrounding this was a wide grass walk bordered by flowers and flowering shrubs and a number of small trees which offered a very pleasant shade.

Everest motioned me to a seat on the other end of the stone bench on which he sat. Without seeming to join us, and making no effort to take part in the conversation, Bayles lowered himself to the ground nearby and sat staring into space and chewing on the petals of a yellow flower he had plucked from the border. Was it always like this? Someone guarding James Everest every minute?

"What did you think of the horses, Mr. Seavering?" the owner of all this asked, as though my opinion might actually be of interest.

"Oh, very handsome. Not that I know too much about horseflesh. I can stay aboard one, and I like to watch them run sometimes—never make any money on 'em, though. Guess I'm a born loser."

"Are you? Some of us are." A perfectly ordinary remark, but when this man said it, it sounded like penetrating insight. What was it that he did with words to imbue them with special meaning—or was it simply his reputation that gave an added dimension to what he said?

"I love horses," he went on. "Rather ride than walk—anytime." And he grinned. "Maybe that's because my feet are always hurting me." He looked down at them, and I looked too, perhaps because of a tiny downward motion of his hand.

"Corns," he said, and turned his ankle to one side, as though curling his toes in his shoe. The leather sole tilted away from the ground, and suddenly I found that I was staring at the space beneath. In the brown soil on which his foot had rested, four letters had been clearly scratched: HELP

My eyes jumped, startled, to his face. And as he saw that I had read the message, he nodded almost imperceptibly, commencing, at the same time, to scuff at the soil with the side of his shoe, obliterating his printing in the earth.

He drew from his pocket a much-used, much-sharpened yellow pencil.

"I'm not sure Richelieu was right when he said the pen was mightier than the sword; violence is still with us, isn't it? Any noticeable victory for the word purveyors is as yet in the future—if ever it does come. But in the meantime, it's words we live on—don't you think?" He blew on the point of the pencil and then rubbed his finger around the raw wood around the lead. A very normal action—who of us hasn't blown on a pencil after taking it from the sharpener, to get rid of the loose carbon and the fine wood dust?—but I thought he was making a point, for me, of removing all trace of earth.

He smiled, tossing the pencil in his hand, and restored it to his pocket. "I'm never without one. Never know when I may need it."

"You write with a pencil, then, not a pen?" I asked, trying, while racking my brains for what to do, to follow wherever he might lead. I was still in shock; still trying to believe that what I had seen was real, had a meaning—an urgent one.

"Oh, my actual writing I do with a pen. Pencil is too dim, too difficult to read later. And I never wish to erase—I cross out, and write in, and mark up, but I'm afraid of losing some first thought, if I should erase; something I may later want part of. But pencils—yes, I always have one handy for writing notes to myself, jotting things down. Any odd little use." And he lifted his foot, looked down, and we both saw that no evidence remained of any message.

"Mr. Everest, I've wondered," I began, taking the first approach I could think of to try to find the right path. "Why do you live in such seclusion? Why go to such pains to keep people away?"

He acknowledged the question with a nod. "I've been asked that before—of course. I've always fallen back on the excuse of wanting no interruption when I write. That's the result, certainly. But my real reason for shutting out the world, by force, was so painful I've never wanted to talk about it. I think I can, now.

"My first book made a lot of money. With most of the proceeds I bought quite a lovely house—for my wife. It was a more expensive house than I could afford, even at that. We were going to fill it, over a period of time, with the things we wanted.

"One night, when I was busy writing on the kitchen table, two men forced their way in. From the exterior, they had assumed the house to be that of someone quite wealthy. They wanted money, or jewels, or furs . . . When they found that all the cash we had came to less than five dollars, and there was nothing else worth taking, they went berserk. They started breaking things. Mr wife objected—not trying to stop them physically, but she made some gesture —and one of the men struck her over the head with a chair . . . She died."

Well, what do you say when you've been told such a story? It was a little late for sympathy when the crime, the sorrow, the loss, were nearly a quarter of a century old. After a suitable pause I said, "What a terrible thing."

He was silent for a moment, and I noticed again that his hair was much lighter than it photographed —he was almost blond.

"My subsequent book and movie sales," he went on, "enabled me to insure myself against another such piece of violence. Though for years it was a recurrent nightmare: the dream of someone breaking into my house, or thugs overtaking Abigail— that was my wife—and me in the street. Time went by, but I continued to buy for myself this physical security." Everest's clear grey eyes strayed over the wall of his enclosed garden, scanned the group of people beyond the glass of the living room's windows, looked up at the Texas sky. "What I did not know for a long time, Mr. Seavering, was that no locks, nor gates, nor guards"—he glanced at Dan Bayles, and away again—"can shut out fear. Perhaps—I've come to wonder—perhaps they shut it *in*."

Bayles turned his head in our direction, and I knew that he was listening.

There was a light smile on Everest's face. "One becomes *dependent*, you know, on one's living arrangements. *Too* dependent, I wouldn't be surprised." Although he did not look at our silent companion, I had the feeling that he was very much aware at every moment of his guard, and that they were playing some kind of game.

Inside the house, I noted, Reg Curtiss had taken up a position by the door to the courtyard, and was keeping the other visitors within.

24

"The death of your wife," I said, "is a story I've never heard before. Obviously it wasn't publicized. Yet the circumstances must have been written up at the time in the papers? How did you—"

"I remained simply James White. No more than a handful of people knew there was any connection between the novelist James Everest and the young man who had lost his wife because of a brutal attack by thieves. My pen name was in those days a well-kept secret.

"After that, actually, I never cared to be James White again—that life had lost all meaning. I became more and more, and finally became exclusively, the writer. A writer who had good reason to protect himself from strangers, from anyone who might force a way, unwanted, into my life."

James Everest stood up, grimacing.

"I'm afraid it would be inhospitable of me to prolong much further the peace and quiet we're enjoying out here, my friend. Not fair to all these other newsmen who've gone to so much trouble to come."

I looked around, and saw Vern and another photographer snapping pictures of us from the other side of the glass. Two other reporters, just then, came out through the door from the living room, with them Everest's sister. Someone else's turn, now, to talk to the great man.

Would there be no further chance to find out what he was trying to ask of me? Or had I imagined the word HELP drawn in the soil? No, it had been quite real, with the P drawn a little crookedly—perhaps because it had been done, that last letter, in haste? And my present feeling of panic was real; I ran a dry tongue over dry lips. The time left, in which I must find out what his message meant, was running out.

I glanced at the guard, Bayles, who at the approach of the others had gotten to his feet. As though magnetized, my eyes went to the gun in his holster; it didn't make me feel any better.

Helene Everest had reached my side, and she murmured, "I'm sorry. It tires my brother to talk to more than one or two people at a time. If you don't mind—"

25

"Yes, of course." But I turned to the man beside me, to whom I was linked now by a conspiratorial bond, and said, "May I talk to you later—before we go? I've had no opportunity to ask you about the possibility of a long article I'd like to write. About your work."

He turned, impatient, from *The New York Times* representative. "An article?" He frowned. "I don't know. Perhaps. Yes, we'll find a few minutes to discuss it, if you wish." And I was dismissed. Surely the brusqueness was cover for his attempt to contact me?

I went back into the house and wandered about the large mission-style living room with its dark Spanish-looking furniture against stark white walls. The ceiling was high and beamed, the chandelier a great spoked wheel decorated with wrought iron and sprouting imitation candles.

The little white-jacketed fellow operating out of the bar offered me another bourbon. As he handed it to me, I said, "Mr. Everest is not having anything, I noticed."

"No. He never have anything to drink at midday. Cannot work in the afternoon then. Before dinner he have a sherry fino. Sometimes two."

"Does he ever entertain? I mean friends, not reporters?"

"Entertain friends?" The face of my informant reminded me somewhat of that of a shrunken head. Not quite so gruesome, maybe. Must be because he's small; small head, and wrinkled. "His friends live here. Live with him." His eyes flitted over the gathering, lit first on Reg Curtiss, standing by a massive plaster fireplace in which you could have roasted a whole steer, then on Dan Bayles, still out in the courtyard. "Mr. Curtiss, Mr. Bayles." He grinned.

Reg Curtiss I could theoretically (if it were not for that word HELP scratched in the earth) have credited as a friend. Not the Bayles character.

"No other friends?" I asked.

"Not now no more. Used to be another, Mr. Carrington. He killed, automobile accident, las' year. That before I come here."

Yes. Walter Carrington. I remembered about the accident. Everest's sister, too, had been in the accident, had been seriously injured. That much had gotten into the newspapers.

We served ourselves from the elaborate buffet laid out in the dining room (shrimp in dill, cucumbers in sour cream, stuffed tomatoes, ham, turkey, meatballs)—all but our host, who was brought a Spartan array of items on a plate his sister carried to him out in the courtyard, where he sat in the company of two of the visitors.

When Miss Everest returned a second time from the dining room, with her own plate, I cornered her. Unwillingly, I thought, she sat down, with her plate on her lap. There was something gypsy-like about her, I decided. Perhaps it was the fierce look of her eyes—dark, almost black eyes, not at all like those of her brother. The nose was like his—aquiline—and there was that indefinable family resemblance, hard to analyze exactly.

"Your brother told me about something I believe he has never mentioned before—not to anyone from the press, certainly."

She hesitated a moment, and I thought I saw in her face a little flicker of fear. "Oh? What was that?" Her voice was all right, but she gripped her plate as if it were trying to get away.

"How his wife died."

"Oh. Did he, really." Maybe I'd imagined her apprehension. Or then again, maybe this subject was safe. (What was the subject, then, that *wasn't* safe?) "No, he's never talked about Abigail's death. Not publicly, I mean."

"What a terrible thing to have happened."

"Did he tell you they beat him senseless? After he'd seen what happened to Abigail . . ."

"He didn't mention that."

"He wouldn't. How did he happen to tell you this?"

"I asked him why he had shut himself away from the world—and so he told me. How about you, Miss —Miss White, isn't it, really?"

She acquiesced with a little nod. "But it's simpler

27

to let myself be called Helene Everest. Most people call me that."

"Don't you find it lonely here?"

"It was at first—a little. But I come and go more than Jamie does. Sometimes I take a shopping trip to Dallas; last year I even spent quite a while in New York. I'm here most of the time, of course."

"Could I ask you about your brother's friend, Walter Carrington?"

"What—" Her eyes turned to me and then quickly away, but I had seen in them a sudden weariness. "Oh, yes, Walter . . ." Her voice and her attention trailed off together, and then she said, "if you'll excuse me—" and got up from her chair, abandoning simultaneously both me and her nearly untouched plate.

Had her duties as hostess suddenly demanded her presence elsewhere? Or hadn't she wished to talk about Walter Carrington? I felt quite irritated with her as she walked away. Probably unfairly, I realized: how was she to know her brother had secretly asked me for help? If the two of them were in such a desperate situation that they must rely on an off chance of assistance from a total stranger, the "friends" and staff surrounding them must all be suspect. And the more I thought of this, the more involved and difficult the situation began to seem.

They were not merely being held prisoner in this splendid isolation; in that case the press would never have been admitted, for Everest would have only to point an accusing finger, and cameras would have clicked and the whole thing—whatever it was—would have been splashed in headlines across papers from Kansas City to Timbuktu.

No, there were intricacies somewhere. To which I hadn't a clue . . .

My cohorts had been going in one's and two's to talk to Everest in the garden. But now the last of them were coming inside, accompanied by the author, and Bayles, too, of course. I crossed over to stand beside Everest.

"Gentlemen, I believe it's time—" Curtiss moved to shepherd us out.

No further chance.

My eyes met Everest's And he did not let me down. "About that article, Seavering—"

It was with very mixed feelings—elation, fear, excitement—that I knew we had made contact again, and to all intents and purposes were back in the garden once more, with his shoe tilted to one side while we both contemplated a four-letter word.

"Could I have a few minutes to discuss it with you? Now?" I signaled Vern, said, "Go on, I'll be along in a minute," and he nodded and went out with the others. I intercepted a look that passed between Reg and Dan Bayles, and saw that Bayles was to ride herd on the group of newsmen while Reg lingered nearby, within earshot of whatever Everest and I might say.

"Just what kind of article did you have in mind?"

"Something about the connection between your life and your work. What influenced you to write on certain themes, what details might have come from life; so little of your private life has been—"

"Actually there's little to know." He was looking at me very directly, frowning; in warning, perhaps? "I'd want to see this article of yours, you understand; approve it before publication. It would appear in *Perspective?*"

"Yes. And certainly subject to your approval. If you could give me a little background, Mr. Everest, some biographical—" Out of the corner of my eye I glanced at Reg Curtiss. He stood with his hands in his pockets, staring up at the ceiling, and listening, I was sure, to every word.

Everest shrugged, and smiled lightly. "I was born in St. Louis, grew up there. My father was an electrician. William White. I had only the one sister, Helene, much younger than I. I went to Washington University, in St. Louis. Didn't graduate, started writing instead. But all of that is known, of course." "He glanced sidewise at Curtiss. "You can simply look it up. Very bare bones." And he added, as though it were a private joke, "But then I'm a very spare writer."

"Perhaps your editor could be of help to me?"

He nodded. "Dwight Percy. You might try."

"Could you suggest anyone else? One of your college professors, perhaps, if—"

"I didn't confide in my teachers; you'll probably not find one who even remembers me."

"Friends, then. Early friends?" (With the thought of Reg standing there listening—but concerned, I would suppose, with current matters, not old ones.)

Gently Everest shook his head. "You've cut out quite a piece of work for yourself—Jack, isn't it? There really *are* no sources for what you want to write. Early friends, you say. There was one. Walter Carrington. He's dead. And there doesn't seem to be anything I can do to help you."

"But there is. If you would sit down with me and tell me yourself how you came to write—"

He sighed. "I'm afraid that isn't possible. I don't talk about myself, I'm not—not *able* to."

Curtiss's eyes came down suddenly from the ceiling and he stepped forward—with much the same manner as a bailiff's, reclaiming a prisoner from the stand. "Mr. Everest is not to be harassed—"

*"Harassed—?"*

"Yes, harassed. I'm here for the precise purpose of seeing that it doesn't happen."

"It's all right, Reg," Everest said softly. He turned again to me. "But as I say, I cannot help you. If you'll let me see what you write, though, and if I find it suitable . . ."

And that was the end of the interview. I was ushered out the door and into the car where Vern, at the wheel, waited for me, and the thing was over, leaving me wondering what the hell had happened. Charades? And was there a prize if you guessed the answer? Or a padded cell? Or a bullet through your head?

"I wonder," Vern said as the two characters at the gate locked it after we had passed through, the last of our little safari to do so, "which are the black hats and which are the white hats?"

I said with conviction, "They're all black hats." There was no doubt in my mind.

# 2

AWAY FROM HOME, HE STILL SOMETIMES WOKE up thinking of himself as a married man—a mistake he never made back on Fifty-sixth Street in his very utilitarian bachelor apartment. And so first of all, today, he had to delete Eloise from his mind.

He pried himself out of bed and wandered to the window.

The glassy blue Texas sky was the same as yesterday. Limitless. Hot.

Before going downstairs to the hotel restaurant for breakfast, he fished from his briefcase a Manila envelope, which he addressed to himself at the offices of *Perspective*, on Park Avenue South in New York, and then he carefully sealed up in it the pages he had typed last night. He took the envelope with him.

He passed up the steak with refried beans which was the breakfast specialty, settling for bacon and eggs, sunny side up. But he was hardly aware of eating them. By this morning, yesterday's little drama seemed like something he must have dreamed, and if it were not for the envelope resting under his elbow as he ate, he would almost have doubted that the scene in the garden had ever taken place. As Vern had said, when he'd told him during the drive back to the hotel yesterday afternoon, it was crazy. "Absolutely crazy."

Vernon Fix would of course talk to no one about it—except, naturally, their mutual boss, Tom Krug. Professional discretion, partly—a possible scoop for the magazine. But even aside from that angle of it, you could trust Vern—absolutely.

And no, Vern had seen nothing amiss during the interview and lunch; had received no pleas nor signals of any kind. The climax of the entire visit, for him, had been those fish in the color photos: the marlin that had been caught down in Mexican Baja. He'd mention them again just before boarding the plane last night.

Having signed his room number on the bill, Jack ambled out into the dusty street (paved, of course, but still it was dusty) in search of the post office. There he sent off the envelope—and felt relieved to have it out of his possession. A nuisance having to carry it around. But he'd had a feeling that to leave it in his hotel room, even locked in a suitcase, would have been unwise.

Had Reg Curtiss had someone at the airport last night counting the visiting newsmen as they'd boarded the plane? Or had he checked by phone with the hotel to find out whether any of them had stayed on? Possibly. Whatever this conspiracy was, of which Everest was the victim, it was obvious that elaborate precautions would have to be taken by those in charge.

Well, he couldn't investigate in secret. He would use the pretext of this article he and Everest had agreed he would write, and search right under their noses. The real question was, would they (who *were* "they"?) try to stop him?

Anyhow he would give the thing a try. For which he'd already gotten Tom Krug's O.K.—by phone last night. Not that he'd told Tom much. Couldn't. It would be up to Vern to fill him in on the thing, which he'd be doing today.

Jack's first step was to call on the editor of the local newspaper, *The Western Spring Gazette*. This turned out to be one Ira Sloper—a tired-looking man with a deeply lined face and lank black hair.

"Howdy," Sloper said over the clanking of a press, giving Jack once again the uneasy sense of having strayed into movie- or TV-land. He had supposed all that Texas talk in cowboy stories was exaggerated.

Jack explained about the article he was trying to write.

"We surely do have our own celebrity out here in this parta Texas. Good copy if yu c'n find anything on 'im. America's greatest living writer. Texan by adoption, o'-course." Sloper, delighted to meet a New York journalist, offered him the run of the establishment.

"Help you with anything you'd like to know—if we've got it. Though anything on Everest himself—well, I've got no 'in' there. Like yesterday's do, we had to get that from our wire service."

"How about your files on Walter Carrington?"

"Oh, Walter." The tired face lit up. "We got reams of stuff on him. Local boy, *loved* publicity . . ."

Jack made himself comfortable at a large table and pored over the material on Carrington, beginning with the early news stories when he'd gone off to college in St. Louis. That was where he had met James Everest, though there was no reference here to the fact; James White had yet to make his mark, and the name Everest had still belonged, at that time, unequivocally to a mountain.

After college, Carrington had made news with his marriages and divorces; with deals in oil and gas. Pictures of a handsome, dark-haired young man smiled from item after item. The more recent one showed him greying, but still fit, looking more than anything else like a movie star. The final batch of stories, then, about his death in the automobile accident which had occurred near Abilene, Texas. In February of the year before. The earliest accounts gave the name of his critically injured companion in the car as Helene White; it must have been run just as it had come in from the wire service. In later dispatches, the newsworthy connection had been picked up and she was referred to as "Helene Everest, sister of James Everest, the writer."

Looking around him for Ira Sloper, Jack found him setting type for an ad.

"There was a Mrs. Carrington, I see, when Carrington died . . ."

"Besides the ex's y'mean. Yep, one of 'em managed to

33

hang on long enough to inherit. Sue Ann Carrington. She's there yet, out at the ranch at Hardy."

He called her—and fortunately she would see him.

"This afternoon? Why, yes, I guess so . . ."

So he took a second drive, in the rented car, across all those bleak hills.

The Carrington place was huge. They had passed it yesterday, he realized—on the way to Everest's. The house, when he finally reached it, could have been straight out of ante-bellum Georgia—plantation style, with two-story white columns all across the front.

He was admitted by an elderly uniformed maid, who led him along a hallway wide enough to hold a cotillion in—and deposited him in a small clutter-filled parlor. There were portraits in oil on the walls, Chinese porcelains in a glass-doored cabinet, inlaid tables covered with bric-a-brac that must have been brought back from a world tour, Venetian glass on the mantel—

"How do you do, Mistuh Seav'ring."

He turned from contemplation of a cloisonné box; disconcerted, for some reason, that he had not heard her enter the room.

She was a pretty, blonde woman, barely thirty, he would guess, with soft, curly hair which was cut quite short, and large blue eyes that looked as though they might fill with tears at any moment; not that they did, for she seemed quite cheerful.

"It's kind of you to see me." He explained a little the type of article he hoped to write, with a link-up between his subject's life and work. "Rather difficult to achieve, as you can guess, because of James Everest's inaccessibility."

"But you say he has approved of your doin' this article . . ."

"Oh, yes."

"Sit down, won't you?" And she seated herself in a yellow brocade chair beside a sampler on a frame.

"Since your husband was Everest's closest friend, Mrs.

34

Carrington, you must know Everest well?" He settled back into his chair—one made of buffalo hide and trimmed with the animal's horns.

"Well, when I was first married, I was at Jamie's house a great deal, with Walter. And Jamie came here, on occasion. He and—and later Helene, his sister. But I haven't seen the Everests socially in—oh, a couple of years. Walter and I were estranged at the time of his death; I was livin' in San Antonio. I came back here only after Walter —after the accident. He left me this house, and the ranch." Her accent wasn't Texas, he thought; more like South Carolina.

With a start he realized he was hardly following what she said. She disturbed him; something about her—

"When you were still seeing the Everests, though—can you tell me about that?"

"Well, it was only Jamie, at first. His sister was at college then. She's much younger, you know. She only came here about four years ago. To stay, I mean—she'd visited before, of course." Jack thought there was a little sharpness to her voice as she spoke of Helene.

"I wondered, myself, why she would choose to isolate herself in such a place, when she's single, still young—"

"Yes, there's that, isn't there?" Definite antagonism in the voice now. "Actually, one reason I haven't seen Jamie in such a long time *is* Helen. We—didn't exactly get along." She didn't say why not. "I haven't been over there since I've been back. Last time I saw Jamie was raight after Walter's funeral. He came to see me, twice, I think it was, to make sure things were goin' all raight. Helene was still in the hospital then . . . But I'm not tellin' you a thing about Jamie, am I!" She gave him a dazzling smile.

"Well, Jamie's hard to know. He's laike—well, you only see part of an iceberg? Not that he's cold, that's not what I mean at all—he's just the opposite."

"I know. He's warm and outgoing, yet when the conversation's over, you feel you haven't even scratched the surface."

"Yes."

35

"When you used to see him, did he have guards with him all the time? Bodyguards?"

"You're talkin' now about the eccentric genius. If he didn't have so much money to throw away on whatever he pleases . . . I think he b'lieves privacy is somethin' you have to buy nowadays, and he may be raight." She glanced about her, and then at Jack, with a sort of bitter smile, as though there were perhaps too *much*—now that she was widowed—of the kind of solitude James Everest had been at such pains to purchase.

"About the guards?" he prompted her.

"Oh, yes. When we went to Jamie's, of course there was that great big old gate, which was locked, and two guards. With Walter at least there was no wait while they checked with the house; anyone else would have to be approved over the phone. And no phone in the house proper, you understand—Jamie won't have one, he says a ringin' telephone would just ruin his writin'. The house phone is in Reg Curtiss's suite. So if Reg doesn't answer, someone has to ride up from the gate to get the visitor checked on."

"Tell me—he didn't keep a bodyguard with him during your visits?"

She dismissed the suggestion with an exaggerated frown. *"Oh,* no. There was always someone—with a gun—by the front door, but he'd let us in and then we were free to come and go in the house."

"Do you know any of the guards?"

But suddenly she was suspicious. She frowned. "The questions you're askin' have nothin' to do with Jamie's literature as a reflection of his life; in fact they seem altogether odd, Mistuh Seav'ring!"

Too late, he saw that they did. "They do have a bearing, believe me. However . . . What's your opinion of Reg Curtiss?"

The large blue eyes had narrowed, and they stared at him distrustfully. "He was merely an employee of Jamie's," she said slowly; reluctant. "I seldom had occasion to speak more than a word or two with him. He's the chauffeur, also the pilot of Jamie's private plane. He uses that to fly down to his home in Mexico."

"I think Curtiss has been promoted. He seems to be running things now for Everest. And according to the little fellow who's bartender and butler, Reg Curtiss and one of the guards named Bayles are Everest's only personal friends."

She was frowning. "Personal friends?" She paused, biting her lower lip. "Who's Bayles?"

"Dan Bayles. Personal bodyguard, seemingly. During Everest's press conference Bayles never left his boss's side, except for a few moments when I finally got to talk semi-privately with Everest while Reg Curtiss monitored our conversation."

Sue Ann Carrington stirred in her chair, more uneasy than before, though no longer, he thought, because of his questions. "Well, of course Jamie's chary of reporters— or of people in a group . . . Dan Bayles. I don't remember him. A big man named Tim used to be chief guard. I b'lieve I heard that he'd left. Jamie's houseman left, too, after Walter died—to come back and work for me; someone Walter had found for Jamie years ago, a man who'd grown up here on Walter's ranch."

"Why did he leave?"

"I gathered he'd been fired—Reg told him he'd been kept on only through Walter's favor."

"What's this man's name? Perhaps he could tell me some things about his years working for Everest?"

She shook her head. "He was killed, not long after he'd come back to the ranch here."

"Killed?" His tone caused her to look up quickly.

"Died, I should have said. A gas heater in his house exploded."

Jack's brain seemed suddenly air-conditioned. "Quite a turnover in personnel in Mr. Everest's household. Except for Reg Curtiss."

She didn't answer.

"You never did say," he pursued, "what you think of Curtiss."

"I don't think I laike him particularly. No special reason."

"Thanks." He smiled at her. "You wondered why I was asking these questions—which don't seem to have much to do with James Everest's literary output. But—"

"Yes, I *did* wonder." She crossed her arms and leaned a little forward. "You almost sounded as though you were plannin' to—to break in. Or somethin'. I couldn't help—"

"I don't blame you. But the questions were apropos. What I'm trying to get at is the—the emotional climate Everest writes in. And I keep coming back, somehow, to the word 'fear.' "

"Fear? Then you're wrong. I've *never* had a feelin' of fear connected with Jamie. In spite of the guards, the precautions, his keepin' people oot. His security system seemed to be somethin' he was maintainin' in almost a spirit of irony—or perhaps I should say in retribution, as though he were sayin' to the world, 'Look, once you smashed up what was mine; I won't give you the chance to do it again.' But fear—no, I've never felt that about Jamie."

"May I quote to you something he said while we sat in the garden, the two of us overseen and overheard by the guard I mentioned, Dan Bayles? He was talking about having shut himself away from everyone, and he said, 'No locks, nor gates, nor guards can shut out fear. Perhaps—I've come to wonder—perhaps they shut it *in.*' "

"He said *that?* The wordin' sounds like him—yes. But not the sense of it."

"It doesn't?"

She looked really dismayed. "Mr. Seav'ring, why have you come here, *really?* Are you writin' an article, or are you a private investigator, lookin' into—what *are* you lookin' into?"

"I'm doing exactly what I told you I am. Writing an article. If you'd like to check on me—"

"No." She dismissed the suggestion with an impatient wave of the hand. "If you wanted to prove to me you're somethin' you're not, you probably could. Checkin' up on people isn't my kind of thing. But I've begun to wonder whether your purpose goes—well, deeper than you said."

"If that were true—and I'm not saying it is—I couldn't tell you, could I? It wouldn't be wise."

"You're sayin' that I should trust you—whatever it is you're doin'."

"Something like that."

"You think there's somethin' wrong. Don't you?"

"I don't know."

"If you think so, why not call in the F.B.I.?"

"On what grounds? A kidnapping, yes. But he hasn't been kidnapped. Whatever newspaper you take, you must have seen the pictures in today's edition—there he is, safe and sound, cheerful and healthy, sitting in the garden of his home yesterday and smiling for the cameras. I was there. I saw him—and so did any number of other reporters."

"Helene, too? She was there?"

"Yes, I talked to her a little. She seemed nervous—reluctant to say much."

"Really? That's not like her." She was frowning again. "Look. I can tell you one thing, and that's that Reg Curtiss can't actually be runnin' everythin'. The ranch—yes. But Jamie's affairs? Arthur Wheelock takes care of those."

"Arthur Wheelock? Who's—"

"He's Jamie's accountant—his 'money man.' Walter oversaw everythin' when he was alive; Art just carried out his instructions, did the dog work. But now he would be in charge . . . of the bookkeepin', the investments—there's lots of those—the ranch payroll. So perhaps he could tell you somethin'?"

"Unless he's been replaced?"

"I happen to know he hasn't been."

James Everest's money man . . .

Whatever all this was about, it was a pretty safe bet that money came into it somewhere.

He had thought of asking Sue Ann Carrington if she'd have dinner with him, but hadn't. The only civilization

39

within a decent distance of the Carrington ranch was apparently the town of Hardy, which, from what Jack had seen of it on the way through, boasted a bank, a post office, and a filling station with eating arrangements adjacent to the service garage. He could not exactly visualize Walter Carrington's sumptuous widow partaking with him of chili and franks over which wafted a fine aroma of lubricating oil and high octane.

So he'd said good-by at her front door, and thanked her. And hoped, he'd said, that he'd see her again during the course of things.

"You have me worried, you know," she'd said. "I think I'll go over and see Helene. It's been quite a while since Walter's death, and there are actually no hard feelin's . . . If anythin's wrong—"

At once he had disliked the idea. "I thought you and Helene didn't—get along."

"Oh, that's all in the past." (It was *something* to do with Walter Carrington?)

"I think you might be asking for trouble, going over there."

"Oh, no." She seemed easy about that. "I live next door, after all."

"This is next *door?*"

"You're not used to Texas, are you? It's quite some distance, I'll agree, to the Everests', but Jamie's land borders mine. Ranches are large oot here, you know."

"A little bigger than I'd thought."

"Anyway, what could be the harm in my droppin' over for a friendly neighborly call on Helene?"

"Don't. It's kind of you to think of it, but—"

"Well," she flared, "they're *my* friends, after all. I'm not doin' this for *your* sake."

"I didn't suppose you were. But in any case, I've a feeling you'd much better not go."

She smiled—belligerently—provocatively. "But it's not your business, is it—what I do. Don't worry about it, Mistuh Seav'ring. I'd never risk my neck, you know, for anyone. I'm much too selfish."

"So you say. I hope at least you're too wise."

40

"You just don't want me on your conscience—isn't that it?"

That was precisely it, he thought as he drove back to Western Spring. The thought of Sue Ann Carrington kept nagging at him.

Oh, yes; he knew why, too. She reminded him in several ways of his wife. No, his ex-wife. Eloise had much the same coloring. Blue eyes, a little smaller than Mrs. Carrington's—or was it simply that they did not open quite so wide? Eloise seemed always to be studying something through narrowed lids. Nothing wide-eyed about her; no. And the hair worn longer, in a different style—sleekly falling along her cheek, covering the nape of the neck. And a certain stubbornness they had in common—Sue Ann Carrington and his wife.

When would he hear that Eloise had remarried? Three years, now, and *that* blow had not fallen. But one of these days . . . People always supposed a marriage broke up because of infidelity—or that at least there was a third party lurking *some*where in the wings. But there were lots of other reasons. Lots. Money, for instance. Well, that was closer to the reason, in this case. Too *much* money. Hers. He'd never been able to get used to how she threw it around, how she measured everybody by it. "Oh, not *you,* Jack darling, you're completely different from everybody I grew up with, that's why I fell so hard for you. You've got class of your own, you don't *need* a pricemark to tell." But he'd had one, all the same. Sometimes he'd felt like an amusing item she'd picked up at some quaint bazaar—or like a gigolo she'd bought instead of hired.

"You're absolutely one of a kind, Jack. You *know* that."

"No, I'm one of many—you just haven't met the others."

And so Eloise still lived up in Boston, and he was his own man again. That Eloise Hutchins should have married a reporter from the *Boston Globe* had never been a feasible idea, anyway. Well, you don't know a thing's impossible till you've tried it, do you?

Arthur Wheelock operated out of a hole-in-the-wall office in Western Spring. Jack parked across the street

41

from the white frame building, walked across the dusty pavement and entered the door lettered in black, BRADY & WHEELOCK, ACCOUNTANTS. He was greeted by a middle-aged woman so fat she hardly fitted in her typewriter chair.

"Afternoon."

"Is Mr. Wheelock—?"

"Yes, he's in, go right on back." She gestured to a door in the rear wall, beyond a pair of desks, both empty. Over against the wall, a man in a green eyeshade (when had he seen one of *those!*) worked at a table, his back to the room.

Jack went on through the door, the kind with frosted glass in the top half, and closed it behind him.

The man at the desk in the back room looked about forty. Broad forehead, round, greenish-hazel eyes, sandy hair beginning to thin, a generous mouth. A big man. His expensively made clothes, more Wall Street in cut than Southwestern, did not match the setting, which was bare, almost shoddy.

The voice was Texan. "Whut can I do fer ya?"

Jack explained about the article. "It's hard to find anyone who knows him well, you see—"

"I c'n b'lieve that! Who put you onto me?"

"Mrs. Carrington."

"Oh; lovely woman. I see her now and again—business matters, you understan'."

"She thought you might be able to help me. I hope you don't mind a few questions about James Everest?"

"Not at all. Not at all. Shoot."

"Just how long have you known him, Mr. Wheelock?"

"Art. Ev'rybody calls me Art. How long've I known Jamie? Must be nearly ten years, I guess, since I first started goin' out there to his ranch. I was the younger partner in our firm—there were just the two of us—and as Henry got older and not feelin' so good, I did more and more of Jamie's work. Just me, now—my partner died, few years back, I do all of it. Got an assistant, of course, do the actual accountin', and get an extra clerk or two in to help, now and then.

"Like you say, hardly anybody who really knows Jamie, is there?"

"You see him regularly?"

Arthur Wheelock screwed up his face, looked ceiling-ward, and said, "Not's often as I used to. Seems to me every time I go out there Reg Curtiss—you've met him? —he tells me Jamie's in his writin' room, writin'. Man works like a fiend."

"Has he always done that? Worked to such a tough schedule?"

"Oh, yes. But seems to me he's gone kind of loco on work ever since Walter Carrington—that was his best friend—ever since Walter died. He don't want to talk to people, mostly."

"You think Carrington's death changed him?"

"Well, I've thought about it, now and then . . . Yeh, I'd say it must have. Don't know what else could of got inta him like that."

"How about his sister? Do you—"

"Helene? Oh, I've never seen much of her. She isn't interested in bunch of figures; makes herself scarce when I come. Besides, she's always out ridin'. She's a horse enthusiast, you know. Right part of the country for *that*."


He learned very little, really, from Arthur Wheelock. And came away feeling that perhaps the man was a little too folksy, a little too round-eyed, for someone who had in his charge millions and millions of dollars' worth of investments.

Though there was no reason, actually, he reminded him-self, that the homespun charm which was a sort of spe-cialty of the Lone Star State should be incompatible with the ability to balance sums in the eight-figure class. Was there . . .

Back in the car parked across from Wheelock's office, he studied the Texas map; and twenty minutes later, he was checked out of the hotel, headed for Abilene.

He used the last of the daylight, before stopping to eat, then had dinner at a crossroads restaurant. The waitress was kind and friendly, but the Giant Special Sirloin was tough. It shone greasily on his plate, under the overhead fluorescents, and the center was purple when he cut into it.

He wondered how many solitary dinners he'd eaten, like this, since he had parted from Eloise. And then wondered what had made him think of Eloise anyway. But he knew that; knew what had caused this damned fit of depression. Sue Ann Carrington had brought back the image of his wife, in sharp-edged focus.

He'd thought he was past letting Eloise bother him—*really* bother him . . .

In the car once more he felt better, the depression easing off. He'd probably just been tired.

All divided highway from here. No sweat.

Hardly any traffic. He settled down to a fast, steady pace. Not so hilly as around Hardy—though all he could see were road markers flashing by, the blur of dirt, grass and weeds at the roadside, and an occasional pair of headlights on the far strip of highway, going in the opposite direction.

He'd almost forgotten how much he enjoyed night driving (didn't have a car in New York—a bother in the city) . . . Had almost forgotten the sense of adventure waiting out there somewhere in the dark, and the sort of bond that could sometimes develop between one driver and the next, as they followed one another for mile after mile —you wondered where the other fellow was going, maybe even felt a pang of disappointment when he turned off.

Like the car behind him now. It had been there for miles. And then he frowned as that fact consciously hit him.

Well, nothing wrong in one car sticking behind another; a lot of drivers did that at night, picked another vehicle and let it set the pace. He increased his speed a little, and the lights of the following car fell slowly behind.

More hills here, more curves in the road. His speed must have dropped, because the other car came up again behind him.

He tensed, as the other driver put on a burst of speed and came abreast. If anyone wanted to force him off the road out here, with no witnesses—

The station wagon pulled past, and moved rapidly away in front, and in a minute or two the taillights had disappeared in the night.

Jack grinned. Too vivid an imagination, he guessed.

Five minutes later he rounded a curve through a deep cut and saw ahead of him a line of blinking yellow construction-warning lights, like a constellation of fireflies. He slowed, as he passed the placard beside the paving, WARNING, CONSTRUCTION 0.8 MILES, ROAD LEGALLY CLOSED.

The highway on his half of the divided road narrowed to one lane—the outer one—and he dropped to under forty. And then just before he reached the end of the barricades, he saw that the lane ahead was blocked.

The Chrysler station wagon that had whizzed by him was parked, its lights off, crosswise of what was left of the road, completely blocking it. As Jack slowed, the other car's headlights were suddenly switched on, and the driver leaped into their beam, flagging him down.

Well, he certainly wasn't going to play *that* game. He swung wide of the figure dancing on the edge of the pavement, swung onto the shoulder; and the man was suddenly motionless—taking aim, Jack could see clearly in the station wagon's headlight beams, which showed the weapon in his hand.

Three shots. Almost at once he felt the loss of control of his car. It slewed back onto the road, unmanageable; left front tire gone.

No possibility, now, of getting away. He came to a halt, a little farther on, and by the time he got out of the car, the station wagon was pulled up a the side of the road, its lights blinding him as he looked back, and the driver was trotting up alongside his captive, in his right hand the heavy revolver.

"What do you want?" Jack asked.

"What yuh got?" came the amiable answer. "And don't try anything frisky, 'cause y'already know this here's loaded."

"Okay. Want my wallet?"

"Not yet. Take off your jacket. Careful; slow-like . . . Now hand it t'me. Now face your car—hands on the

45

roof, head down, feet apart . . ." He frisked him from behind.

"Now take everything out of your pockets and put it on the hood. Right there. And pull your pockets inside out."

He did as instructed, and meanwhile the other emptied the pockets of the suit jacket on to the hood. "Over here—" He motioned Jack to move a few feet away while he examined one item after another in the headlight beams.

It was the first chance he'd had to get a look at the man's face; looked vaguely familiar, at that. Just where—

"Any secret compartments?" He was going through the wallet now. Broad shoulders, hollow chest, lumpy face, not much chin . . .

Jack shrugged. "The usual—in the bill section. Nothing in it."

He found that there was nothing under the little flap, and nodded; took all the money out and pocketed it. Abruptly he looked away, along the road behind them. There were lights in the distance—a car or cars coming this way.

"Right *now!*" he said sharply. "Unlock your trunk and get your spare out. Put it alongside the car, in plain sight. And don't get cute fella'—" he added.

And so when eventually three cars, at varying intervals, passed the two vehicles parked on the shoulder, all there was to be seen was some Good Samaritan helping another motorist change a flat.

The Good Samaritan took Jack's suitcase and the Olivetti—"Cute, eh? Don't hardly weigh nothing—" and went through the glove compartment.

"That's it, I guess . . . Oh, say, you don't wear a money-belt, I suppose—" And Jack demonstrated that he did not.

"Well . . ." the stranger looked at him speculatively. "Have a good trip." And as Jack clenched his jaw, he added, reasonably, "Well, you've got your credit cards; take you anywhere."

"Thanks."

The other set down the suitcase, which he was carrying in the left hand, and the typewriter, which he had under that arm, and reached into his pocket. Dropped something in the dust at his feet. "There y'are. Five dollars. Pin money."

Again hugging the typewriter under his arm, he picked up the suitcase and backed off, still holding his revolver on Jack. He threw his booty into the station wagon, started it, and doused the lights, so that as he swung in a U-turn across the dividing strip and back onto the road in the direction of Western Spring, there was no opportunity to get his plate number.

He'd spent the night in a motel at the edge of Abilene.

Now he talked, in an office that smelled of new paint, with Lieutenant Carl Haver of the Abilene police. And he made no mention of his brush of the night before with a highwayman. Although the whole episode was clearly supposed to have looked like a plain and simple holdup—*Stagecoach* in modern dress—it seemed probable that what his man had been looking for was any trace of a note that might have been passed him surreptitiously by Everest; or, equally, anything he might already have written for his "article" that would indicate whether this project was genuine or a cover for something else.

But it was safest in every way for Jack not to send the police nosing around in Western Spring and putting up the backs of whoever had dispatched the operative in the station wagon. He thought he knew where he previously had seen the man, too—in the lobby of the hotel in Western Spring.

Now he took up only old business with the Abilene Police Department; nothing current.

"Always drove too fast—that Walter Carrington," said the lieutenant. "Character around the state; everybody knew him, seems like. In everything. Cattle, oil, cotton, politics—you name it, he had a piece of it. Women, too. Don't know how many wives—lost track." The tall, massive police lieutenant wrinkled his well-tanned brow. "Like I say, he always drove too fast, and this was no

47

exception. Brakes failed on a curve, and he ran straight into a concrete pillar where they were building a highway overpass. Killed instantly. The woman with him was thrown out, critically injured."

"James Everest's sister."

"That's right. Her name was something else. White. Helene White. She was in the hospital a long time, finally pulled out of it."

"There was no possibility, I suppose, that it *wasn't* an accident? Car tampered with, anything like that?"

Haver frowned. "You have some partic'ler reason for asking?"

"No, it's just that I like to look at all possible angles."

"Well, I'll *tell* you. If there'd been anything not quite right about that car, we'd have found it here in the Department." He stared stonily at his visitor.

Jack spread his hands. "I'm sure you'd have found it if you were looking for it—*if* there were anything wrong. I just didn't know whether you'd felt there was reason to look."

The lieutenant pushed across to him the report he'd pulled from the files. "The boys checked out everything. It's right there."

Jack's eye ran down the page. Nothing unusual. Just sudden death—a very ordinary thing. He nodded, looked up. "I didn't want to start anything, Lieutenant. Just wanted to cross off the possibility that anything could have been wrong over and above mechanical failure."

"Speed—that was all. As it too often is in that bad an accident."

But he'd noted the name of the garage to which the wreck had been towed, and he hunted it up. Just in case.

"Scrapped," a black-handed young man in coveralls told him. "Long since. Man, that car was *tot*aled."

Next the hospital, where a little over a year ago Helene White had spent several weeks.

He talked to the head nurse—short, grey haired, efficient. Miss Emily Cone. "Oh, yes. Miss White. A lovely girl."

"Did her brother come to see her while she was here?"

"Mr. Everest. Oh, yes. He came regulary. He has his own plane and pilot, and he flew here from his ranch."

"Did he come alone to the hospital? Or did someone else come with him?"

"Alone?" She screwed up pale eyes behind her glasses as she tried to remember.

"I understand that Mr. Everest never goes out in public. Dread of being overwhelmed by autograph seekers, I suppose. I just wondered if he came alone here, or whether he had a bodyguard with him."

"Oh; I understand." She nodded her grey head with its neat white cap. "There was no guard with him. Though another man came up to the floor with him some of the time. I think it was the pilot. Sometimes the pilot would go in to see Miss White for a few minutes and then go down to the lobby to wait till Mr. Everest was ready to leave, to fly home again. But no guard. Of course it's very quiet in a hospital, you know. He would hardly have been rushed off his feet here by his public. Just sick people and their visitors."

The doctor, then—who had attended Helene. Jack called his office and was sandwiched in between appointments. Found the new, mostly glass professional building, and parked in the lot behind it.

Dr. Frank Neilson was tall, stooped, grey, with a thin face.

"Were you able to talk privately wth Everest, Doctor? He never goes anywhere nowadays without a bodyguard along, and I wondered—"

"Well, there was no bodyguard with him *there*, not in the hospital. That would hardly be necessary."

"You talked with him privately, then, without—"

"Of *course* I talked with him privately. When his sister almost died, there at first, we talked quite frankly about her chances of survival. Certainly no one else was present."

49

"He didn't—Everest didn't at any time talk to you about being in danger, did he? Himself, I mean—not his sister."

"In danger? Why, no. He wasn't even in the accident." Dr. Neilson smoothed his grey mustache.

"I know that. I was referring to this—well, almost fixation he has about keeping people away. Shutting himself up behind guards, at his ranch. I was there myself—a couple of days ago—with a contingent from the news media; surely not an alarming number of people, no more than seven or eight. Yet there was an armed guard with Everest every moment. You'd think he could trust a well-screened group from the press not to attack him physically? Especially when we'd all been frisked—"

"Frisked?" The doctor's face lit up in sudden glee.

"Yes, frisked. What I'd like to ask you, Doctor, is whether you think the man's perhaps a victim of delusions. Paranoiac."

Neilson laughed. "No. I talked at length with Everest—several times. We may not share too many views on how the world is going—or ought to go. But James Everest is quite sane. No delusions, I assure you. Eccentric, I'd say, to a degree. But don't you have to be a bit eccentric to become a writer? I think so.

"I assure you—time and again, while his sister was in the hospital, we talked quite normally, with *no* guards around, and he was not peering over his shoulder for possible attackers—nothing like that."

"I see."

"And as for shutting himself away from everyone, at his ranch—oh, my, I'd do that in a minute if I didn't have my practice. Your patients *never* leave you alone, you know —not a moment to yourself, not even in bed. They call. And if you go out, there's always your answering service, you see, reaching out to pluck you from wherever you've taken refuge—someone's broken their arm, or has a cold, or a *headache,* by God! And you newsmen, now—you say he had an armed guard there? Can't blame him for that. Lot of people would like to drive off the press with a shotgun, I expect. And the frisking business sounds to me

50

more like a little leg pulling, for his own satisfaction." He sighed. "No, James Everest's just able to afford what we'd all like to have. Privacy. And for a *writer*, he's a perfectly sane man."

He made one more stopover on the way back to New York.

Lousy connections. Change at Dallas, naturally. Arrived late evening in St. Louis—in time to go to bed at a motel.

Everyone to whom he talked the next morning at Washington University—an attractive campus with grass and trees and a mixture of impressive buildings, both Gothic and contemporary—was very cordial.

A professor in the English Department, to whom he was turned over, welcomed him into his office and listened to his questions.

"We bask in what reflected glory comes our way because of having been his alma mater. But the truth is that no one here even remembers him. He seems to have passed through the university like a disembodied spirit." Sadly, Danton Carroll shrugged his hunched shoulders—pouted his thin lips. "The college doesn't even have any of his manuscripts. He seems to be keeping them under lock and key, along with himself."

Professor Carroll took him to the library to see their collection of Everest first editions, and to the alumni office, where they examined a thin folder of newspaper clippings for the most part no different from the ones Jack had gone through in New York before leaving on the trip to Texas. Except for one, which he read through with care. It was from the *St. Louis Post-Dispatch;* a feature story on last April's annual Everest interview. Though it was mentioned that Helene Everest—who had put in a brief appearance during the reporter's talk with the author—had only recently come home from the hospital after recovering from a near-fatal accident, there were no sinister overtones in the writing. A photograph of Everest at work in his writing room accompanied the story.

Probably there had been no secret message last year. Everest had not yet grown so desperate as to attempt one.

One thing he got from the college records was the address of the house where the Whites had lived. He found it—one of a row of small brick bungalows, their yards terraced several feet above the level of the street.

A tall black woman in slacks and a purple tee shirt came to the door. "Someone who knew Mr. Everest? When he was a boy?" She smiled. "Some of the neighbors told me I'm livin' in a famous person's house. We've got a copy of every one of his books. My son has. Paperback—"

"Anyone still live around here who knew the Whites?"

"Only one left, by now. Lady that lives across there. Miz Spense."

Mrs. Spense turned out to be a white woman, old and dried up, with frizzy dyed hair through which the scalp showed. "The White family. Yes." The name served as password to get him inside the door, which at first she'd opened on a burglar chain.

She seated him in an overstuffed chair, one of a three-piece suite, in the twilight of a living room with drawn shades.

There wasn't much that she, either, could tell him. Jamie had been such a quiet boy; kept to himself. Always reading. Except that he did love horses, she remembered. "Will—that was his father—Will used to take him someplace out in the country, where he could ride."

"Is there anyone I could talk to who was a friend of his?"

"He only ever had one friend, that I knew of. Little Jew boy, I can't recall his name. But he died. Years ago. Jamie's sister, now—Helene—she always had friends around. But all that was so much later, Jamie was already gone from home then. When Helene was born he was twenty years old and married."

He got a little information about Will and Ellen White. Something, anyway, to use as background for his article.

But no answers to any of the questions that were bothering him.

He was exhausted after the flight home, late in the afternoon.

His apartment looked wonderful to him, though the room seemed subtly to have changed shape in his absence. Eldyce had been in yesterday to clean, he deduced —the framed lithographs were all crooked on the walls— her way of informing him that she had dusted.

He unpacked the few items he'd bought and dumped in an airline bag, after his suitcase was taken; then made himself a bourbon highball. Glanced wistfully over the contents of the refrigerator. (Dinner on the plane had been both poor and small.) Nothing but some old boiled ham, looking slightly green through its plastic wrapper; a tired loaf of bread; and a lone egg. He resigned himself to an empty stomach and took his drink into the dinette, where he settled down at the old Royal standard typewriter he kept on one end of the table to type up the scribbled notes he'd made on the plane.

(Damn that character who'd taken his Olivetti! He had a tape recorder, naturally, that he could carry with him on trips, but he preferred to see what he was thinking, not play it back . . .)

He ended his account of the day's interviews with his conclusions, as of the tired, disbelieving moment, about the Everest Project.

Everest's present situation would seem to date from sometime after Walter Carrington's death. During his sister's stay in the hospital in Abilene, Jamie Everest had still been free. But after that . . .

There had been the personnel changes—how many, he didn't know. But the chief guard, Tim, from Carrington's day, had left. To be replaced by Dan Bayles. The houseman—who had been there for many years, who would have known pretty much everything that went on—had been fired and replaced by Shrunken Head. And soon after had died. Because of a faulty gas heater? Such an easy death to arrange.

Brake failure? Easy, too, to arrange with a little careful sabotage.

Highway robbery? . . .

# 3

A SLIM, DARK-HAIRED GIRL WHOSE NAME WAS Linnet Emries stood quite still in what nowadays passed for sunlight in the city of New York. Oblivious of the Fifth Avenue traffic behind her and of the pedestrians passing in two meandering, interwoven streams at her back, she was looking through the plate glass window of the Scribner Book Store. The whole window was devoted to the anniversary edition of *The Kingdom Lost*. A dozen copies—white, with leather trim, and boxed—strikingly arranged. Blow-ups of reviews ranged behind them, and stills of the two movies that had been made from the book —the first version, from the late forties (she'd seen a revival of it at a movie theater on upper Broadway), and the recent remake starring Erin Bruce. And gazing back at her from a camera portrait centered in the display space were the translucent grey eyes of James Everest. She knew, of course, even though it was not a color photograph, that the eyes were grey. Just as she knew the hair was not black as it appeared, but light brown.

The pain that struck through her was as fresh as though their parting were recent; it had been so unexpected, coming across his picture here, almost like meeting him face to face.

*With a new preface by the author,* promised a discreet ad in Lydian type.

She left the window, pushed her way through the door into the store. There would be something in the preface, surely; something between the lines—

"*The Kingdom Lost,* please—the new edition," she said

to the woman clerk. Not that she didn't already have a copy, years old and suitably inscribed, at home.

She paid, waited for her change and for the beautiful little book to be handed to her.

When she had it, she retreated to a corner of the store, where with fingers become annoyingly clumsy she fumbled the volume out of its box and turned to the preface.

Although every novelist, either successful or as yet unpublished, yearns for lasting fame, and as he labors with such love and diligence over each of his brainchildren, hopes that he is producing a classic, no one—least of all his writer—expected, when this little volume was accepted for publication twenty-five years ago, that it would find a niche all its own in the hearts of the young. I know that it did this. But I cannot take credit, as a writer, for the reception accorded my hero, Lons Fell.

The clear-eyed sadness that is really compassion in the young, and the hope that is the other side of the coin of fear held doubtfully in the hand of the under-twenty—these things were mine because of my age, when this tale was spun. So I gave them to Lons Fell. And it is these things, and others like them that older people have forgotten . . .

Linnet Emries read on—disappointed. Why would she have thought there could be a message for her?

She slipped the white-bound book with its gold lettering back into its box, the box into the bag.

She wanted to know what he thought *now*. Not what he had thought twenty-five years ago. Now. What he thought and what he wanted. But it wasn't there . . .

Did longing for her seize him ever, a sharp and sudden pain? She hoped so. She hoped he suffered the tortures of the damned . . .

She made her way among the book-laden tables, pushed against the glass of the door, and went out again into the street.

"Vern told me—yes," said Tom Krug, his boss. He'd finally showed up at the magazine after being stuck all morning in some meeting. "I wondered if he could have been exaggerating?"

"Afraid not."

The big, energetic man with the rangy frame, balding head, and bifocals looked up at him from behind his overloaded desk.

"Tell me about it, then. Just as it happened." When he had heard it all, he said simply, "God!" And Jack knew he was torn—between distress at Everest's plight (whatever that might turn out to be) and delight at the scent of a major scoop.

"What a story—if we're ever going to be able to use it. And God, we're certainly going to try! You're on special assignment, Jack. Go ahead and do the article you and Everest agreed on—"

"Yes indeed. But do you know what bothers me? Both of Everest's visible custodians heard us discussing it, so they know I intend doing something of the sort; either they expect to stop me, or there is next to nothing that can be found out—even if I knew where to look. Or for what."

"Oh, you'll think of someplace to look." Krug gave a half smile. "May end up just falling over it, you know."

"And breaking my neck?"

The place to start was with the man's editor. Dwight Percy.

But there he hit a snag. A maddeningly impersonal voice informed him over the phone that Everest's editor was not in his office at the publishing house; he had taken some time off, and could not be reached.

Fuming, he wrote a letter, marked *Personal* and URGENT. Took it over himself to Mackenzie & Company, of which Percy was Editor-in-Chief, so that it could be forwarded to him at once—wherever he was.

He wondered how long it would be before he got a reply.

Fifty miles from New York City, at his home in New Canaan, Connecticut, Dwight Percy read intently the first installment of Everest's new novel—three chapters of which had arrived in today's mail. Except for the big German shepherd Cap, he was alone in his sunny library.

He finished the last page of manuscript and laid it down with a sigh of satisfaction. Jamie was still turning them out as good as ever. Maybe even better, this time. Dwight could not have been more pleased.

He felt better today. Much better. There were more and more days, as the time since his operation grew longer, when he was almost his old self—except for the pains from his incision, where they had split him open like a shelled pea pod, and the pains in his leg where the sections of blood vessels had been removed for use in his chest. Wonderful what these heart surgeons could do now. He hadn't believed, really, that he was going to die —who of us can truly believe that he is mortal? But with the danger past, he found that even with the pains left him by the surgeon's knife, he savored each day as he had never done before.

He glanced around at this room of which he was so fond. It had been made by knocking out a wall between the back parlor and the sun porch, and the windows, on three sides, looked out from the wooded ridge over a view of the Connecticut hills. Books crammed all the wall space and overflowed onto table tops, the big kidney-shaped desk and even onto chairs. Opposite Dwight in the shelves next to the hall door was the collection of first editions, his special love.

He switched on the dictating machine that sat atop the desk. At the sound of Dwight Percy's voice, the big black and tan dog lifted his head. Perceiving that his master was not speaking to him but to himself, Cap dropped his muzzle again onto his paws and with a heavy sigh closed his eyes.

"Jamie, it's excellent. And you *are* determined, aren't you! I must admit that you were right and I was wrong. If you hadn't written me of your preoccupation with Poe, however, I would never even have suspected his influence in the formulation of your theme. The idea may have begun as Poe, but it's coming out Everest. I should not

58

have worried that you might produce anything that was only a rehash of someone else's work . . ."

Jack went fruitlessly to talk with an acquaintance in the F.B.I.

"Nothing we can do," Ken Murtagh told him. "No possible reason for us to enter the picture. There's no kidnapping—the man's in his own home, happy as a clam, to all appearances, giving out interviews and posing for pictures for the papers. Where's there any crime that's been committed?"

"Yeah. Sure."

"Not that I doubt your story. Couldn't have been a practical joke, though?"

"No. And I've already got the opinion of a doctor who knows him: says Everest couldn't be a paranoiac."

Ken Murtagh did one thing for him—he checked the names of Reg Curtiss and Dan Bayles with the F.B.I. files. Nothing on them.

Not under those names, anyway.

"You've tried to reach him at home, I suppose . . ."

It was Friday—of what had been a very busy week—and Vern Fix had dropped into his office.

"Yeah, I did. Found out, at least, that he lives in New Canaan. Unlisted phone number. I don't suppose he's there, anyway." He broke off. "Say, isn't it today you take off on your vacation?"

"This evening. Got my flight booked to El Paso."

"El Paso? I thought you were heading for Florida— some deep-sea fishing."

Vern was grinning at him. "I'm going to Mexico. You know those pictures we saw down at Everest's ranch—"

"You're going *there*? Baja?"

"Been reading up on the place—it's fabulous. Possibly the world's greatest sport fishing. And then the scenery! I should get some marvelous pictures."

"How do you reach—what's its name, Cabo something? —from El Paso? I could bet Everest picked the location because it's so remote—"

"Oh, you can get there by air. But I'm renting a car at the border. Drive down through Mexico and see a little of the country. There's an overnight car ferry—goes twice a week—from Mazatlán across the Gulf of California to La Paz, on southern Baja. From La Paz it's only an eighty- or ninety-mile drive down to Cabo San Lucas."

"Sounds like a lot of trouble to go to for a few fish."

"Not at all. I even get two vacations for the price of one. Gladys and I always planned to drive through Mexico someday; never made it."

Vern propelled himself loose-jointedly out of his chair. "Well, I've got lots of stuff to get out of the way, still. But I wanted to tell you where I'm off to." A quick grin made his homely face more than ever that of a gargoyle. "I'll have one mounted—one of my fish. So you'll believe me."

"You'd better. Those fish stories of yours—"

"Oh, and I'll try to get a few shots of the Great Man's retreat down there—if I can get near it."

"Would you? I could use one with the article. If it ever comes off."

"It will," said Vern, lingering at the door. "One way or the other."

"What do you mean by that?"

"I mean you'll come up with a bona fide article in any case. But the other—this hypothetical prisoner business—"

"You don't believe in it . . ."

"By now, uh-uh. You haven't come across a single thing that bears out your theory, have you? I mean anything concrete?"

Jack glared. "No."

"Well, then—"

Before he could answer, Vern was gone. Leaving him feeling like—well, he could take his choice: paranoid or an idiot.


When he got home that evening, there was a letter from his wife in the mailbox.

His ex-wife.

He tore it open, steeling himself against what it might contain.

*Dear Jack,*
*Before it's in the papers, I thought I ought to let you know I'm being married ...*

He stuffed the note back in its envelope. Finish reading it later.

He felt a little numb. That was all. Rather as though someone he hadn't seen in a while had died. Had a little trouble getting his key into the lock of the apartment door. Not paying attention, he guessed.

It was Sue Ann Carrington he was thinking of as he opened the door. Good thing, wasn't it, that he hadn't seen anything more of her. Another rich, stubborn, capricious blonde—enough like Eloise to be her sister.

There certainly was such a thing as a losing combination.

# 4

ON MONDAY, DWIGHT PERCY PHONED.

"I have your rather curious letter here . . ."

Jack took the train out, for an afternoon appointment. Changed at Stamford and took the tiny two-car local to the end of its short line. And from the station, a taxi to an old, authentic New England house, white clapboard with black shutters, the first story almost completely hidden by giant rhododendron.

A sign on the door said "COME IN" and so he knocked and went in. And almost went right out again as a large black and tan German shepherd materialized, growling, in the hall.

"It's all right, Cap," a voice called from somewhere to the rear, and the dog turned and walked back toward the voice, stopping every few feet to look over his shoulder, making sure that his owner's visitor was coming. He led Jack to the last door at the back of the hall, beyond the staircase, into a sort of sitting room and study whose windows looked out over a view of wooded hills.

"Thank you, Cap. I think this is Mr. Seavering," said the stocky man with a white crew cut and handlebar mustache. He sat in an adjustable reclining chair next to a square table covered with stacks of manuscript. Cap padded up to him and sat down and received a pat on the head.

"How do you do, Mr. Percy. I wondered for a minute there if I might lose an arm on the way."

"Oh, no. Cap wouldn't do that. You see, I haven't been well for some time. Cap takes care of visitors—when my housekeeper's out, that is . . . Here, sit in this chair—it's comfortable."

It was. The large, green-upholstered overstuffed chair molded itself around him as he sank into it.

"You're doing very well with that magazine of yours, I see." Percy gave him an approving nod. "I wondered, when it was started a few years ago, how you could make a go of it when other magazines have been folding all over the place—and with the competition, too, in the news magazine field. I'm glad you still seem to have your heads above water."

"Thanks. That's Tom Krug's doing—he's a real dynamo."

"Now." There was an inquiring grin beneath the handlebar mustache. "What *is* this about? Your letter intrigued me, I must say—"

"Well, I've just come back from interviewing James Everest . . ."

"Yes?" Percy cocked his head—polite, waiting.

Jack hardly knew how to start. Maybe head-on? Shock value . . .

"Have you had any reason to believe, Mr. Percy, that at some time since the death of Walter Carrington, James Everest has been taken prisoner by his guards? And is being held?"

*"Held?"* Dwight Percy's face was incredulous. "Held *prisoner?"*

"That's what I'm asking."

Percy looked at his visitor as if he'd suddenly perceived himself to be in the presence of a madman. "You can't be serious!" Jack had a feeling that if there were anyone besides himself and the dog in the house at the moment, he would have summoned help.

"All right, I'll start at the beginning." But there was no thawing of the frosty countenance opposite as he told of the interview, and of the private talk with Everest in the courtyard—complete with his traumatic viewing of the word HELP scratched in the earth.

Percy's face twitched with contempt. "That's enough. Of all the low-down reporter's tricks—you're trying to put

63

together some piece of sensationalism, I suppose, to boost circulation of that little magazine I was congratulating you on. Why you'd bring *me* such a story, I can't imagine! Didn't you know James Everest's publishing house would give any canard like that the lie, at *once?* I'd have thought you were an experienced enough newsman to know that!"

Jack was standing now. Angry. "It's no lie, Percy. No hoax. And I'm *not* trying to use it for any sensational purpose. I came here in good faith, to tell you what happened, because believe it or not, your number-one author needs help!"

The dog Cap was making a low growling sound, deep in his throat.

"No, Cap. It's all right!" Cap's master pulled open a drawer of the overloaded table beside him. Took from it a sheaf of clippings—shoved them into Jack's hands. Pictures of Everest, of course. The pictures that had been taken the week before.

"Does *this* look like a man held prisoner?" He jabbed a forefinger. "There. And there. And his sister—there, Helene, looking perfectly normal. *Nothing* wrong! How could there be, with representatives of the world's press right there, taking down everything that happened, photographing everything they saw!

"Get out of my house, Mr. Seavering. And don't try to sell your crazy story anywhere or you'll be in trouble; I'll *see* to it!"

Angry and disappointed, Jack left. Escorted by a police dog of whose present intentions he was not entirely sure.

The one man he'd thought could help him most . . .

*Perspective*, with a picture of James Everest on the cover, was on the stands today. Jack eyed it, automatically, on his way out of Grand Central as he headed back to his office. One of Vern's photos, of course, and a good one. His account of the interview, too, was in there. Maybe that was the end of it?

Because the undercover Everest operation was now hopelessly bogged down.

* * *

It was Tuesday morning, and he was working over the opening paragraph of the promised Everest article. For all the good this was going to do.

"Jack?" His research assistant, Flo, appeared in the doorway, a pencil stuck, like the bone ornament of some primitive time, into her Afro hairdo.

"There's a girl here who wants to see you."

"What about?" People didn't just wander into the magazine offices off the street; visitors were screened.

"Your Everest article. She's a friend of the family or something."

"Oh? Send her in!"

His first thought about the girl, as he took in the long, dark hair falling sleekly almost to the middle of her back, was that she must be a college student. And then he saw that she was older than that—though not by much.

He found himself placing a chair for her. "Just what was it—"

"My name is Emries. Linnet Emries."

She had strange blue eyes that seemed to gather and reflect, intensify, the light in the room.

"I hope this isn't an imposition. But you see, of all the articles that have just appeared about James Everest, yours was the only one that mentioned Helene White. And so I wondered if you could help me."

"In what way?"

"I've been worried about her, and unable to find out anything."

Help from an unexpected quarter? "What's your connection with Helene White, Miss—"

"Mrs.," she swiftly corrected him. "Why, Helene is my best friend."

"Tell me about her—would you?" He leaned forward, wondering if Project Everest was, after all, still alive.

She was nervous, and in some way defiant, as though expecting to be challenged. (Why?)

"My family moved to St. Louis when I was twelve, and I met Helene in school. She's been my closest friend ever since—though we haven't seen each other in the last few years. But we kept in touch. Long letters. Until—oh, a little over a year ago."

"And then?"

"Well, I heard nothing from her for a while after the automobile accident—when she was so badly injured?"

"Yes. When Walter Carrington was killed."

"That's right. And then when she did write, you'd have thought from her letter that we were acquaintances only —not friends. It was cold, formal—and all her letters since then have been that way. Not like Helene. I've wondered whether she could have suffered some kind of brain injury in the accident—or a nervous breakdown afterwards? Because after all this time, when she should be completely recovered—"

"Have you inquired of Everest? Whether she—"

"It's much too touchy a subject to tackle by mail. What would I say, 'Look here, I just happened to wonder whether your sister is off her rocker—?' And if she isn't—"

"But you thought I might be able to reassure you."

"Yes."

"I'm hardly a judge of whether she was quite herself; not knowing what she's like. If you could tell me more about her . . ."

But Linnet Emries's description of an impetuous, joyous, vital young woman was no match to his own recollection of a stiff, unfriendly creature unmistakably ill-at-ease in his company.

"Your Helene White hardly seems to be the one I met." He turned from her; opened a desk drawer. The pictures Vern had taken . . . yes, there was the envelope. He shuffled through, put the two photographs of Helene White on top, and handed her the sheaf of glossies. "Here."

"Oh." She was looking at the shot Vern had taken through the window of a group in the courtyard: the noon sun cast harsh shadows on the faces of Everest and his sister. She glanced at the second print, and then held it closer. The picture that had been snapped in the dining room.

"Look as if she has changed very much?" Jack asked carefully.

"Not a bit." She studied the photo again. "Of course I can't see her expression, since she was half turned away from the camera. It would be the look in her eyes that would tell whether something, basically, is—is wrong?" She started leafing through the rest of the shots.

The idea of an impostor, which he had, however briefly, entertained, was at least disposed of.

"There are no more of her. The rest are of Everest."

"They're very good," she said judically, considering them one by one. Yet he had the impression that there was some further reaction, something more personal, that she was withholding.

"You *knew* Everest, of course?"

She looked up. "Why do you put the question in the past tense?"

"Because I've gathered that either he has no friends now, or they no longer come to see him."

"No one?" she asked thoughtfully.

"He sees only his sister, I believe—and the hired staff."

She frowned. "There *is* no one else now, I suppose, since Walter's death. Except his editor."

"Dwight Percy. Who's been ill for quite some time ... But you know Everest well, you were saying?"

"Oh, yes." She laid aside the pictures. "Though I've seen him only occasionally over the years. He's so much older than Helene, you know. He was long gone from St. Louis when my family moved there; already famous. But every couple of years he'd come home to visit."

"You saw him then?"

"Yes, I saw him. I'd heard so much about him—Helene worshipped him, certainly—and I'd read his books. Helene and I tagged along, goggle-eyed, I expect, after Jamie— and Walter. I seem to remember that Walter Carrington always came with him."

"Everest used actually, then, to leave that security setup of his; I didn't know he ever had."

"The—oh. You mean the ranch at Hardy, with the guards. That's to insure his privacy, when he's writing. It's necessary—he's almost a cult, you know; all the young people who idolized him. If he didn't shut himself away, he wouldn't have a private moment."

She believed that, he supposed.

"You say he did bring Walter Carrington with him, to St. Louis. As a sort of bodyguard? I understand he was quite a tall, athletic type."

"Oh, that's not why he came!" She regarded him with hostile eyes. "You talk of Jamie as if you thought he was *afraid*—physically afraid—to come out of seclusion and—and even walk down the street. That's not so. Walter came with him because he was his best friend; they were always doing things together. And I imagine Walter had friends, himself, in St. Louis. He'd gone to college there, it's where he and Jamie met."

"Yes, I know. Tell me—have you been to Everest's ranch?"

"I visited there four years ago, over the Christmas holidays."

"Was that the last time you saw Everest and his sister?"

"It was the last time I saw Jamie. But Helene and I were both still going to school, then, in New York. I saw her often. She graduated from Barnard that spring, and went back to Texas, to stay. Her parents were both dead by then, and the ranch was the only place she could call home. Jamie has an apartment here, but he almost never uses it—his real home is at Hardy."

"When was it you last saw Helene, then?"

"Three years ago. She came up from Texas to be maid of honor at my wedding. Since then there have only been the letters."

"Three years. You didn't see her last year? She told me she'd spent awhile in New York."

Linnet Emries looked almost as if he had struck her. "In New York? She couldn't have been here! She'd have called me!"

"She distinctly said she'd been here then. When I asked her about finding life on the ranch rather lonely. Though I'd say her not calling you fits in with the difference in her letters, doesn't it?"

68

"Yes—it could. But it's very strange. I wonder what reason she—"

"Mrs. Emries—" He hesitated. "I'd be very much interested in seeing her letters."

"Why?" What long, thick lashes she had, he noticed.

He smiled. "I thought you wanted my help?"

"Not *that* much help. Helene is my worry, not yours. If you're thinking of her letters as a prospective mother lode of biographical material on Everest, you can forget it. I'd never show them to anyone who works for a news magazine."

He leaned forward earnestly, to explain. "Look. I haven't told you yet why I'd like to see the letters—aside from trying to help you with your quandary. I'm doing a second article on Everest, about the connection between his life and work. With his reclusive habits, you can imagine how hard up I am for material. But: I would use nothing that's in those letters without your absolute say-so; and in addition Everest's to approve the article before it's published. Nothing would get through to the printer without the agreement of all concerned."

She shook her head. "They're much too private."

He propped his head on one hand and sighed. "This isn't a scandal sheet we put out here, you know . . . How about letting me see only the recent letters. You've already told me they were quite impersonal."

"Then why would you want to see them? They'd be useless to you for research."

What a maddeningly difficult young lady! He wished, certainly, that he could tell her; tell her of Everest's message, scratched in the dirt. He couldn't risk it. A girl he knew nothing about? Who had materialized without notice, from nowhere? He had no idea what he was up against in this thing; Reg Curtiss, aware that he was investigating Everest's life, might even have recruited this girl to find out whether he was onto anything. How did he know she was what she said she was? That was one reason he had to see the letters.

But the two of them seemed to have reached an impasse.

"I suppose," he said, "the reason you're concerned about the letters is that there's a great deal in them about Walter Carrington. She was in love with him, wasn't she? But that side of things is no affair of mine—what I'm interested in is sidelights on Everest. You could extract parts of the letters, couldn't you?"

She gave him a rather bitter, thoughtful smile. "I'm not at all sure Jamie wants any sidelights cast on him or his life. He much prefers to remain an enigma." Adjusting the strap of her shoulder bag, she got to her feet. "I'm sorry I've wasted so much of your time, Mr. Seavering. I really don't know what I expected to find out." She turned to go.

He stood, too, and came around the end of the desk. "Look. Wait a minute. I know I haven't answered what you asked me, about Helene White. I can't. Except to say that even before you came to see me I was convinced something is wrong down there at Everest's place." She checked, her hand on the back of the chair. "Not just with Everest's sister; something more."

She looked around at him. "Like what?" she asked softly. And he had the almost subliminal impression that this was the question she had come to ask; not the one about Helene.

"I don't know what. Nothing you can put your finger on. You don't believe in a sixth sense?" Close enough, wasn't he, without betraying James Everest's confidence? He must tell her something, in order to get a look at those letters—and a chance to talk more to her of what she knew; or his investigations had reached a dead end. "It was an impression I got; something that I could feel, almost tangible, yet I can't describe it."

"You don't have ESP, I suppose?"

"Definitely not."

She walked away. But at the door she turned. "When would you like to look at the letters?"

At five o'clock he went uptown to her apartment. It was on East Seventy-third Street on the second floor of a brownstone.

"Come in," she said, and let him into a large room, very sparingly furnished, and except for the dark, polished floor, done all in white. A painting, in splashes of orange and brown, a Persian-looking wall hanging, and a set of shelves built into the wall and filled with books and assorted art objects provided the only decorations in the room. The effect was contemporary and uncluttered—and for some reason not what he had expected.

She had placed a small stack of letters on the glass coffee table before the coach.

"These are from before—" She indicated two fat envelopes. "And these are the recent ones." Four of them.

He looked at the early ones first.

There were detailed accounts of where Helene had gone with Walter, what they had done, what he had said, what Jamie was doing, how his work seemed to be going. A wealth of information about her daily life. Written in a very personal vein.

The later letters, then. Very short. Stilted. Practically nothing in them. She read a lot. What could Linna recommend that she might enjoy? . . . She was reading constantly nowadays. Yes, she had Linna's new book, Jamie had ordered it for her. The drawings were delightful . . . Two of the letters—the last two—mentioned riding every day.

No clues to anything.

"Strange," he said. "The contrast."

"Yes. What do you make of it?"

"It's as if she'd had a complete personality change."

"Isn't it!" Linnet Emries rose from her chair to stand restlessly by the mantel, leaning lightly against it.

"Or," he added, "as if you'd had a falling-out—the two of you."

"In that case she wouldn't bother to write."

"I suppose not. Though actually I wondered why she did write—the letters being as they are. No camaraderie; no mention of auld lang syne." It was almost as if someone had *made* Helene write the letters.

She came and sat beside him on the couch. "What did

71

you mean, this morning, about something being wrong at the ranch?"

But that was Jamie Everest's secret; and his. "I wish I knew," he said. "That's why I wanted to see the letters, in case I could pick up a clue to something. But on a first reading I see nothing."

"Surely you had more than a hunch. You said you were convinced, even before I came to see you, that something was wrong . . . Something happened, or you saw or heard something when you were at the ranch. You're holding out and won't tell me."

"All I can tell you for certain is that Everest himself seemed to want to keep in touch with me, using this projected article of mine as a pretext. That's atypical behavior for him—isn't it?"

"That's not all, surely?"

He spread his hands. "I hope to know more when I go to see him again, to get his approval of my article. Because he so clearly intimated that there was something behind the conversation we had, something he wanted me to know, or perhaps something he hoped I would find out on my own, in connection with writing the article."

"You're talking in riddles."

"I know. And believe me, that's not generally my style. You see I'm looking for answers, and that's difficult when I don't know what the questions are. You may be able to help me."

"With your article, you mean?"

"With that, yes, and also with whatever's bothering Everest." But he'd have to get behind the guard she had up before he'd learn anything. "By the way, what's the book of yours Helene refers to in one of her letters?"

"I'm an illustrator. Children's books." She got up and crossed to the shelves beyond the fireplace, and he followed. She picked a slim little volume from a row of books and handed it to him.

He smiled at the drawings—cozy firesides, homey kitchens—and at a world where children, dogs, cats, oversized hamsters, and large, friendly caterpillars were ap-

72

parently allied against all the adults, who were shown only from the knees down.

On a shelf above the books, propped between a Chinese ginger jar and the bronze figure of a bull, was the framed photograph of a young man in naval uniform.

"My husband," she said when she saw him looking at it. And added harshly, "He wasn't killed in the service—he survived that. He died in the crash of an airliner."

"Oh." Some instinct told him that sympathy would make her angry. "How long were you married?"

"Two years, just about." She replaced the book on its shelf. "Can I get you a drink?"

"I'd love one." And as he settled into a large, comfortable modernistic chair next to the fireplace, he knew that the letters and the children's book had told him what he needed to know. Linnet Emries was just what she'd said she was. Not someone sent round by Everest's captors to probe.

Wednesday morning's mail brought him a letter from Texas, written in bright blue ink on pale blue paper engraved with her name and address.

*Dear Mr. Seavering,*

*You must realize that when you were here I had doubts about you, and about your purpose here. Not now.*

*I did go over, and asked to be let in to see Helene. No dice. I never got past the gatehouse.*

*"Miss Everest is not feeling well," was the message that came back from the house when the guard telephoned. "No visitors."*

*I doubt that she is sick—she never is (I don't count her stay in the hospital last year—it wasn't an illness. And if she weren't a very tough horsewoman she wouldn't have survived that.) Curiosity would have made her see me, if it were up to her; and my connection with Walter.*

*Yours quite sincerely,*
*Sue Ann Carrington*

Not exactly solid information. Conjecture only. Yet what *wasn't* conjecture in this Everest matter?

He was remembering how he had felt alternately attracted to and put off by this very beautiful woman, when his phone rang.

"Dwight Percy, Mr. Seavering. I'd like to talk to you. And—my apologies for last time."

And so he again took the train out to Connecticut, and a taxi to the big white house, where he was admitted this time by the housekeeper, a motherly looking woman in her late fifties. Cap, at her side, wagged his tail.

Dwight Percy, receiving him in the same room as before, rose from his chair to shake hands. "I'm very sorry about the other day! Very!"

"You've changed your mind?"

He looked at Jack quizzically from under the heavy grey brows. "Would *you* have believed some brash young man who came in and tossed off a story like the one you told me?"

"Probably not." He grinned, and sat down in the same green chair as before, opposite Percy.

"I've had some inquiries made about you, since then. I hope you won't take that amiss—I had no choice. Ours is a conservative publishing house. Sensationalism doesn't go. We couldn't have some supposed scoop for your magazine involving one of our authors—some hoax. But what I've learned about you convinced me that any information you might have brought me would be reliable, insofar as you yourself knew. Leaving me no alternative but to believe this bizarre tale of some arcane message from James Everest."

"Well, that's a relief; you were my best hope as to any clues that might exist."

Dwight Percy nodded his rather heavy head, with its spiky white hair and the handlebar mustache—which made him look English, though his accent was not. "What have you done, then? So far?"

"Well, I did look up a few people while I was still in Texas. Walter Carrington's widow; Arthur Wheelock."

"Art Wheelock? Yes, I've met him a time or two when I've visited Jamie at the ranch. Handles all the finances."

Jack told him about the chat with Wheelock, and a little of his talk with Sue Ann Carrington. Then the trip to Abilene—though he left out the episode of the highwayman that had occurred en route; maybe no connection at all.

Percy agreed with the Abilene doctor. "No, Jamie's not paranoid. That's out."

"How long since you've actually seen Everest, talked with him yourself?"

He shook his head. "It was quite a while before Walter Carrington's death. The fall before, it must have been. So if you're right about something's having gone wrong since then, I'm no help to you. I've not been well. Had a heart attack, awhile back, and was out of commission for a long time. Jamie and I have had to handle things by mail or by phone—since he refuses to come north."

"I thought he had an apartment in New York—"

"Had. Penthouse. At one time it was a convenience for him. But he doesn't like New York; and he hasn't the apartment anymore—building was torn down a few months ago."

"So you haven't seen him, then, the last year and a half?"

"Doesn't seem that long, but it must be . . ."

"When did you have your heart attack?"

A pinched look on Percy's face. "Last year. It was on New Year's Day, as a matter of fact—never forget it! I was up in Vermont—invitation from one of my authors."

"January. I was wondering, you see. This organization that runs things for Everest would have known, wouldn't they, that you were ill—and that they could count on your not getting in their way for a while?"

"Of course they'd know." Percy threw him a shrewd look from under his bushy eyebrows. "You're convinced, I've gathered, that Walter's death was planned. And with me out of the way already—"

"You. Also, there was the chief guard, Mrs. Carrington told me—"

"Tim Donan?"

"Who doesn't seem to be there now. Mrs. Carrington thought she'd heard he had left."

"I'm not surprised. He probably left when Walter was killed. He was devoted to Walter."

"This man Dan Bayles appears to be chief guard now. And the former houseman was not only fired but died soon after in a questionable sort of accident."

Percy's head perked around with a quick, startled movement.

"Space heater exploded and killed him."

"Oh, *no!* Where did you find that out?"

"From Sue Ann Carrington."

"I see. Did she think—"

"She hadn't felt there was anything suspicious about how he died; *I* did. Anyhow, I wondered."

"Yes." Percy stared speculatively at the green vista beyond the windows. "Ought you to have taken Mrs Carrington into your confidence? Granted, you found out some things. But will she keep her mouth shut? If this combine should accidentally learn through her what you're up to—"

"But I had to start someplace. I tried not to let her know just what I was doing—I did use my cover: that I'm doing an article on Everest. But I'm afraid I told her more than I wanted to." He drew her letter from his pocket and handed it over. "She went over to try to see Helene. I'd told her not to."

There was a thin smile under the copious mustache. "You can't tell a woman anything—don't you know that?"

Yes, he knew that. Had learned it the hard way, from his wife.

Jack told him what little else there was. His talk with Ken Murtagh—and, no, the F.B.I. had no reason to enter the case (*what* case?); and no, they had no record of Curtiss or Bayles.

Linnet Emries, then, and Helene White's letters.

"Yes, curious—" Percy said. "Say, I've got something here—let's have a look at it." Pushing himself up slowly out of his chair, he shuffled over to a file cabinet in one

76

corner, opened a drawer, and brought out a folder. He sat down again and leafed through the newspaper clippings it contained. "Here." He handed one to Jack.

It was from a Dallas newspaper. Last November, Helene Everest had granted the paper an interview on the subject of her famous brother. She had been in town, she said, to attend a concert and do her Christmas shopping.

He scanned it. Nothing that hadn't appeared about Jamie before. It was more about Helene herself, with a photograph of her examining Everest's latest book, which had come out at about that time. "I suppose Reg Curtiss was right there with her while she gave the interview—bodyguard and censor."

"Very clever, if that's what they're doing: she's seen, at different places, free as a bird, but escorted by Jamie's personal pilot. Speaks of her brother, of course, who's busy at home, writing—and yes, he is fine . . ."

"Unless the interviewer pepped up what the girl said, there—" Jack pointed to the clipping—"she doesn't sound like the same zombie that wrote letters to Linnet this past year. I'm having those checked, incidentally by a handwriting expert; the early against the late ones."

"Why?" Percy raised his eyebrows a trifle.

"In case someone else wrote the later set. When I see, though, that Miss Everest is giving out interviews, like this one—you know the girl, I suppose?"

"Of course I know her."

"Linnet Emries, too, saw the photos of her . . . I don't know why I keep thinking there's some sleight-of-hand—"

"I certainly don't see how! But the handwriting should tell. Let me know the results?" Percy cocked his heavy head to one side—apparently a characteristic pose. "And I hope, Jack, that you're not telling this Emries girl any more than you have to, either."

"As little as possible. But you don't get something for nothing."

"I know." He said it feelingly, as though the fact were only too well borne out by his personal experience.

"And now—" Percy took from the table beside him a file folder. Opened it. "The moment you left here, the day before yeserday, I started rooting through my correspondence with Jamie. And was appalled. How *stupid* I've been! He's been trying to tell me something, and it didn't get through to me at all!"

He thumbed through a mass of pages closely written in a small, pointed script. "They censor his mail; that would be obvious. So he's tried to frame messages that look as if they're about his work." Dwight Percy drew out a page and read from it.

" ' "The Cask of Amontillado" sent a chill to the marrow of your bones, didn't it, when you were a boy? Imagine it updated. You think such a story incredible today? Not like me, you say? Think again, and you will see how apt it is. A lifetime of endeavor has brought me to a point that Poe, the master storyteller, could so easily have foreseen. To quote from—you won't believe the source—Snoopy, I have "written myself into a corner." And Poe seems the only way out.' "

He handed the page across. "My God! It doesn't sound like him, you see. And he's never—in his letters—had hidden meanings; goodness, Jamie comes right out and says what he means. Well, I thought he was cracking up; burden of overwork or something. I never dreamed . . . Until your visit, with your little bombshell."

He handed Jack another page. "More Poe. 'The Tell-Tale Heart' . . ."

"Could I have copies of these?"

"I'll have them Xeroxed for you." He glanced at his watch. "Mrs. Groves—that's my housekeeper, whom you met—is expecting you to stay to lunch by the way. And so am I. Otherwise we'll never finish."

Frowning, Percy rubbed the end of his nose. "You're being very careful with notes, tapes, and so forth, that you've made in connection with this business? They're not just lying around where someone could get at them? If the wrong person should—"

"Don't worry. Everything on 'Project Everest' is securely locked away. No one at the office, even, can lay hands on it."

"Good. Good. Because if there were any kind of newspaper scoop on this thing, Jamie's life could be endangered."

In the hall a large asthmatic clock chimed three-quarters of the hour—a quarter to one. Percy heaved himself out of his chair and led the way into the dining room. He was perfectly able to get around, he explained; he was just taking things easy for a while yet. "As of next week, the doctor's even letting me try a few hours at the office!"

The large and elegant dining room was traditional, with white wainscotting, quite a collection of paintings, and a magnificent beige and blue Oriental rug occupying most of the polished floor. A pair of built-in corner cupboards was crammed with fine china, and there were two antique sideboards which Jack could guess held more.

Percy sat at the head of the table, Jack near him at his right.

"I pretty much rattle around in here," he remarked as they started on the chowder Mrs. Groves had brought them. "Used to entertain a great deal, even after my wife and I were divorced. Not the last few years, though. Got tired of all that. You have a family, do you?"

It was suddenly painful even to mention her. "My wife and I are divorced. She lives in Boston."

"Ah. Yes, too bad, these things. My wife took the children, too, of course. They grew up away from me. Married, now, I never see them."

Their common private woes seemed to Jack to form a sort of bond between them. Though it was much worse, he was sure, to be left all alone in a big pile of a house like this with a lot of furniture and china and silver that belonged to another life than to be snugly established in a bachelor apartment in the city.

"Yes, that's a Courbet," said his host as Jack studied the painting directly opposite him on the wall—a still life, not to his taste, but beautifully done, of a dead rabbit lying on a kitchen table in the company of a crock, an onion, and a bottle of wine. Every hair of the rabbit looked real. "That's if you're interested in art. Not everyone is, certainly. Even Jamie—loves good literature, and music, and scenery, but never has cared one way or another about a

79

good painting. Says he'd rather have a beautiful view out the window." He looked around him, at the oils that hung there.

"That's a Monet, and that one, an obscure Dutch painter—"

Mrs. Groves took away the soup plates and brought in the main course—broiled sea bass, served with a salad and homemade rolls.

There were some things you didn't get with a bachelor apartment . . .

During most of the meal his host talked of Everest. Jack had wanted background material; well, here it was.

"When Jamie came to us with his first book, he was only a boy. Nineteen. He had this tremendous talent I felt mustn't be wasted in easy success, because he was capable of so much. I became something like a father to him, I suppose. He and his own father were never close—how could they be? I don't suppose Will White ever read a book in his life, other than a high-school textbook. He sent his son to college to learn business administration, believe it or not! No wonder Jamie dropped out; after we accepted his book, he never went back."

One recollection followed another. It became clear that Everest and Percy weren't merely author and editor; they were great friends.

"Happens like that sometimes," Percy murmured. "A really rewarding relationship, both ways."

He had often gone down to the ranch at Hardy, in past years, or to Everest's Mexican place. Until his heart attack.

"Extraordinary country—Baja. You have the desert and the sea, side by side. Harsh but beautiful. Seven- or eight-hundred-mile long peninsula, just sticking down into the Pacific from the California coast. Rugged mountain terrain, most of it still quite inaccessible—though all that'll change when they finish the highway I understand they're putting in to link up the northern and southern halves of the territory. Have a plethora of tourists then, no doubt. But as of now you can only reach the southern part by plane or boat—might as well be an island!"

"I thought there was some kind of highway." Vern, he remembered, had mentioned it. "From the north on down—"

"Oh, yes. A modern highway, a sort of loop, from La Paz on south. But as I say, much of the territory is still primitive, can't be reached except, I suppose, by burro. Lots of places the roads just peter out in the desert, and unless you have a native handy to tell you where you are, you haven't a hope of finding your way—even wth a four-wheel-drive vehicle and your own gas and water. People have just disappeared, in the interior—lost; their water supply ran out; and they died.

"Well, Jamie flies down there, naturally. Has his own plane. In fact Cabo San Lucas has become quite a Mecca for the air-age famous who want to get away from it all. Some plush resorts there; have their own landing strips. Some of the movie people who own planes go down. We had one of them at Jamie's place that last time—Erin Bruce. Helene invited him. Don't know where they find young men who look like that—he doesn't even look real, you know. No dumb bunny, though. I was surprised to find that he's an excellent photographer. Took some fine shots of the mountains and the cactus, and some that Jamie liked very much, of the fish he caught."

"Oh, is that who took the pictures. I saw them at Hardy. Everest's got them displayed on a wall by his studio."

Gently, Percy smiled. "I told you. A painting he doesn't care for—but a snapshot of a fish? By all means!"

After lunch they settled again in the big, comfortable library. Dwight stared thoughtfully at his guest.

"Your article, of course, must be one that will pass muster both with Jamie and with whoever's in charge, down at Hardy. What kind of start have you made? Got an outline?"

"No, but I can whip one up in five minutes."

"Really? And how about the article itself?"

"I'm used to working under pressure. A news reporter isn't like one of your quality authors, with seven drafts. My stuff I've got to get *down,* right now. I do what I can to try to pull the right phrase out of the air when I need it but—" Actually he was short-changing his profession, with what he'd said; he qualified for his job because he could do with lightning speed what others might sweat over for hours.

Percy was looking pleased. "And you've enough material to put together a satisfactory piece?"

Jack smiled at him. "With what you told me at lunch, yes."

"Well. The sooner the better, with the article, Jack. Don't you think? It's your passport in to see Jamie again, isn't that so?"

"That's what I'm counting on."

"Giving him, we shall hope, a chance somehow to slip you the information on what must be done. So that we can act."

"Yes."

"When will you be ready? To go back down to Hardy?"

"A day or two."

"Good."

"Could I have something like a written okay from you on this project? It might help get me past that famous gate."

"Why don't I call Reg Curtiss right now? Tell him I feel this thing is important? He'll have to go along with us then."

"Fine!" Jack grinned.

"Pass me the phone, will you?" And as Jack did, he shooed him away. "There's an extension in the next room. Go listen on that."

The first door on the right, down the hall, stood ajar. Jack pushed it open and went in. Though it looked more than anything else like a room in an art gallery, it was obviously a bedroom, the one Dwight was using, because books and a couple of manuscripts overflowed the night table by the bed. The phone was on the floor—no room for it anywhere else. He picked it up and set it on the bed; lifted the handset to his ear. Dwight was still dialing the call.

The paintings in here were good ones—the bullfight scene over the mantel looked like a Goya. And the one over Dwight's bed, surely, was an El Greco? A portrait of some church dignitary, in a robe of purplish, other-worldly red.

"Reg? Dwight Percy. How's our author?"

"Fine. Working. How's yourself?"

"Okay, Reg. Thanks. I'm going to be well enough one of these days to come down there—"

"Great, Dwight! I didn't know you were that much better."

"Listen—you remember this writer, Jack Seavering, from *Perspective* magazine? He was down there for an interview—"

"Sure. I remember him."

"He's written an article about Jamie's life and work. Jamie gave him the green light on it while he was there, but wanted to see it before it goes to press, to okay it? Seavering's got it done now, wants to bring it down. Can Jamie come to the phone and get this firmed up?"

A laugh at the other end. *"You* know how hard it is to get the boss to a telephone! He's working. Won't talk to anybody. But listen, does this fellow have to come down here? Why can't he mail the—"

"No. As Jamie's editor, *I* say it's essential that Mr. Seavering come in person. After all, he could print this thing the way it is, and the hell with whether Jamie or his publisher likes it, you know? Better to let Jamie handle it himself and see that the *wrong* thing doesn't get in print."

"I get your point. Matter of fact, I remember Jamie telling the fellow he wanted to see it. So, okay, tell him to come ahead."

"When?"

"'Anytime. Anytime at all."

"Fine. I expect he'll be there in a couple of days. Tell your boss I called and you wouldn't let me talk to him."

"Sure will." Reg Curtiss hung up.

Jack found Dwight Percy waiting for him with a funny little grin. "Thought I'd just shake him up a little with that suggestion about my coming down soon. Couldn't tell whether it bothered him or not."

"Will you be able to travel soon?"

"Not if I know what's good for me, according to the doctor." He looked thoughtful. "You know you may be taking some kind of huge risk in going down there to talk to Jamie again . . ."

"Sticking my head in the lion's mouth?"

"Yes."

"I don't see what else I can do. And I'll probably come away knowing nothing more than I did the first time . . . What *is* the hold they have over him?"

Dwight Percy was studying him. "Do me a favor," he said quietly. "Be very careful?"

"Oh, I will." It was good to have Percy on his side, at last.

"Wish I could go with you. This heart surgery I had went fine, you know. I'm feeling better every day. But any kind of trip—"

"Wrong thing, anyway, for you to come. If they've counted on your being out of the picture, your suddenly appearing in Hardy could be a good way to get yourself killed."

Percy gave him an odd look. "We're both so sure, aren't we—that this is a lethal matter. That Jamie is in the hands of—unscrupulous enemies."

" 'The Cask of Amontillado'?"

Jack saw the grey shadow that passed over the face of Jamie Everest's editor.

# PART TWO

# 5

AS FAR AS THE EYE COULD SEE, THERE WAS NO one. And there was nothing. Only the endless rolling land, with its covering of tough grass. Not even any cattle on this side of the range.

She wondered how far she had ridden. And where the boundary lay, between the Carrington ranch and the Everest ranch. She'd come on a fool's errand, of course. Helene no doubt still rode every morning, as she always had. But not in this direction, nor at any great distance from the house, either. If actually, as had begun to seem possible, she was a virtual prisoner, she was no doubt restricted to some area where an eye could be kept on her. But, well—it was curiosity as much as anything that had brought Sue Ann out here.

The ground became rocky and uneven, and she slowed her horse to a walk. A rabbit, starting from some scrub just ahead, zigzagged in long leaps to a new hiding place.

It was early, not yet eight. The morning sun shone at her back. Later she would be glad of the protection of her broad-brimmed hat.

And could it just be, she wondered, because of Jack Seavering that she was doing this? For some reason, whatever she would learn on this expedition into dangerous territory seemed twice as interesting, in prospect, when she imagined herself telling him about it.

He'd ordered her not to go—not even to drop by for a neighboring visit. Worried about her. How nice . . . Well, it had been the failure of her first attempt to see Helene that had triggered this one. Walter had always said she was stubborn, and she was.

From the next rise she could see the wire fence that marked the property line, running north-south across the land. She rode on toward it, down an arroyo that cut between the hills.

She took her horse right up to the barbed wire, showed him the ground, and patted his neck. Then she rode off a little way, turned Diamond, and put him at the fence.

They were over. And on Everest's land.

It was some little time later, as she tried to make her way by dead reckoning toward the ranch buildings, that she heard the sound of a motor, beyond a curve of land to her left. She turned the other way.

But she had gone scarcely a hundred yards when the motor noise became abruptly louder, and she looked over her shoulder to see a Land Rover coming down the slope behind her.

She reined in.

The vehicle came alongside, and its driver got out. He wore jeans, and a shirt that hadn't been ironed. The creased face under his ten-gallon hat had been browned by fifty years of sun.

"Just what d'yu think you're doin', miss?"

"Good mornin'." Her heart beat uncomfortably fast. Yet what could he possibly do, beyond running her off?

"What you doin' here? You're trespassin', you know."

"No, I *don't* know. I'm Mrs. Carrington and I've a perfect right to be here."

"Oh. Mrs. Carrington." He took off his hat and scratched his scalp. "Well, this ain't your land, this here, and I'll bet you know it ain't." He settled the hat back onto his rather small head. "Your property's the other side that fence you don't seem to've noticed."

"Well, I'm a friend of Mr. Everest's," she lashed out, her voice high with indignation, covering the fright, "and you've no business—"

The man reached out and took hold of the bridle. "Listen. You're goin' back, just like you come. You're gettin' off this here property. You want to see Mr. Everest, you come through the front gate. Now *git!*" He pulled, with

88

a vicious jerk, on the near rein, causing the startled Diamond to half rear, and then he hit him a resounding thwack on the rump. Horse and rider went flying over the ground, back in the direction from which they had come.

Sue Ann felt weak from anger. That some of the weakness might be from relief she would never have admitted —for now that the encounter was over, it was obvious there could have been no actual danger, none whatever, in her riding over to Jamie's. Or trying to.

Her horse dropped to a trot, and Sue Ann glanced over her shoulder. With annoyance she saw that the Land Rover was following her. Damn the man!

But at least she had proved something—and that was the impossibility of getting in to see Jamie or Helene.

The character in the Land Rover trailed her all the way to the boundary line. She jumped the fence again, and rode on, feeling very let down. She had really hoped for some adventure; hoped even more to outwit the guards in the security system and learn something that would either prove or disprove Jack Seavering's theory that things were amiss.

And she was sorry, really, not to have had a chance to see Helene. It was so everlastingly lonely out here at the ranch. Her eyes scanned the horizon. To the right and to the left. Nothing in sight. No buildings, no people. There were just the grass and the things that lived in it—rabbits, snakes, birds. On a distant slope a small herd of Walter's Brahmins grazing.

She looked around as she became aware of the far-off sound of a plane. Jamie's plane—she recognized it. She wondered if it was coming in or had just taken off.

It was a few moments later that she felt the first pang of alarm. The plane was unmistakably coming in her direction; flying low.

Surely they didn't think it necessary to watch her clear to her own stables to make certain she didn't trespass again?

The plane flew over her, and she scowled into the sun as she saw it bank and turn, heading straight back at her.

It would have to be Reg Curtiss. And then it occurred

to her that Jamie might be aboard, he might be waving to her in greeting. She prepared to wave back.

But as the small red and white airplane drew near and its body tilted downward, she was seized with a premonition of disaster. This was no friendly greeting—the pilot was going to buzz her. Diamond would be scared out of his wits, the horse would go mad!

She must dismount. But before she could translate the knowledge to action, the plane was upon them. Sue Ann thought for a moment it was going to crash into them— it seemed only feet away. In the same moment Diamond neighed in terror, reared, and as his front hoofs touched the ground again, bolted.

Sue Ann hung on. No one could have stopped the bay gelding, not till he had run out his fright. But the animal could break a leg on this terrain.

She wondered where the plane was. Turning, to make another run? And just then Diamond stepped in a hole and went down.

He came low over the area where he'd seen them last. First he saw the horse—riderless, standing head down. He had to sweep three times over the stony slope before he found her. She lay crumpled in a quite impossible position.

He flew back to check, around noon, and again had trouble finding her—especially since the horse was gone. Spotted her, finally, still in the same position. He was quite sure by then that she was dead.

That afternoon (Friday again? Already?) Jack had a call from the handwriting expert.

"They're all the same writing. I can show you if you like."

So he went over to the offices of the outfit whose business was the certifying of questioned documents, and their Miss Smithe explained to him how she had arrived at her conclusions.

Back at his desk again, he called Percy and told him.

"Um," said the gruff voice in his ear. "I didn't expect anything else. Did you?"

"No. But at least now I can be sure the Miss Everest I met is the right one, they haven't trotted out some substitute. I did wonder, from what Mrs. Emries told me—and from the letters themselves."

"Yes, strange. Jack, you'll reassure Mrs. Emries, I trust —we certainly don't want her airing any dangerous speculations, even this far from Texas, before you've found out what's going on."

"I quite agree!"

"When are you leaving for Hardy?"

"Tomorrow. My article's three-quarters done. Finish it tonight."

"Good. I haven't had an easy moment since this—since you first came to me, you know. If anything happens to Jamie . . ."

"I know."

"Jack—"

"Yes?"

"Take care, now . . . I still wish I were going along . . ." A thread of wistfulness in the last words.

"Soon enough, Dwight. You'll make it down there before long, don't worry. And I'll keep you posted on what happens."

Next he called Linna Emries—Linna seemed to be what she was called—and asked if he could drop by to return her letters.

And he told Flo to get him on a plane to Texas.

"You could have mailed them." She was wearing a cream-colored dress that set off her blue eyes and dark hair.

"Yes, I suppose I could." He folded his raincoat and laid it on the white cushion seat of a chrome chair, one of those modernistic, thirties-revival pieces of furniture.

"Tell me what you've decided. Any clues to—anything?" He hadn't mentioned to her he'd suspected the later letters of being forgeries. Now he explained. And told her that they weren't.

"Forgeries?" Frowning, she looked down at the packet with two rubber bands securing it. He'd placed it on the lamp table by the couch. "Why would you think they were forged?"

"It seemed to be a possibility. I was wrong."

She walked away from him, to the window, and looked down into the dark evening street. "I don't know what to think of this game you're playing. With Everest? With me?" She turned to face him accusingly. "What are you after? And are you even on his side!"

"I'm on his side; I can tell you that much."

"Oh, sure!" Anger made her voice a little unsteady. "All this talk about Everest, but you've just been pumping me. You don't tell me anything you know! You know enough to suspect someone of forgery, and you won't even tell me why!"

"I don't know anything. I'm only trying to eliminate some of the possibilities."

"But you're looking for something criminal? You think there's some kind of a plot?"

"That's one of the possibilities I haven't eliminated as yet."

She stood quite still, looking at nothing. "Yes," she said at last.

"What do you mean, 'yes'?"

"Everything would be explained . . . Everything." (What did "everything" include, he wondered. Surely more than Helene's letters, from the way she'd said it.) "Jamie is frighteningly rich, of course; it would be quite worth someone's while. And he has put himself out of range of the protection of the law—hasn't he!"

"That's right."

"With Walter dead . . ." The lightning progression of her thought outstripped its utterance, and she stopped.

"That's it, isn't it?" She stepped close to him, the better to compel a straight answer from him with those extraordinary blues eyes. He could feel the excitement in her, like an electric current.

"Isn't . . .? I don't know what you're trying to say," he countered, hanging onto caution.

"It's a conspiracy to control Jamie's fortune—and to keep him there, writing and writing and making more money. Isn't that what you've been getting at?" And when he didn't answer at once, she gripped him by the sleeve. "Isn't it?"

"The thought has crossed my mind." Well, she'd figured it out for herself; he hadn't told her. He shouldn't, he guessed, have introduced forgery into the conversation.

"Supposing you're right," he said. As she let go of his arm, he quashed a sudden unexplainable impulse to reach for her. "How do you explain the fact that these conspirators allowed a bunch of newsmen to interview Everest? Taking quite a risk, weren't they?"

"Were they? With Jamie and Helene serving as hostage for each other? I'd think the interview would be the best insurance in the world for any such conspiracy. For its safe continuance."

"You're only guessing, you know—about there being any kind of plot." The same thing Vern Fix had so infuriatingly said to *him;* and his F.B.I. friend, Ken.

"I'm guessing, and you had a hunch. That makes two of us." She seated herself on the wide, white-painted sill of the window. "How well does my theory match yours?"

"Pretty close," he said with regret, aware that Dwight would not approve of his admitting it. Too late now to do anything else.

"They were both guarded every minute, when you were there?"

"That's right. And as far as talking privately to either of them—well, a guard was at all times within earshot of Everest, listening to every word he said. His sister had very little contact with any of us. She was kept busy attending to the serving of lunch, and hovering, I would say, over Everest, seeing that he was all right, and personally bringing him his plate. I succeeded in talking to her for a few minutes, but she seemed nervous and distracted, and then she left me quite suddenly in the middle of a sentence, with no explanation."

"That's not like her. She's quite outgoing and enthusi-

93

astic. I'm sure she would have been delighted by the chance to talk on and on to any one of you—about New York, or your work, or anything at all."

"She could have been warned, I suppose, not to talk to us." He tried to remember whether any of the staff had lingered near her, with an ear to the conversation. Shrunken Head? Damn, he couldn't recall.

"There was no chance, either," he added, "for one of them to slip a note to any of our group. The attempt would have been seen." Still, he did not tell her of the silent, dusty plea for help.

"You do believe it," she said. "You really do . . ." She looked up at him intently. Yet she hardly saw him, he thought—the focus of her eyes was on something far away. "What's your estimate of the physical danger they're in?"

"They'll not be harmed—for a while yet. Unless some-one—anyone—rocks the boat. And that includes you and me."

"And the police, I suppose."

"There's nothing to take to the police. There's no evidence that any crime has been committed."

A shudder passed over her, and she hugged herself as if she were cold, grasping the creamy wool of her dress with slender, tapered fingers. "Incredible, isn't it?" she said. "*If* it's true. That they've been seized, and are being held, like that!"

"He set himself up for it. I think that's one of the things he tried to tell me."

Now that they had made common cause, there was no problem of her holding back whatever she knew. But he must get it all this evening; tomorrow he would leave for Hardy.

She showed him a few more letters, the older ones, but there was nothing in them that would help. One was a letter of sympathy, written shortly before the automobile accident; Helene had just learned of Pete Emries's death.

"Did Everest also write you," Jack asked, "as she said

94

he would? Because it was at about that time, or a little after that—"

"No," she answered rather shortly. "He sent me flowers."

When they'd finished with the letters, he took her to dinner.

He knew just the right place, over on Third Avenue. A steak house, with the look of an English pub—more to his taste than the run-of-the-mill restaurants with continental cuisine that were so common in this part of town. An almost forgotten feeling, entering the place with a girl. His hand touched her side, as he followed her through the door, felt the curve of her rib cage beneath the cloth of her coat. Hell, I'm not an old man, he told himself; why am I always alone?

"I'm sure I don't have to warn you," he said when they sat at a corner table with drinks before them, "not to talk to anyone—no matter who it is—about this Everest business."

"Anyone but you?" she flashed. "Of course not. I can't imagine who I'd talk to about it, anyway. I don't see many people."

He had assumed her to be the center of a throng of devoted friends. "By choice?" he asked. "Or don't you know many people in New York?"

"Both. After my husband died, I lost track of the few couples we'd been friendly with. No common ground. And the friends I'd had when I was in art school, before my marriage, are scattered. It's easy to—well, just drop out."

"I know. I changed location, with about the same results. Used to live in Boston. Then my wife and I were divorced, several years ago, and I came down here. The only people I know are on the magazine. I see them during the day, and that's it."

"Do you have children?"

"No. Luckily, I guess. Incidentally, how did you get into the children's book field?"

"A friend of a friend liked my drawings and introduced

me to someone. I've done several. Keeps me young in heart, I suppose." But Jack thought she sounded a shade cynical.

He laughed. "I don't think you're exactly old, as it is!"

"Twenty-five." She shrugged. "And some years are a lot longer than others, you know."

Yes. The last year of his marriage had seemed, he remembered, more like ten.

"It wasn't Everest who launched you in the publishing world?"

"No."

The rest of dinner was spent on the setup at Hardy. Everything she could remember about the staff at the ranch at the time she had visited there. The daily routine of the household. The stables. The plane. The private landing field. Everest's working habits, and others. Helene's schedule. Walter Carrington—and his wife. Walter's place in the scheme of things. Art Wheelock, Everest's accountant? She hadn't met him . . .

They talked on over coffee and a brandy. "Now that you know everything I can tell you, what good will it do? There's no way, is there, no possible way, to get them out of there?"

"Who can say? It could be that the whole scheme depends on no one's knowing of it. Once the knowledge is out—but first I've got to find the joker in the deck—whatever this hold is they have on Everest."

"You haven't much more time to finish your article, have you?" She consulted her watch. "Oh, do you know it's late? Almost eleven."

He could work straight through if he had to. Nap on the plane.

He walked her home. Stood with her in the second-floor hall while she unlocked her door and flicked on the lights.

She didn't ask him in. "Good luck," she said. "Where will you be staying, down there?"

He told her.

"Will you call me, to tell me what happens? If you don't, I'll call you."

"I'll call." He knew he'd grab at any chance to keep in touch with Linna Emries.

"Good night . . ." He went fast down the stairs; he was pressed for time now, to finish the article.

# 6

IT WAS JACK SEAVERING'S THIRD SHOCK OF THE day.

The first had been the news, on the front page of the paper he had picked up in the Dallas airport, that Sue Ann Carrington was missing—somewhere on the Carrington ranch. Her mount had returned to the stable without her, the day before.

The second had been the telephone message, waiting for him when he checked into the monolithic hotel in Western Spring in mid afternoon. It had read: SORRY, CALLED TOO LATE TO REACH YOU IN NEW YORK. EVEREST GONE TO MEXICO. YOU CAN SEE HIM CABO SAN LUCAS, B.C., signed CURTISS.

He had said "Damn!" very quietly, had then made inquiries about flights to southern Baja (not the easiest place in the world to reach), and made a reservation for a flight in the evening from Midland to Tucson, and one on the plane, in the morning, to La Paz, Mexico. (Lucky; that flight was scheduled only three days a week, and Sunday was one of them.) After that he had gone to see Ira Sloper, and had learned from the editor the singular fact that when Sue Ann went off the day before, she had loaded her horse into a horse trailer and driven halfway across her ranch before unloading the animal and riding away on it.

"Horse came back on its own," Ira had told him. "It had fallen—dust on its coat. Had an injured leg."

"What direction was it she took off in?"

"West." West. Toward Everest's place, he remembered. Now the third shock. Tired and hungry—travel always

98

made him ravenous—he was crossing the hotel lobby on his way to the elevator when he noticed a girl leaning against a pillar, apparently waiting for someone. She was slender, her hair long and dark; funny, he thought, you could be hundreds of miles from home and see someone who looked so much like—then with a jolt he realized the girl *was* Linna.

He changed course.

Catching sight of him, she pushed herself away from the pillar and waited, with a casualness he thought a bit overdone.

"Oh, you're back."

"You have no business being here! None!"

She fluttered her thick lashes at him. "Well, that's my affair!"

"No, it's not; it's mine." He looked at her in exasperation. "You're going home on the next flight I can put you aboard."

"No."

"Listen. We've got to talk . . . Come on, I'll buy you a drink."

When they were settled on a black leather banquette against the mirrored wall in the hotel's bar, he sighed. "Why? Why in the world did you come?"

"Because they're my friends."

"I know that. But it just won't do. You'll foul everything up."

"Thanks."

He ordered drinks from a buxom cocktail waitress in a see-through blouse and mini-mini skirt.

"Remember, I have a perfectly good excuse for going to see Everest. It's all set." (He certainly wasn't telling her that the meeting place had been changed!) "For you to tag along—well, it doesn't fit in. It's much too great a coincidence for Helene's dear friend to just happen to arrive at the Everest place at the same time I—"

"We'd look like a posse?"

"Something like that." A hypothetical prospect, of course; since she didn't even know where Everest was.

"Much as I appreciate your intentions, and your moral

99

support, you are *not* coming along on this caper—that's what it is, you know."

They sat in not-very-companionable silence while he considered the problem of what to do with her.

"You read some newspaper or other today, I assume—"

"Yes. I know. Walter Carrington's widow is missing—and you had talked to her about the situation at Jamie's ranch."

"Exactly."

"Her horse probably stepped in a gopher hole."

"I don't think so." He told her about the horse trailer.

"So she was probably trying to reach Helene and Jamie."

"And someone intercepted her."

"You don't know they did, Jack. Any number of things might have happened to her. She may have nothing worse than a sprained ankle and is sitting out there somewhere, waiting for help."

"They'd have located her, if she's alive—if she's still out there; she'd have found some way to signal. They've searched by plane as well as on foot and on horseback. I'm convinced she's either dead or incarcerated. In any case, Linna, you can see why I won't have you taking part in this operation."

She gave him a tight, determined smile. "You have nothing to say about it."

"Well, I'll warn you—if I get the chance to lock you in your room and go without you, I will." He hated simply running out on her, leaving her stranded in Western Spring while he went on to Mexico, but he had no choice.

He was still trying to argue himself into a proper state of regret that she had come, when two men entered the bar. As they made their way among the tables to the far side of the room, Jack recognized one of them—a barrel-chested, swarthy-faced young man wearing black-rimmed glasses. He was an AP reporter, and he'd been on the Everest interview.

Jack excused himself to Linna and went over to his table. "Hi, Douglas," he said. "You covering the story on Mrs. Carrington?"

"Yes. Had you heard? They found her." And Douglas gave him the news he'd been dreading. "I just got back from the ranch."

"That's rough." Jack's voice didn't work too well. "I knew her. Met her once, that is . . ."

He went back and sat down next to Linna. Their drinks had come. "He's an AP reporter."

"And he gave you some bad news."

"They've found Sue Ann Carrington. Dead since yesterday, of a broken neck."

If he'd never gone to see her . . . she'd be alive.

"I'm sorry. You liked her, didn't you?"

"I felt as if I knew her—better than I did, really. She reminded me of someone." Like thinking of Eloise dead, thinking of her lying there all that time, her head twisted at some horrible, impossible angle.

Linna said softly, "It wasn't your fault—you mustn't think that."

"Well, I know I'm not going to have the same thing happening to you," he said harshly. Maybe the fact that Sue Ann *wasn't* just sitting out there with a sprained ankle would convince her? "You're going back to New York."

"No." At the odd resonance of her voice, he looked around at her, sitting beside him on the banquette. Her intense blue eyes could have been those of a zealot.

"Damn!" He felt real anger now. "Okay, I'll tell you." There was no other way. He just couldn't leave her here, alone, uninformed, to wander around Western Spring poking into Everest's affairs and maybe stepping into a nest of vipers.

He told her, at last, about the message scratched in the dust.

She put clenched knuckles to her lips and stared at him. "Oh."

"So you see? I haven't been merely guessing. And Everest trusts me. He's counting on me. I can't afford to have you jeopardizing our plans."

"What plans?" Her voice was a little shaky. "Have you actually made any?"

101

Well, she had him there. "So far, nothing beyond the hope of getting another secret message from Everest. Until I know what's hanging over their heads so that neither of them dared to speak up, even with a bunch of reporters gathered around—well, I can't make a move for fear of doing some fatal kind of damage."

"So you need me. For one thing, two heads are better than one. And then I know Jamie and Helene—as you don't."

"Making for an extremely dangerous situation. After all, I'm an outsider, simply working on an article, but if an old friend turns up, so very coincidentally—"

"Don't worry. You can explain me easily enough—we met as a result of your hunting up background material, and I was so helpful you took me on as a temporary assistant."

He looked at her sourly. "You always write your own references?"

She shrugged. "They probably won't let me in, anyway."

He wondered, again, just what was back of her presence here. And her refusal to be argued or frightened into giving up didn't make sense.

"You haven't told me the real reason you're in this with me—have you?" he accused her.

She just looked at him.

"Girls don't risk their lives for their female friends—or their friends' brothers."

"Don't they?"

"No. Actually, I have no reason not to believe you're in the pay of the people who are holding Everest; that you were sent to spy on me and find out what I know." It was possible—though he didn't believe it.

He watched her expression shift to one of incredulity.

"All those letters from Helene could be fakes; I found out the whole bunch were written by the same person, but was that person Helene White? All the details you've given me about the Everests—you could have been rehearsed. I don't even know you're who you say you are—

102

are you really Linnet Emries? Your picture wasn't on the jacket of the book you showed me . . ."

He thought she wasn't going to answer. Slowly the tears welled up in her eyes. God, not that old feminine trick! She turned her head and blinked them away. "You think I'm the *enemy?*"

"I don't know."

"No wonder you're a newswriter!" She ran the back of her hand under one eye, then the other, and looked slantwise at him with an expression of exasperation. "You extract the truth no matter how you have to do it!"

He hardened his heart; this was hopefully a rescue mission, not a romance—what did it matter whether she liked him or not, whether he hurt her feelings—

She didn't seem to be angry, only wounded. "I don't go around confiding the innermost details of my life to people, after all; who does? But I suppose I should have told you, since you're so vitally involved in this 'Project Everest'? as you call it . . . You see, Jamie is the love of my life."

"Yes—I wondered." Why had he pushed her to tell him? Now that he knew, he wished he didn't.

"Everything I've told you has been true; I just left out the part about Jamie and me. It happened when I visited the ranch—four years ago last Christmas. We fell terribly in love. It happened before we knew what hit us."

She seemed reluctant to go on.

"But you married someone else," he prompted her.

"Yes. Jamie sent me away. He said he was too old for me. I was only twenty-one then, and he was forty—almost twice my age.

"The year after that I married Pete Emries—though we had very little time together, he was still in the navy during most of our marriage. Pete's dead, so that part of my life is over. It seemed we hardly even got acquainted. And how I feel about Jamie—well, that's never changed."

"Thanks for telling me—at this late date. But the situation is still the same. I do not want to take you into this —this adventure, with me. And clearly, from what you

103

tell me, Everest, even more than I, if that's possible, wouldn't want you to go."

She said nothing about acquiescing to his wishes and giving up. "What time are you seeing him?"

"I haven't an appointment. But they're expecting me any time I show up." A colossal understatement—leaving out any mention of his flight later this evening to Tucson, the night he would be spending in an airport motel, the flight to La Paz tomorrow, and the further trip on to Cabo San Lucas at the southernmost tip of the Baja peninsula.

But they *were* expecting him.

He had waked in the morning in Tucson, not with the thought of Eloise—as happened so many mornings—but with a delayed-action jolt. Ah, yes. It was like a new disappointment handed out fresh today. Linna. She was committed to Jamie Everest, had been all along. And he should have known it. A man who could charm the birds out of the trees—

It was after he had thought of Linna that he remembered about Sue Ann. And was sorry she was dead . . . Why hadn't he thought first of her? Such a terrible thing, her being killed like that; alone, out in those bleak hills.

He was relieved when the Airwest flight left Tucson without Linna's somehow magically appearing. Though he didn't know how she could possibly have gotten there. Unless she truly were a spy, and therefore watching his every move, she'd have had no way of knowing until this morning that he was gone.

They had dined together and he had said good night to her in the elevator. He had then checked out—leaving a note at the desk to be given to her this morning—and had driven to the airport.

*Dear Linna*, his note had read,

*I told you I'd lock you in your room if I could. Failing that, I've left wouthout you anyhow.*

*Everest is not at the ranch. Please believe me, this is not some kind of trick. I had a message from Reg*

*Curtiss and I am to meet them where they are now.*
*Sorry, this does not include you.*

*Wait for me, I'll be in touch. Stay out of trouble,*
*and I mean this. Don't do anything.*

*Jack*

Not that he had much hope of her doing as he asked. But at least he imagined there wasn't much harm she could come to when Everest and his guards were no longer in Texas.

And then he wondered. Had Helene stayed behind at the ranch . . .? If she had, and if Linna went questing about . . .?

But that didn't bear thinking of.

One good thing, he reflected, as the *No Smoking* sign in the airplane was turned off—Vern Fix was in Cabo San Lucas, so there would be two heads instead of one to pit against the enemy.

He had called Tom Krug from Tucson, before checking out—got him at home, it was Sunday. "Vern must be there by now, isn't he?" he'd asked.

"Got to be. He intended to take the car ferry this past week, across to La Paz, and he planned to stay ten days at least. Said he'd telephone me from Mazatlán when he gets back, and he hasn't yet."

"Do you know where he's staying?"

"No, but it's not that big a place, is it?"

It undoubtedly wasn't.

He'd phoned Dwight, also, and tried to reassure him about how things were going—though the news of Sue Ann's death had clearly upset him badly. He'd made the same connection Jack had, it would seem, between the "accident" and the combine's precipitous flight from the country.

"I'm afraid for Jamie now, after this . . . Aren't you?" came the question gravely over the phone.

"No more than before." But he lied, not wanting to add his worry to that of a man in such uncertain health. "The fact that they've asked me to come on down would indicate they're still conducting business as usual."

"But, Jack—" The voice was urgent. "If they thought Sue Ann Carrington knew something, they could easily figure she must have learned it from you. Go to Mexico now, and you may only be walking into a trap!"

He knew that, of course.

# 7

THE HOTEL CABO SAN LUCAS CLUNG LIKE LICHEN
to the rocks above the Pacific. The ocean beyond had
grown dark, in the last light of day, and the mountains
up and down the coast glowed lavender and purple as
Jack walked along the palm-fringed drive to the main
building.

He passed through the vine-covered entrance and into
the spacious open-sided lobby that overlooked the swimming pool, with its waterfall, and beyond that the hotel's
private harbor, where he'd earlier noticed a long sleek
yacht riding at anchor.

"Where can I telephone?" he inquired of the clerk in
the little office—the same man who had assured him
when he'd registered that no one named Vernon Fix was
staying here, or had been.

"But we have no telephone," the lanky Mexican quite
happily explained—in the same tone he would use to tout
the benefits of the climate or reassure a guest that indeed
the water was safe to drink. "This is a remote area, you
understand. No television, either. We do have shortwave
radio communication. If it is extremely important—"

"The man I wanted to call lives here in Cabo San Lucas.
James Everest, the writer."

"Oh, yes. Señor Everest. I'm afraid you will have to go
to his house to speak with him. There is no other way."

"You know where he lives?"

The young man nodded. "Everyone knows the house
he lives in. It is a few miles along the coast, where there
is a small private cove for his boat, and he has made a
landing strip for his plane."

"I see. Well, thank you." He headed back to his room. He would descend on them with no notice. But tomorrow. Too late, today; he'd be unable to see the layout of the place in the darkness.

He was glad he'd decided to take a car and driver from La Paz, instead of waiting all afternoon for the air taxi. A long drive—eighty or so rugged miles—down here to the very bottom of the peninsula, but the car was going to come in handy.

His driver was still parked in front of the long, tile-roofed building where Jack had been given a room. He stopped by the blue Chevy to speak to him. "Miguel, I want you to do something for me—if you will."

"Yes, señor." He could not have found a more willing driver—cheerful, eager to please, and though the boy couldn't have been more than eighteen, he was a fountain of information; on the way down it had been impossible to shut him off.

"Will you go into the town and see if you can locate a friend of mine who's staying somewhere in the area? Some hotel or motel."

"The Hacienda, perhaps."

"Well, try there. His name is Vernon Fix. F-i-x. If you find him, bring him back with you. Okay?"

"Okay." Miguel's white teeth showed in his thin face, and he at once started the engine, revving it up as if it were an airplane, and took off along the dusty drive that wound, between young palm trees, out of the compound of long, low buildings that comprised the hotel. Jack turned to the nearest of these, and two at a time took the outdoor stair to the second-floor gallery which was the way to his room.

It had been Miguel who recommended this hotel. "Famous all over the world. A place for rich people." Jack had interpreted that as local Baja pride and assumed that at least the beds would be comfortable. But already he had discovered that Miguel knew whereof he spoke. Three private planes had arrived in the last half hour, almost knocking tiles from the roof as they came in over the hotel to settle on the landing strip behind it. Now he sat in the cocktail lounge—a terrace gouged into the rocks above the beach—watching the expensive people.

It was their manner, more than anything, that identified them as the very rich—that utter ease of bearing which was unmistakable. (He knew it from before; his wife's friends had it.) The cut of their clothes, too—though he counted four men who went barefoot without looking sartorially remiss. Here informality was chic.

Jack glanced again at the portly white-haired man with the brown circles under his eyes; the face was familiar. He was holding court, the center of attention for the little group at his table, which included several young men and an exaggeratedly curvaceous blonde wearing a diamond ring Elizabeth Taylor would surely have thought quite decent. Oh, yes—he recognized him now; the man was Martin Case, one of the last of the great old-time Hollywood directors, whose memoirs had been a recent and sensational best seller.

He wondered what Linna would be doing. Where was she, even? And as he looked past Case, at the steps built against the stone wall opposite, he saw her coming slowly down them.

She wore a long pink and navy dress with a fringed shawl, and she seemed different because her hair was up. She was looking at the view—the dark expanse of water and the curve of shore beyond the parapet at his back. Then she caught sight of him.

He waited—endlessly, it seemed—as she made her way toward him. The prospect of his solitary evening was suddenly transformed.

"I'm glad to see you." He pulled out the other chair at his table for two. Nothing he could do about it, she was here.

"Now that's a little hard to believe."

"When I can't see you I worry about you." He resumed his seat. "A tequila sour for the young lady," he told the waiter.

"How do you know that's what I wanted?" she said frostily.

"When in Rome . . . I'm sure you'll like it. How did you get here?"

"On my broom." Not even a tinge of amusement in her, though.

"I didn't want to walk out on you like that—"

"Then why did you?"

"We've been over that. Look—how did you know where he'd gone?"

"I guessed. Partly. After I got your note I phoned the ranch. Naturally they wouldn't tell me anything—only that Miss Everest was away, and Mr. Everest also. So I tried Arthur Wheelock—his accountant? *Anything* rather than just sit and wait in the hotel! I thought he might know where they'd gone. He wasn't there. His wife said he'd left yesterday to go fishing in Mexico."

"Oh. Well, if I ever had any doubt that he's in this thing—"

"That's right. You said you didn't trust him . . ."

"No." Why he hadn't, he wasn't sure. That wide-open, genial countenance, with almost the hint of naiveness or stupidity? It was that, he guessed: no one with even a touch of stupidity would be trusted with the handling of millions of dollars. So his manner was a lie.

"I don't like it, Linna. The whole pack are running from something."

"An arrest for murder? Sue Ann Carrington's death?"

He grimaced. "So you're finally seeing it my way."

"I always did. But surely you wouldn't expect me to have agreed with you about the danger. You mightn't have let me come." She gazed demurely into her drink. "I had to fly via Los Angeles, by the way. Then the air taxi from La Paz." She was glancing around at the people, as he had, and he saw her do a double take.

"Why does that man look so familiar?" She was not looking at Case, the movie director, but at an incredibly handsome blond giant leaning against the bar. His feet were bare, and he wore neatly pressed bluejeans and a patchwork shirt.

"Oh. Well, movie stars often don't look quite the same off-screen—or so I've been told."

"You're right—that's Erin Bruce, isn't it!" With what seemed to be a real effort, she tore her gaze from this vision of male pulchritude. "He knows Jamie and Helene."

"Yes, Dwight mentioned him. Though he didn't say how—"

"When he starred in the remake of *The Kingdom Lost,* he went to Texas to talk over the role of Lons Fell with Jamie. Also, Jamie had done the screenplay for them that time, and the director wanted him to come on location with them while they were shooting. He wouldn't, of course. In the end he sent Helene as sort of liaison."

"I know he's visited Everest's hacienda down here. Took some pictures; Everest's got them framed, on a wall at Hardy." And he wondered what luck Miguel was having in locating Vern. He stood up. "I'll be right back," he said, and crossed the red tiled floor to the bar.

"Mr. Bruce—"

"Yes?" The blond giant turned his head, but with no glimmer of interest in his deep-set blue eyes; his world was undoubtedly filled to overflowing with strangers plucking at his sleeve.

"My name's Seavering. We have mutual friends—the Everests."

Now the interest was there, but guarded. "You know Helene and Jamie?"

"I'm working on an article on Everest, for *Perspective.*"

A chill came at once over the handsome face. "I don't talk to reporters and such when I'm on vacation—Mr. Seavering." His tone was overly polite. He started to turn away.

"I'm not looking for any quotes from you. My article's finished. I wanted to offer you a non-professional invitation to have a drink with us. The girl I'm with is an old friend of Helene White's."

Erin Bruce knew which girl was meant, because he picked up his beer and prowled over to their table. "And you are—?" he said, looking down at her, not waiting for Jack's introduction.

"Linnet Emries."

111

"Linna? You're the chick from St. Louie she used to talk about." He ducked his head in acknowledgment, padded around her chair, and sat on the low parapet; set down his beer on the table. "How *is* Helene?"

"I was going to ask you. I haven't seen her in several years."

"Nor have I. Last time was right after we made *The Kingdom*. She'd told me how great the fishing was down here, so I came on down and stayed with them. Must have been over two years ago."

"What's Everest's place like?" Jack asked. "This one, I mean."

"You haven't been there?"

"No. Just got here this afternoon."

"Oh, well, it's a charming house."

"Fortified?"

Erin Bruce smiled. His teeth were beautiful and white, and he had almost as many of them as Charlton Heston. "Thoroughly," he said.

Erin Bruce had not eaten dinner with them; he had promised to dine with Martin Case and his coterie. So Jack and Linna had cebiche and rare steak and fruit pudding together in the big cathedral-ceilinged dining room. When they finished, Jack found Miguel waiting to report.

"Your friend Señor Feex did not stay in the town. Not at the Hacienda. Not at Bajo Colorado, either."

"Well, I know he's here someplace. Where else is there?"

"The only place left is on the other side of the town, far out. A fishing camp."

"Good. We'll try it tomorrow. You have a place to sleep, Miguel?" But he needn't have worried; Miguel had been here before and had friends in the town, with whom he would stay.

Now Jack sat with Linna on one of the steps of the long walk that zigzagged down to the beach below the hotel. Exuberant Mexican music was still being played in the bar, and at this distance the fact that one of the violinists—or possibly two—was playing somewhat off key could hardly be detected.

"Try doing without me tomorrow," she said, "and I'll go separately. Which would look very queer, you know; it might foul everything up."

"It might be quite dangerous. For us all."

"That's why I'm counting on your doing it my way."

"You don't hesitate to use duress, do you?"

"No."

He stared off at the dark shape of the mountain on the other side of the little bay where the yacht rode at anchor, and then up at the stars—so many more of them in this sky so far from the lights and pollution of the eastern seaboard. "The princess to the rescue of the prince in the tower. Rather of a switch on the old version . . ."

She was silent for a moment. Then she said, "I'm not throwing myself at him, you know. This is strictly a rescue operation. We were friends before we were anything more than that. So we're still friends."

"You don't believe that or you wouldn't be here. When it finally dawned on you that he was being kept prisoner, your very next thought was that that explained why he'd never made a move toward you after you were widowed. Isn't that so! He sent you flowers, you told me, and nothing more. And that's why you came—to see if there isn't still something going between the two of you, despite the fact you hadn't heard from him."

"I don't like people telling me what I think, or why I do things!"

"Too close to the truth?"

"It's none of your affair!"

"It's become my affair," he contradicted her. "And I'm glad, really, that you'll see him. I hope you find you've simply been cherishing a girlhood infatuation all this time. He *is* twenty years older than you. That's too big a gap."

"Nineteen years. And I don't care in the slightest what you think."

He couldn't help himself. "I wish you did," he said.

She looked around at him.

"Linna . . ." He put his arm around her shoulders and

kissed her. He wondered why she'd come to matter to him so much; all they'd done, since they'd met, was argue! He wasn't even sure he liked her.

Yet at this moment he didn't want to let her out of his sight or out of his reach, ever.

She spoke very quietly, when he let her go. "My preference is still the vintage wine."

He escorted her back to her room, across the compound from his. And stubbornly kissed her again. She clung to him, surprising him and catching him off guard, because he was fractionally too late remembering that he was only a stand-in for Everest.

"All ready for tomorrow?" he asked.

"Of course."

The scent of some flowering thing was sweet on the air. She detached herself from him, and the light by her door shone full on her face. She was afraid, he saw; that was why she'd hung onto him.

She opened the door and went in.

What was it she feared—the danger? Or coming face to face with Everest after so long?

# 8

SHE FELT FEVERISH THIS MORNING. HER LEGS were weak, her head felt hollow, and her pulse was racing. Nerves, Linna told herself.

Miguel, the driver who had brought Jack Seavering down yesterday from La Paz, picked them up at the hotel a little after ten. They turned to the right, on the road which ran along the coast.

The land was desert, with scrubby growth; silvery-looking bushes seemingly without leaves, cactus in great variety, from little spiny ones and low-growing forms with yellow flowers to the branched candlestick giants. Buzzards wheeled overhead, and mountains were blue in the distance. They passed a small settlement, and then there was only the empty country on either side of the two-lane pavement.

It was about three miles to where a rutted road left the highway, wandering between barren dirt hills toward the water. This would be Jamie's place. They turned off.

First of all they saw the small landing strip, a piece of ground to the left, leveled off. A pickup truck stood by the runway. Either the plane wasn't there now, or it was parked in some shelter out of sight. Next they rounded a low hill and there before them was the boat—quite a large craft—riding at anchor in the little bay.

They passed a native house, a thatched dwelling set in a yard neatly fenced by lengths of branches from small trees or bushes, placed vertically and fastened at the top to a rail. Beyond the house stood a larger building—a garage, apparently, semi-open, with room for several cars. The only vehicle there now was covered by a tarpaulin, and the near end of the shelter had been converted for use as a stable—two horses stared curiously at them over a barricade.

Now they came within sight, on the far side of the private harbor, of a cluster of walls and red-tiled roofs crowning a hill that dropped off precipitously into the sea. A high tower, rising above the rest of it on the seaward side, gave the place almost the look of an old Spanish monastery.

"He can certainly pick 'em!" Jack's tone was one of exasperation.

"Pick what?"

"Impregnable, isolated locations to live in."

At the base of the hill, the rutted track became a flower-bordered drive, ending in a stone-paved circle set into the hillside at the front gate.

"All laid by hand, like the Roman roads." But Linna was so bemused she scarcely heard him.

A Mexican boy was using a hose to water the palm trees that edged the stone paving. Bougainvillaea trailed over the wall by the gate, a cascade of scarlet flowers. "Broken glass. Set into the top of the wall," said the voice at her elbow as they got out. "Naturally."

She felt almost disembodied as they stood in front of the heavy, round-topped wooden door in the high white wall and Jack pulled on a length of braided many-colored fibers that rang a sweet-toned bell.

A wizened face appeared at the square of grillwork let into a panel of the door, and Jack stated his errand.

"Shrunken Head," he told her when the man had disappeared.

It was Dan Bayles who let them in. Linna had been out of his range of vision until he opened the door, because when he saw her, he was evidently taken aback. "Who's she?"

"Oh, I'm sorry. She's my research assistant. This is Dan Bayles," he added to Linna—conveniently omitting her name altogether.

Bayles hesitated. "I guess it's all right," he conceded reluctantly. And proceeded to close, bar and lock the door in the wall behind them. They stood in a little hillside garden with a path through it of long shallow steps leading up to the house. Bayles made a motion to Shrunken Head, and said, "I'm sorry but—" and while the little man frisked Jack, he himself held out a hand for Linna's bag. It was then that she first realized he was wearing a gun. It struck an odd, discordant note with his vacation attire of knitted shirt, shorts, and thong sandals.

"You're sorry, of course, but—" she said to him sweetly as he riffled through her belongings with strong, hairy hands.

"If you'll follow me." They went up the steps and entered the house through wide double doors that stood open, flanked on either side by planters filled with flowers. Bayles turned to Linna. "And your name was . . .?"

"Mrs. Emries."

They passed first through an entryway with some carved wooden cupboards, and then into a high-ceilinged room that on the right overlooked the little bay with the boat in it, and straight ahead, on the long side, gave through an arrangement of three archways onto a cloistered courtyard containing a swimming pool.

"Eli will tell Mr. Everest you're here," Bayles said.

She walked across to one of the arches and looked out at the pool, and beyond the open end of the courtyard, the ocean, sparkling below in the sunlight. There were no screens or glass, though heavy shutters were folded back against the wall: the whole of the room was open to the outdoors, while being sheltered from sun or rain by the loggia without. The loggia ran around three sides, and under it were lounges, and chairs and tables for outside living.

Dan Bayles lounged with his back to a wall, looking at nothing—ready for anything that could conceivably take place.

Jack studied the big fireplace of rough stone, the skin of a mountain lion stretched on the floor before it, the heavy X-shaped chairs with leather sling seats and leather backs, grouped around the hearth. Linna prowled restlessly the length of the room, touching things—the top of a sawbuck

117

table, a painted earthenware bowl, a lantern of Mexican tin, a chunk of obsidian. The waiting was unbearable . . . How would he look—

He came through one of the arches, walking quickly. He checked, as he passed into the room, and came to a standstill.

Before he moved forward, she already knew she shouldn't have come. He didn't want her here.

His look, his voice, were quite impersonal as he greeted her; oh, cordial—yes; charming—yes. But that they had ever lain in each other's arms, ever said those things that . . .

"How very nice to see you. I didn't know Mr. Seavering was bringing anyone with him . . ." But at once he turned his attention to Jack. "How are you? I'm so glad you have finished that article. And sorry you had to come so far to show it to me."

"No trouble. Good to see you again. As a matter of fact, I'm glad of the chance to see something of Baja. My assistant, here, too"—he nodded at Linna—"has been delighted with the trip."

She wished she could sink through the floor. To have believed all this time that he still thought of her . . . Two brief weeks—the measure, she understood now, of an infatuation meant to be forgotten.

"I didn't know she was assisting you." Jamie was looking at her questioningly. "I thought she'd just come along for the ride."

"No, she's been—"

She felt movement behind her, and the eyes of the three men told her, even before the sound of footsteps on the tile floor, that someone else had come into the room. She turned, as Helene stepped quietly up beside her.

Her friend had not been told that she was here—didn't know that the female guest whose face she hadn't seen was Linnet. And suddenly Linna realized why it was that Jamie had been so distant. Neither the guard Bayles nor the little man Eli knew she was an old personal friend; and it was a secret better kept.

"How do you do, Miss Everest," Jack said.

Surely Bayles was too far away to catch a whisper. "Helene," she said softly, "don't be surprised, don't, but—"

Too late it struck her as odd that Helene was so tall. Tall than Linna; two inches too tall. Her memory couldn't be so bad . . . There was something wrong altogether about the familiar profile—the aquiline nose, like Jamie's, the flare of the eyebrow, the distinctively curved forehead, the determined set of the chin.

The head turned, the eyes met hers, and the shock was chilling. She was face to face with a total stranger.

There was surprise in the woman's face; but then, there would have been in Helene's, no doubt. A moment's puzzlement in the eyes that were placed too close together; then a little glow of triumph.

"Linna!" Her face lit up. Head-on, the resemblance had almost disappeared—the nose was too broad, the lips thinner, the cheekbones not the right shape. The wrong Helene smiled at her with a grotesquely different personality, and Linna felt as though trapped in a dream where identities changed without notice or reason.

Helene . . . Where was Helene?

She was caught in the woman's embrace, with an arm across her back and fingers biting into her upper arm. "Say nothing!" The words were hissed to her ear.

She caught a warning look from Jamie—a frown and an almost imperceptible shake of the head. "Quite a surprise for us both, isn't it, Helene?" he said. "I gather Jack Seavering enlisted her as a helper while doing his article."

Dan Bayles had come away from the wall, his hand resting on his gun in its holster. Linna started to open her mouth, but no sound came out, and as she pushed herself away from the ersatz Helene, Jamie turned easily toward the guard, made a small motion of one hand, and spoke, head bent, with Bayles, so low that no one else could hear him, ending with a reassuring pat on Dan's shoulder —the kind one gives to a faithful and understanding employee.

Bayles drifted off, frowning, to stand as before, shifting his gaze watchfully from one visitor to the other.

119

"I can't get over the surprise!" The close-set eyes were fixed upon Linna. Fierce and gypsy-like, Jack had said; Linna hadn't understood how he could think that of Helene. "It's so wonderful to see you." The tone was warm, but the face of the speaker was cold and appraising.

Whoever she was, she had done her homework—she knew enough about Helene's friends to recognize one.

Linna swallowed. "Yes, it's been such a long time." How strained her voice sounded; she must try to be natural. Though where was this masquerade taking them all?

"Well, now that you're here, you must stay. Mustn't she, Jamie?" (Ah, yes! She mustn't escape—not now!)

He was watching her, with the old look that used to turn her blood to water. "We'd like you to." He had hoped, hadn't he, to keep the woman in the dark as to who Linna was. But that attempt had failed.

"Well, she can't—" Jack Seavering started to say.

"Why can't I?" She had no choice. She would never be allowed to walk out of here alive with what she'd found out—the secret of their hold on Jamie, the secret that Helene was held as hostage, not here, but in some other place.

"There's no reason, surely, Mr. Seavering, now that your article's done, that you can't go on back with it and Linna stay here with Jamie and me. We haven't seen her in so long . . ."

"It's settled," said Jamie.

"What can I say?" Jack spread his hands and shrugged. "Best research girl I ever had!" He gave a little laugh, disguising a bit the bleakness of his face. "Easy come, easy go."

She wondered if he guessed the truth.

His companions were coping well—Jamie Everest bitterly noted—with the surprise of Linna's turning up. Though Art Wheelock still might have Dan's hide for letting her in. If either Art or Reg had been here, it wouldn't have happened.

Nothing short of dire emergency would have taken the two of them from the scene today—the emergency, he imagined, being the necessity of finding out what was going on back in Hardy. They'd flown to where there was a telephone.

Lucille had dragged Linna off somewhere, ostensibly to talk over the things best friends talk over; no doubt, though, to warn her about the importance of keeping her mouth shut. Dan had taken Seavering for a tour of the premises. And Eli, his black eyes sunken into his wrinkled face, watched while Jamie, seated at a table near the pool, went over the article that would appear in *Perspective*. There was to be no chance that he would write a message in invisible ink (what would he use, lemon juice?) or tape some call for help to the bottom of the table for the reporter to find.

He looked up from the page on which he was marking suggested changes. "Shouldn't you be fixing lunch?"

"Plenty time yet to cook the white-wing doves. The soup is already made." Eli rolled between his simian palms the handle of a twig broom.

Jamie shrugged. "Lucille will check this carefully anyhow, you know. For any kind of secret message. You're wasting your time." He went back to work—annoyed, because Eli frequently gave the uncomfortable impression that he could read minds. His own was so deeply concentrated on the words he was trying to conceal, in plain sight, in Seavering's article, that he feared the little man might start receiving brain waves.

He had made slight progress with his task when he heard Eli brushing at the tiles with his broom, and turned to see Seavering and his guide coming from the tower— the tall, square structure, on the right of the courtyard at the seaward end, that housed his writing room. They'd probably gone up there for the view. His guest paused, some distance off, reluctant to interrupt his work.

He pushed his chair a little back from the table. "You've done very well with your article."

"I had the best of help." Seavering came around the corner of the pool and seated himself on the other side of Jamie's shaded table beneath the loggia. Dan lowered himself to the paving at the edge of the pool, where he sat

121

staring into the space above their heads, and Eli slipped off to the kitchen to get on with the lunch for which Seavering had been invited to stay.

"Linnet Emries was a great asset, of course." Jack's tone was casual, but he watched Jamie intently, waiting for any sign or message.

"And Dwight, I see." Jamie indicated the pages under his hand. "How is he doing? I can't tell from his letters; he'd never let me know if—well, if that operation wasn't the success he'd hoped."

"He seems to be doing okay. Slow recovery from a thing like that, I'm sure. He says he can't do too much for a while yet; no trips, for instance. He looks fine—hale and hearty."

"Good. Glad to hear it. You got on well with him, I imagine."

"Oh, yes. Though not at first. He didn't seem to agree with my—my approach."

So Dwight had found it hard to swallow the story Jack Seavering had brought back from Texas. Until he'd thought about it and put a few things together? "I'm not surprised. You know how editors are about their authors —touchy, very protective; an author's a valuable property."

"We agreed eventually. He ended up seeing things entirely my way."

Jamie smiled, and gave a sigh of relief. "I thought it would work out." What a load off his mind just to know that at last Dwight had been informed of what had happened. For so many years he'd depended on Dwight, had shared with him his thoughts and feelings; Dwight had been almost like another self, though an older and wiser one. To have been cut off from him since his heart attack and subsequent state of precarious health had been a terrible hardship; and to have had his alter ego unaware, all this time, of the fate that had befallen him and Helene had been almost as miserable for him as the captivity. Though to admit as much seemed weak, to him. What was it that was so important, that he must have it from Dwight? Sympathy? Perhaps not that, exactly—wasn't it just need every human being has, to be in touch with another human being, somewhere, who understands? The all-important bond between people.

He saw Linna, with Lucille Garvan, coming up the steps from the terrace below the courtyard. At the top she stopped to examine the two stone figures which were copies of primitive Mexican ones. Touched one, curiously, with her fingers.

Almost unbelievable, having her actually here. She stirred his senses, disturbed him, fillled him with tenderness. Watching her, as she walked toward him through the strong sunshine, he felt as young again as he and Abby had once been. She came to stand beside him, and he reached out and took her hand.

"Linna . . ." Whatever anyone did now, Linna was to share his fate. Lucille had made that quite clear. If only she hadn't come . . .

What had gone wrong?

His hand was steady as he opened the door of the Chevy and got in beside Miguel, but he felt that unless he kept an iron grip on himself, his fingers would tremble visibly.

The warm shore breeze was cold on the nape of his neck.

"Back to the hotel," he grated. "Mrs. Emries is staying on here."

He cast an eye back on the wall; what could be seen of the house; the sheer rock face dropping from house to sea on the bay side; the boat; the stretch of rough, pebbly shore; studying everything, and impressing it on his memory. Because he would be back.

As they regained the highway, he hunched in the car seat, the dry wind from the desert blowing in his face, and started going again over every detail he could remember of what had taken place, in hopes of singling out some clue. A clue to anything, but most urgently the reason they had kept Linna.

She knew something. Or they were afraid she knew something . . .

They passed the cluster of dwellings by the highway; almost to the hotel. There was a flurry, to their right, as a half-dozen buzzards, disturbed at the approach of the car, took off from their perches in a pair of scrub trees.

"Miguel—" he said. "When you've dropped me at the hotel, would you go on and try to locate my friend at the fishing camp you mentioned?"

"Of course, señor. Señor Feex."

"Yes." It was imperative that he get hold of Vern with out delay.

He must also find Erin Bruce. But there he was out of luck. When he asked at the hotel office for Bruce's room number, he was told he'd gone deep-sea fishing.

Damn! "When will he be back, you think?"

"The boats come in, oh, four o'clock, four-thirty." The same young Mexican who had so happily explained to him yesterday about the no telephone.

"Thanks. Oh, and I have a message from Mrs. Emries." He relayed the request that a maid pack up her things. "She is to be a guest at Mr. Everest's. Someone from there will pick up her bags." Helene's instructions; Linna wasn't to be allowed outside the gates. "And just add her bill onto mine."

What was it, he speculated on the way to his room, that had been wrong between Linna and Helene? Superficially, their conversation with one another had seemed friendly enough, but he had sensed that it took an effort, on both sides, to keep up what he had finally decided was a totally specious cordiality. He wondered whether Helene had been opposed, always, to a match between her brother and Linna—and now that he thought of it, he could recall, both this time and the last that they had met, her being perhaps overly attentive to Everest. She hovered. Not that he suspected her of incestuous leanings; but given a possessive nature and a good case of hero-worship, she could well be hostile to any attempt to supplant her.

It had been she, certainly, who suggested that Linna stay. That needn't mean she had wanted her there, but rather, if he'd figured it right, that inviting Linna to stay

124

had been the only way of allowing one Jack Seavering safely to depart so that he might still help them.

As to Linna and Everest—if Helene had ever entertained a hope of breaking *that* up, she was doomed to bitter disappointment.

Or would be, if any of them survived long enough for it to matter. The sudden flight from the United States had boded ill, he was sure; time was running out.

His last glimpse of Linna was one he couldn't rid himself of. Linna standing with her arm touching Jamie Everest's, her fingers intertwined with his. Why did he have to have met the girl, ever!

In his room, with the bright, hot afternoon sun beating down beyond the shade of his balcony; and the ocean sloshing against the rocks below, he drew the *Perspective* article from its Manila envelope.

"You've read 'The Gold Bug,' of course?" Everest had tossed off the question during a discussion of current novels, and the allusion had gone quite over Dan Bayles's head.

Poe's story, Jack well remembered from his boyhood reading, had been about a cipher.

He leafed through the pages he had written on Everest's life and work, considering each suggestion, deletion, or addition Jamie had made. The message was here somewhere, in code.

He would have to have done it in such a way that his keepers could look at it and decide the corrected copy of the article was innocuous. Lucky that it would have been only Dan Bayles checking it—not the razor-sharp Reg Curtiss. Curtiss, Jamie had explained, had taken Arthur Wheelock, who was a guest at the hacienda, to the mainland on some errand in the plane.

Jack started, now, by noting down on a sheet of hotel stationery every change that had been inked in. "Zest" had been underlined, "many" deleted, a paragraph mark put before the word "Subsequent"—(or after the word "style."?) . . .

He didn't suppose even a copy of "The Gold Bug"

125

would help—Everest couldn't have expected him to lay hands on one here in the Mexican wilds.

He plodded on. And could make nothing of what he copied off on the sheet of paper.

He kept seeing Linna as she had looked at lunch, which they'd eaten under a pergola on the terrace below the courtyard, overlooking the wide expanse of ocean; her strangely blue eyes bluer than the water beyond; the belligerence with which he was now so familiar quite gone —replaced by a meekness that didn't suit her at all. In Everest's company she seemed to become another person —almost a docile child.

She's Everest's girl, stupid, he told himself. Forget her —except for getting her out of there.

At lunch he could have rushed Bayles, and gotten his gun. He was sure of it. He'd signaled as much to Everest, when Eli had gone back to the kitchen and they were four to one. But Jamie had shaken his head.

No. So that wasn't the way.

He must find out why not. Add period, capitalize the "u" of "under" . . .

And today would have *seemed* the most auspicious time for a try, with Curtiss and Wheelock away.

He wondered if he would ever again see her alive.

He had copied down all the changes, and now he tried to find some meaning spelled out by using the first letter of each marked word. All he got that way was "zmsurt," to start with. He tried putting the last letters of each together; that way, reading from the top, he got "tyerde" or possibly "tytrde," or, reading backwards, Chinese style, the same word came out "edreyt" or "edrtyt." No go.

He focused on the wall decoration above the desk—a pair of triangles in brown and turquoise straw, like a bas relief. Gazed out the open sliding glass door at the chain of amethyst mountains coming down to the sea, farther along the coast. Everest's place was over that way.

He sighed and came back to the problem before him.

Midway of the article, the word "held" was underlined —"some critics had *held* this to be true." Used whole, it could certainly apply to the situation. But none of the other whole words worked. His eye went again down the list of words he'd copied. And was caught by an acrostic.

> mirroring
> expended
> x-ray

mex. Short for Mexico or Mexican.

Maybe there was a different code for each word of the message.

He leaned intently over the desk.

He had decoded another word. s-o-m-e. It stared up at him from his worksheet. He had gotten it by substituting "o" for a period Jamie had put in. The word "carnal" had been changed to "sensuous"; then there had been the added period; "several" had been struck out and "most" written instead; "nirvana" was crossed out in favor of "eternity." Taking the first letters of the words Jamie had deleted gave him a word beginning with *c* and ending with *sn;* not likely. But the first letters of the words he'd put in—disregarding the period for a moment—made s—me. Since a period was really a very small circle—*some?*

*held some Mex*—the middle part of the message.

There had been a period added earlier, hadn't there? He went back; it had been the period itself that mattered, not the word before or after it. So?

"zmsurt" became "zmsort." God, no! He struck his forehead with his clenched fist and almost stabbed himself in the eye with the pen.

He must be on the right track. If a period meant the letter "o," then it was a matter of interpreting Jamie's marks in perhaps some offbeat way.

Marks. Proofreader's marks. The proofreader's mark for "insert period" was a circle with a dot in it, placed in the margin. Wasn't it? And Jamie had actually put the mark there, looking very like an "o," the first time he'd inserted a period; not the second time, because it might have been too easy for Dan to pick out the word "some."

But "zmsort?" As he look back, he saw his mistake, and a thrill coursed down his spine.

He had broken the code. The mark ¶ for paragraph. It was the mark that was important, not the words between which it was placed. "P" for "paragraph."

"zmsort" became "zmport." (This was progress?) How about "import"? He looked back at the first underlined word. "*Zest*." And broke into a beautiful smile. "Zest" was Or maybe "important"? Or—Feverishly he looked at the to be italicized. "I" for "italics." The word was "import." next two corrections on the manuscript. Jamie had inserted the word "original." Farther down, he had written in the margin, "relevant? or not?"

"o" and "r"? If in each case he used the first letter.

"importor." But was that how you spelled the word? He thought it ended with "er", not "or"—

He was so engrossed in the decoding that the knock at his door actually caused him to jump.

"Come in—" He turned and saw Miguel. Hadn't the boy gone out to the fishing camp as instructed?

"Señor—"

"Yes. He glanced at his watch and was flabbergasted to discover how much of the afternoon had passed while he worked. It was nearly four-thirty.

Miguel had a half-smile on his face. Was that good or bad, or did he always smile no matter what kind of news there was?

"Your friend, Señor Feex, was there, at the Posada de Baja, but he has gone."

"He was? He stayed at the fishing camp?"

"Yes."

"Where is he now?"

Miguel shrugged his narrow shoulders. "The manager tell me your friend only stay part of one day. He has left on Wednesday night."

But Jack had the impression that something had been withheld—some further piece of information.

All that distance Vern had come; all those marlin and

128

bonito and sailfish out there waiting for him; he'd not have left so fast except for one reason: He'd found out something. "What else did the manager tell you?"

"He said he was surprised, because Señor Feex said he come for the fishing and he did not stay to fish."

"He must not have."

Again Jack caught Miguel's hesitant glance. There was something more.

He frowned. "Something was wrong, Miguel, or he would not have left so soon. He did come here to fish. What is it you haven't told me, because you don't know whether you should mention it? It may be important."

There was a glint of humor in the brown eyes. "Your friend left in the middle of the night, with his car and all his things, without paying."

For a moment Jack was stunned. Yes, Wednesday. Five days ago. And yesterday Tom Krug had told him, when he phoned, that there'd been no word from Vern.

In the middle of the night. Without paying.

Whatever it was he'd learned here that was so important, he'd never gotten out to relay it to anyone else.

He thought of Vern the last time he'd seen him—his face wrinkling into a smile. "I'll have it mounted," he'd said. "So you'll believe me!" And he was afraid for his friend.

"Close the door, will you, please, Miguel? I've got to talk to you." Miguel closed the door and stood uncertainly in the middle of the room, undecided as to whether or not he should sit down.

"Listen, Miguel, I need your help." Walter Carrington; the houseman; Sue Ann; now Vern Fix? To hell with pussyfooting around at this stage of the game.

"First of all, my friend would not have left without paying. He was abducted. Kidnapped." And he told Miguel exactly what was going on at the Everest hacienda —as far as he knew it.

His driver's face expressed suitable shock. "I talked with the boy you saw. The boy was watering the trees, you remember. Also I talked with his sister. She brought me tacos and beans to eat."

129

"From the house?"

"Not from the big house. From her house—we passed it before we got to the house where the man lives. Rosalia said to me that it is very strange, her mother and Rosalia and her brother have worked for the man and his sister for a long time, but now they are not permitted to be in the house, and can only work outside. They say it is because there is something wrong with the señorita, she has some sickness of the mind. But does that not sound crazy, when Rosalia and her family have always cleaned and cooked and watered the trees—"

"It fits. If Mr. Everest and his sister are being kept prisoners in their own house, the servants would have to be prevented from finding out what's happened or they'd help them escape."

"Señor, that is the truth."

"Will you help, Miguel? To try to get them free?"

Miguel was frowning. "Señor Feex was trying to free them, perhaps?"

"No. He was only looking around, expecting to take some pictures of the house—he's a photographer. In fact, if he disappeared on Wednesday night, Everest and his sister weren't even here at Cabo San Lucas then, they were still in the States."

"You think they kill him, señor?"

"I don't know." What he did know was that Vern wasn't being held prisoner at Everest's house—not, that is, unless he were hidden away; bound, gagged, and locked into some little room well out of sight. Because he'd had a personal tour of the place only today. "Miguel—you mustn't tell anyone what I've told you. No one, understand?"

"Yes, I understand."

"And we must try to find out what happened to Mr. Fix." He described Vern for him. "And carrying a camera."

His driver shrugged. "Half the *norteamericano* tourists who come to Mexico also carry a camera. But if I hear that anyone has seen him—"

130

"I'd like to know what he took pictures of last Wednesday. Or at least where he was that day."

"I will find out what I can."

But first Jack sent him to check on the returning fishing boats.

He went back to decoding.

The word "sister" emerged—again the "i" coming from italicize; the word "complete" had been underlined.

Importor—sister held some Mex

The word "importor" still looked queer to him. Maybe Everest was one of those writers who can't spell. "Importer," then.

*What* importer? Was importer right?

"Zest" italicized: i

"many" deleted: m

¶ sign: p

⊙: o

~~related~~

"related" was crossed out but restored. The word for this proofreader's instruction—though not written in the margin—was "stet." "Stet" for "let it stand." s

Not *importer.*

*impostor!*


Erin Bruce, instead of relaxing under the hot shower he'd been looking forward to after a day of salt spray and sun, sat bolt upright on the couch of his suite's duplex living room—listening to the darnedest story he'd ever heard.

If it were a script for a movie, he'd turn it down on grounds of its credibility. But coming from a reliable journalist like Jack Seavering of *Perspective,* it had to be believed. Besides, in these days of piracy and extortion on an international scale—diplomats, businessmen, airliners seized either for political blackmail or for personal gain—anyone unlucky enough to be sitting on a fortune of his own was asking to be taken.

And because of Helene this outlandish conspiracy now concerned him.

"Here's the corrected article, and my worksheets." Jack

131

handed him a sheaf of typed pages and several sheets of hotel stationery covered with notes. At the bottom of one was printed, in large letters, IMPOSTOR; SISTER HELD SOME MEX VILLAGE.

"That's a writer for you! Both of them in mortal danger and he uses a semicolon!" Erin waved the sheet in the air.

"Anyhow, finally I know why he couldn't blow the whistle on his captors when all those newsmen were there. If he had, Helene White, wherever she is, would have been killed as soon as her custodians got word of it. Everest's hands have been tied all this time."

"So now all we have to do is find her, and then get the authorities to swoop down on Jamie's group here before they learn we have her safe. Shouldn't be that hard—since there's no phone system here, I don't know how they could be warned."

Jack Seavering dropped wearily into a chair. "Great. Sure. I admire your confidence. But we're not exactly in possession of a complete shooting script. 'Some Mex village'—but which? Where? Could be in Yucatán for all we know."

"I saw her last week," Erin said quietly.

"You *what?* You told me you hadn't seen her in a couple of years."

"Hadn't seen her to talk to. But last Tuesday, when I flew down from L.A.—only feasible way to get here, as you may have noticed, is in your own plane—I flew over Everest's place, just thought I'd see if they were in residence. I made a pass right over the pool, and she was there. Waved her arms like an Olympic gymnast."

"Oh, my God!" Jack Seavering's tone of anguish caused a tremor of alarm to pass like gooseflesh over Erin's skin.

"What is it?" he asked. Seavering looked as grim as death.

"A friend of mine, photographer for the magazine, name of Vern Fix. He'd seen your photographs of Baja, including Everest's giant marlin and all, and he was so enthused he came down here last week for some fishing. Well, he's disappeared. Gone."

"But what has that to do—"

"He promised he'd take some pictures of Everest's place while he was here. In case I could use them in my article."

"Oh."

"If he was hanging around with his camera and found out that Helene was there—"

"How did he disappear? From where?"

"From the fishing camp where he was staying, the other side of Cabo San Lucas. Left in the middle of the night, with his car and gear—took off without paying, which he would never have done."

"Probably realized he'd stumbled onto something dangerous, and got the hell out."

"He no doubt realized, all right, but what worries me is that he hasn't turned up elsewhere. He was to call our mutual superior at the magazine as soon as he returned to the mainland. Four days after he took French leave, my boss hadn't heard from him. That was yesterday."

"Maybe he's still on Baja somewhere."

"Dead or a prisoner, then?" I've got my Mexican driver trying to find out what he can. But go on, you haven't finished telling me about seeing Helene." Rough, thought Erin. Sounded like something might really have happened to this papparazzo type. "After you'd spotted her from the air, did you go over there?"

"Yes—the next day. It'd looked to me like the welcome mat was out; but the guard told me the Everests weren't here. I mentioned some girl waving at me, and he said, 'That's Rosalia. She works here.' "

"Rosalia. So you concluded you'd been mistaken? Who was the guard?"

"Big guy, tall, thick-set. American. I think he may have been on duty at the ranch in Texas when I was there."

"No doubt."

"And I'm sure it was Helene I saw. One of these Mexican girls might wave, a bit shyly, at a plane, but I doubt it. This semaphore reaction wouldn't have been Rosalia's style."

"Obviously, though, Helene isn't here now." He gestured at the scatter of paper, with the message, on the

133

couch. "I doubt that Everest has ever known where they were keeping her; they wouldn't have told him for fear he could manage to get word to someone. Even if he guessed that she has been here, he'd have no way of knowing where they've taken her now." He paused; narrowed his eyes in thought. "You know, I wonder if they didn't originally have her stashed in Jamie's New York apartment. The 'impostor' told me, when I met her in Texas, that last year she'd been in New York. She was speaking as Helene White; why mightn't it have been Helene, not her, who was there—"

"Sounds logical. Just move her from one of Jamie's strongholds to another? I'm sure that one's barricaded off from everything—"

"Well, that one doesn't exist anymore. Dwight Percy told me they've torn down the building."

"So they had to bring her here. But then why would they suddenly come down here with Jamie and upset their own arrangements?"

"My guess is they're here to lie low. I think they murdered a woman who was trying to pry into things. Walter Carrington's widow—"

"Murdered! What happened to her?" But the shock in his voice was not for the late Mrs. Carrington, a woman he'd never met; it was for the possible fate of Helene.

"She was thrown from her horse and killed. But I doubt that it was an accident." The reporter's face was grim. "My fault. I started her wondering what was wrong with the setup at Everest's ranch."

It was Erin, now, who got up and paced; thinking of the lively, imperious face of the girl who had turned him down. Twice. (Luckily the fan magazines had never gotten hold of *that* piece of information!)

"If only I'd insisted, the other day; pounded on the gate and made them let me in!" He hadn't believed, even then, that it was any Mexican servant girl he'd seen. He'd thought only that she'd chosen not to see him.

"They wouldn't have let you in. No way."

*Some Mexican village,* they'd told Jamie. But was that logical? Or even likely? Erin looked out at the palm trees

134

shading the stone terrace beyond his living room, realizing quite painfully that the passage of time had done nothing toward obliterating his feelings for Helene White.

"But where is she now?" he said to Jack Seavering.

# 9

JAMIE—LOCKED, SINCE HIS VISITOR'S DEPARTURE, in his writing room at the top of the tower—saw the plane return. It settled on the air-strip, and the noise of the engines dropped and died away.

So they were back. Late. It was almost sunset.

He'd done no writing this afternoon. He'd sat, in the small tower room, trying not to beieve what every line of reasoning told him they would do with Linna. Because Art was going to have to cut and run . . .

It had been on the trip down that he'd discovered how the land lay.

Only day before yesterday, was it? Seemed like an age ago already . . . The little plane had been filled with anger. Art Wheelock, up front with Reg, hunched in his seat in a cold fury; his famous geniality had somewhere met with sudden death. Lucille, in an ill humor, was needling Art; apparently no one had told her why they were abruptly going to Mexico, not even Reg—who was, besides the money, her stake in all this, though she hadn't succeeded yet in tying him down.

At El Paso, they landed to refuel. When they took off again, Jamie saw that Lucille had somewhere picked up a newspaper. It was folded neatly and stuck in the edge of her seat.

"May I?" he asked.

"May he see my newspaper?" she asked Reg in her waspy voice.

But it was Art who answered. "Of course."

The headline jumped out at him—shattering in its impact. There were so few people he knew, or had even seen in years; she was one of them.

## MRS. CARRINGTON FEARED DEAD

"I see they haven't found her," Lucille said. But no one answered.

Jamie knew well enough that whether or not they found her, she was dead. Art and Reg had known it yesterday—they had quarreled violently about something. And the stink of rats leaving a sinking ship had been inescapable. Frenzied preparations to leave; Dan and Eli dispatched ahead of the rest of them to Baja. That something catastrophic had happened was evident. As of now, it would seem that someone had killed Sue Ann. But why?

"Is that why we left?" asked Lucille. "Because Mrs. Carrington—"

"No, it's not, and shut up," Art snapped. He turned, the whites of his round eyes showing all around the blue of the iris.

"Shouldn't snarl at Lucille," Reg said. "She's not hired help, she's on a percentage."

"Then she ought to be more careful what she says. When there's *no* connection between Sue Ann Carrington falling off her horse and—well, Christ, Lucille, this is just a fishing trip." As he sometimes did with those who knew him well, Art had dropped the Texas drawl. He had come to Texas from the East, a long time ago. From New Jersey.

"But sort of impulsive, wasn't it?" Lucille persisted.

"Not as impulsive as all that," Art said. "Carefully planned. And as for Mrs. Carrington—I'm saying prayers for her safe return. She happens to be my best client—or was—excepting Jamie."

So Art had taken over the management of Sue Ann's money! Jamie hadn't known. If she was dead, her share of Walter's estate would go to Walter's children by his first marriage, and right out of Art's hands. There would be an accounting—suddenly, unexpectedly—for which Jamie was positive Art was not prepared.

137

"If she's dead, I may as well go out and slit my throat. Or," Art added with a glance at Reg, "maybe yours."

That was it, then. Reg. Reg hadn't known. And Reg had killed her—or at least had caused her death.

Reg took his attention from the controls to rake the man beside him with an angry stare. "I should of guessed. It's obvious, isn't it, that you'd have wormed you way into her confidence after Walter died."

"Probably part of the original plan, Reg," Jamie said wearily. "Art wouldn't have told you for fear you'd expect a cut."

A muscle that tensed, changing the set of Reg's jaw, told Jamie he had scored. Ah, yes, when thieves fell out!

"You should have told him, Art," Jamie went on. "Then he'd have known better than to have allowed—shall I say? —anything to happen to Sue Ann. He engineered it, didn't he? Some way."

Reg turned and frowned at him. "You've got too much imagination, James. Save it for your books. I had nothing to do with whatever's happened to the gorgeous Mrs. Carrington."

Jamie didn't believe him.

Now he waited; heard the truck coming from the airstrip with Art and Reg. Unless Art had already fled?

Since lunch, Jamie had known for sure what had happened to Sue Ann—Jack Seavering had told him. So now there would be the accounting. And if Art Wheelock were exposed, he'd have to run for it—presumably to some country from which he could not be extradited.

Footsteps on the stairs. The key turned in the lock.

"What kept you? I thought you were coming back early?" he asked coldly as Art Wheelock stepped into the room. He could imagine Art's fury at having been detained, for whatever reason, so that he and Reg had not been back in time to welcome Jack Seavering.

"I understand you had guests."

"We still have one. I'm sure you've heard?"

"Lucille was quite right to keep her. Couldn't possibly let her go."

"Of course not. Not yet, anyway."

138

Art turned sharply on him, as though suspecting Jamie of possessing some bit of knowledge not shared by all of them. "What do you mean by that?"

"Only that you'll have to let her go eventually. When you get around to having to save your own skin."

Art snorted.

"Find out how things are going in Hardy?" It hadn't been difficult to figure that was why the two of them had taken off at dawn this morning for the mainland. Put in a call to his wife, and another to his assistant, and find out what kind of questions were being asked in his absence— by the police, the bank, or the lawyers for Walter Carrington's estate.

"I had some business matters to take up with my office." Art strolled over to the nearest window to look out at the view.

"Like 'On with the cover-up, and damn quick about it'?"

"Go right on making cracks; maybe I'll cut your throat a little sooner, just to shut you up."

"Not today, though. Too soon. Look, I'd like to spend some time with Linnet Emries. No skin off your nose, either. There's no reason you have to keep me locked up." They'd been good, always, about leaving him free to wander—within limits, of course.

Art stood by Jamie's writing desk. He picked up a sheet of paper, the first page of chapter six that he'd been working on this morning; glanced it over, frowning.

"Checking the quality of today's golden egg?"

Art laid it down, and sat on the corner of the desk. "Now listen, you'd better not get impulsive, just because your darlin' Linna is here—I've read all those letters you know, that she wrote your sister after the big romance. And having seen her just now, I know you didn't let her go out of any lack of interest. So if you think you're going to pull anything, and get her out of here—"

"I'm not so stupid as to try."

"Good. You'll play for time, instead, eh?" Art smiled. "By the way, you didn't pass any high signs or messages to your magazine friend?"

"How could I? Dan and Eli watched me every bit as carefully as you could have wished, and Lucille checked the manuscript of Seavering's article after I'd gone over it; just to make sure I hadn't scribbled something in the margins in invisible ink."

"So she said. And is Seavering planning on coming back?"

"If so, he didn't mention it."

"When's he leaving Baja?"

"I really don't know."

"You don't think he's going to come back to try to take little Mrs. Emries away with him after all?"

"I'm sure he was convinced of her delight at the opportunity of staying on with such dear friends."

"Good." Art got up from the desk.

"How about giving me the freedom of the house again?"

"Why not?" He shrugged his big shoulders and started for the door.

Jamie waited till the sound of his feet on the tower stairs had receded, and then he followed him down.

Under the arcade belonging to the guest bedroom wing be came upon Reg, sitting in a lounge chair and staring moodily at the pool.

"You missed the party," he said to him.

"So I hear. Bit of engine trouble. Had to get it fixed."

"Too bad."

"Too bad we got it fixed?"

"Oh, I'd hate to think of my plane falling into the drink. Especially with both of you aboard. Where's Mrs. Emries?"

"Locked in her room."

"Well, let her out."

"Orders not to."

"I told Art I wanted to talk to her."

Reg nodded. "He says you can see her at dinner."

A little flutter of fear. "She's all right, isn't she?"

"Mint condition."

Jamie leaned against one of the loggia pillars, looking down at the red-headed bastard who was his pilot.

He had been trying ever since their arrival here to have

a private word with Reg, but this was the first opportunity. There was no one else in the courtyard, but just to be cautious, he asked: "Where's Art?"

"Gone somewhere in the truck." The sound of the pickup's engine being started, below in the drive, bore him out.

"Ah," said Jamie. "You and Art still friends, Reg?"

"Don't have to be friends. We have our arrangements all worked out. I get *my* cut, he gets his."

"You don't think he should have been giving you a percentage of Mrs. Carrington's money? Not fair, was it? He's had that all to himself, while *my* money you've had to share—with him, with Dan, with Lucille, with Eli, with whoever guards my sister—"

"Never mind, James. I'm looking out for my own interest."

"Sure you are. But is Art? Sufficiently? He doesn't confide in you, does he? Or he'd have told you about cooking Mrs. Carrington's books. Doesn't that kind of bother you?

"And has he let you in on what he's going to do next? Now that he's in trouble over this Carrington thing—and he is, you know. Or will be—"

Reg shrugged. "Tough on him. I should care?"

Reg still sat, and Jamie still stood, leaning against the pillar. He looked down at his pilot and summoned up an almost friendly smile. "You haven't thought it out very well. Art's through. Got to be. His handling of the Carrington affairs will never stand the scrutiny of the courts. That means he's through manipulating my money as well, because he'll have to run for it; you all will—"

"All?" Reg straightened in his chair, raised his right hand as though to swear to something. "I was never so shocked in my life, Your Honor," he said to the nearest empty chair, "as when I found out Mr. Wheelock was a crook. None of us suspected, Your Honor. Not Mr. Everest, or Miss Everest—"

"You'd never get away with that. You haven't the brains, you or Lucille, to go on with this thing without Art."

An odd, foxy look came over his pilot's face. "You think Art's been running this show? You're wrong. He's only the money man."

For a moment Jamie had a chilling vision of some syndicate, behind the scenes, making decisions, sending out orders, banking his money. But that couldn't be what Reg had meant; fancying himself as leader, Reg himself was trying to take over from Art. The killing of Sue Ann would point to that—clearly an action he'd taken on his own.

"But, Reg. When Art runs for it—and we both know he'll have to—he's just spiteful enough to see to it that you get stuck with a murder charge. Had you thought of that? He'd figure you earned it by bringing this whole Carrington mess down on him."

Reg gave a little laugh. "I never laid a hand on her."

"But you caused her death."

"Don't bet on it. Or on there being any murder charge. She just fell off her horse—headfirst, no doubt." He got up from the chair in one easy motion. "Another thing I wouldn't bet on, if I were you, is any help from that magazine character who was here today."

Jamie kept his face just as it had been. "You think we've been passing signals back and forth?"

"We know you have. That's why he was invited to come here. I'm sure he'll be immobilized without causing us any trouble at all."

Jamie's stomach had grown cold. How long had they known about Jack's efforts on his behalf? "You're mistaken, you know." He felt almost ill.

Reg grinned his most amiable grin. "Tell that to old Art. For laughs."

"I would. But he's gone, hasn't he?" Gone to do what? He'd been asking in detail, hadn't he, about Jack Seavering . . .

Across the road from the hotel, Jack walked along the edge of the unpaved landing field with Erin.

"It's a Beechcraft Duke. Great little plane—land it anywhere."

"Well, you're going to have to!" Jack looked at Erin's

trim aircraft, with its twin engines and long, sharp nose. It was parked in the company of several other small planes, beside the runway.

Erin Bruce was a continuing surprise to him. The conceited Hollywood prettyboy they'd met yesterday had turned out today to be something different altogether. He even had a different name. Probably every fan magazine reader in the hemisphere knew that Erin Bruce had been born Aaron Blumberg, but it was news to Jack. "The quintessential goy," he had said of his screen image; smiling.

There was no other course open to them but to take the gamble they had decided on. But Jack was worried.

"You've no idea, you know, just how tough a situation you may be getting into."

Erin only looked pleased. "With good Jewish brains you can lick anybody."

"In this case you might also need a revolver—don't you think?"

"No. A high-powered rifle. If they get close enough for me to use a revolver, we're lost."

"I hadn't analyzed it that precisely. Not my field, this action game."

"No, mine. Been through the dress rehearsal for this many times. I don't suppose you saw a potboiler of mine caled *Mission to Tangier?* Final scene very like what we're figuring on."

"Only this'll be real."

"I know." He showed the dazzling array of pearly teeth. "I've been going through the motions for so long, it'll be a relief to have something be real for a change."

"Sure. Real bullets, real blood," Jack said dryly. "Great."

They stood in front of the white plane with its black markings. Erin put a hand on his shoulder. "Do you believe, ever—really believe—that your life could be snuffed out? I don't."

"I know. Sudden death is what happens to other people. But lately—"

"Yeah—there's lately, isn't there? Or so you tell me."

143

Soberly, as he opened the door of the little plane, "Jack—"

"Yes?"

"You do think we're right? She's there?"

"Got to be."

Jack watched him take off and come around in a huge circle, heading north; watched till the plane disappeared in the late-afternoon sky.

He wandered back, then, to the hotel. Nothing he could do, really, till Erin returned—with or without Helene.

He went down to the cocktail lounge and sat on the wall of the round terrace beyond it. Ordered a drink—feeling lonelier, he thought, than he ever had in his life. The Mexican band—a group of violinists and two very fine trumpeters—was giving a rousing rendition of "Guadalajara." Only last night he and Linna had enjoyed the same number together, after Erin Bruce had left them to join his movie friends.

Two tequila sours and he decided to go and have dinner. As he crossed the cocktail lounge past the large table which seemed to be reserved for the use of Martin Case and his hangers-on, Case nodded to him in greeting—assuming, probably, since he'd seen him with Erin Bruce, they must be acquainted.

He went on up the stairs that hugged the rock wall, and across the open-sided lobby toward the dining room.

"Mr. Seavering?"

"Yes?" He recognized the smaller of the two Mexicans who took turns minding the office—a wispy little man.

"Did your friend find you?"

"What friend? When?"

"He didn't tell me his name, and I did not know it. He is not a guest of the hotel. I informed him of your room number, but I suggested also that you might possibly have gone to the cocktail lounge."

"Evidently he missed me." A small hope. Vern? "What sort of man?"

"From the States. Tall man."

"Thank you. Perhaps he's waiting for me in my room."

But Vern was not waiting in his room. Nor was anyone

144

else. He even checked his balcony, leaning over to examine the shadows underneath it, and there was no one.

Nor was there any sign, as he returned along the outer gallery of the building, and up the length of the drive, of Miguel.

He went in to dinner.

Sitting alone at a table for two, he wondered—had his caller been someone from the Everest place?

But he clung to the possibility that it could have been Vern. If Vern's life were in danger, he might very well be staying out of sight . . .

Linna said hardly a word at dinner. She was too angry.

They dined, as they had at lunch, outside. By the light of torches, now, which were stuck into the planting beds. Their light seemed, more than anything, sinister; it was almost as though she'd been transported to a savage past where she and Jamie had fallen into the hands of enemies.

She listened in astonishment as Jamie talked to his captors, needling them with an air of exaggerated politeness. Undeterred by the fact that the villains of the piece were listening, he expatiated to Linna on his situation. "Why not?" he said. "Now that you've met Lucille, how much you know besides hardly matters." He turned to Art Wheelock. "She's here for the duration, is she not? Whatever that may be?"

Art bowed politely in her direction. "And we're charmed to have you here. De-lighted."

"The longer the party goes on, the happier Art will be. The rest of them, too. If you've wondered why they didn't simply hold me for ransom and take off at once with a lump sum, the reason, naturally, is that they get so much more this way." Jamie smiled pleasantly; it could have been someone else's money, someone else's life, he was discussing. "Over such a lengthy period of time, Art has been able to liquidate more and more of my holdings. Who knows that I'm not reinvesting?

"Then things like the sale of the movie rights to my latest book; and the paperback deal. None of that money was banked in my name for more than overnight; it's in

Swiss or South American accounts, I imagine, in the names, fake or otherwise, of the present company. So much better than a suitcaseful of ransom money whose serial numbers are on record."

The very fact that they let him talk on, explaining it to her, was terrifying. For she saw that they would never let him go alive.

In New York, or even two nights ago in Western Spring, a rescue operation had been easy to believe in—a matter simply of finding out what the hold was on Jamie, then calling in the authorities. But now—

Art Wheelock left the table first—to Linna's relief. Then Dan Bayles. When Reg had finished his dessert, he rose, cat-like, and said, "If you two kids want to chat a little, go ahead. Just sit here at the table."

A safe enough place, certainly. The dining terrace was perched at the top of the cliff that fell away to the water. And to make it perfectly secure, broken glass had been set into the top of the parapet.

Reg and Lucille settled, with cigarettes, on the steps leading up to the cloistered courtyard, watching them—Lucille with her close-set eyes, Reg with his clever ones.

Jamie's hand closed over hers. "I'm so sorry you've gotten caught in this thing."

"Don't be sorry. I'm not." She returned the pressure of his fingers on hers.

He just shook his head despairingly.

"Jamie, where *is* Helene?" With all that he'd said at dinner, he hadn't touched on the subject of his sister. "Do you even know whether she's—she's alive?"

"She was—three weeks ago. Periodically they hand me a page torn from a weekly magazine, or a portion of a newspaper—something with a date on it—on which they've allowed her to write a note."

"Have you gotten any inkling of where they're coming from?"

"They never let me see the envelopes. And they wouldn't let her say, of course. Originally they told me that Lucille's brother was keeping her on a farm somewhere. Though I don't even know whether Lucille has a brother, or her brother has a farm. But when we came to Baja, I strongly suspected they'd had her here—lately, at least. Her room still smells of her perfume. And those two horses stabled in the car shed? They're new." He smiled a little grimly. "Nothing too good for the prisoners, you know. Especially as it's our own money. Art tried to tell me our Mexican family is boarding the horses for someone, but I didn't believe that. He finally admitted that Helene had been here. But he says *no* one could find her now—they're holding her in a village in some remote section of Mexico."

"Do you believe that?"

"It's as likely as anything else they might do . . ."

"Do you know, I saw photographs of Lucille, in New York, and didn't realize I wasn't looking at Helene. She's a *fantastic* double! At least from the side."

"Ah, yes. Lucille." He said it bitterly. "Reg used to mention her once in a while—this girl who was married to an old buddy of his. He said she looked so much like my sister."

"Oh. Before the plan was even thought of."

"Long before. First time he ever saw Helene, he mentioned the resemblance."

"Where's Lucille's husband? Part of the conspiracy?"

"She shed him, apparently. Reg promised her better things."

Linna glanced around at the two warders at the top of the steps, sitting very close together. The flame of a lighter as Reg lit another cigarette for Lucille.

"Was the plot something hatched after Walter was killed? Or—"

"Oh, no. There's nothing to prove it, but judging by the magnitude of the scheme, and its effective organization, I'm unable to believe that any part of it was due to chance. They saw the setup and the plan was born. But they had to put Walter out of the way before they could take over. Walter oversaw everything for me, you know . . . Whatever it was they did to his car—tampered with the brakes, I suppose—was done when he was out of town, so that no suspicion would fall locally. What they didn't know, or

147

found out too late, was that Helene had gone with him. They were very upset when she was almost killed. Because she was an essential part of—" He broke off as Reg got up and came slowly down the steps toward them.

Linna wondered what had become of Wheelock and Bayles; not that she longed for their company.

"Sorry," Reg said. "Curfew time."

Jamie walked with her to her room, next to Lucille's on the second floor of the guest wing. They went up the stairs at the end, and along the balcony, with Reg trailing behind them.

"You'll have to be locked in, I'm sure."

"In this crowd, that's a privilege! What about you?"

"That's my room—across, with the balcony. But they can't lock the balcony doors, so I've been sleeping in the tower, where I write."

The prince in the tower, Jack had said . . .

"Oh, Linna, my dear!"

But it was as though a stranger stood in her place when he kissed her. She was aware of no emotion, no response; and the lack seemed frightening.

When Reg had locked her in, she walked to the window that overlooked the ocean far below, silvered in the moonlight, and put her hands on the ornamental grillwork shutting her in.

Had it been too long? Or was it the memory of Pete Emries, going unloved to the day of his death because of Jamie, that stood in her way now . . .

Miguel, parked in the drive below his room, was waiting for Jack when he'd finished dinner.

"See anyone hanging around my room, Miguel?" The whole of the second-story gallery, with the doors that opened off it, was visible from here.

"No, señor. Not since I came, which has not been very long."

"Have you found out anything about Mr. Fix?"

It seemed he hadn't. He had asked the taxi drivers at the hotel, since their duties might have taken them almost anywhere, and after dark he had gone back to the house where Rosalia lived, on the Everest place—there were no guards except at the hacienda itself.

But Rosalia had not been able to tell him anything about a man, with or without a camera, loitering in the vicinity in the recent past. Nor had her brother Emilio, nor her mother.

"Do you know, Miguel, whether Miss Everest only arrived last week with her brother? Or had she been there earlier?" He had been unable, when they were laying out battle plans, to locate Miguel to tell him to find out; he and Erin had made their tactical decision purely on faith and guesswork.

"Señorita Everest has been at the house for a long time, with a man and his wife, *norteamericanos,* taking care of her."

So Erin had been right!

"The man's name is Teem, Rosalia has told me."

"Teem? . . . Oh, *Tim!*"

"Yes, Teem."

So much, then, for the loyalty of Everest's former head guard. The one Percy had thought so devoted to Walter Carrington.

"Did Rosalia say anything about Miss Everest's leaving recently?"

"No, señor. Though Teem and his wife went away last week. Two men from Señor Everest's ranch came and took their places. Rosalia's mother does not like them any better than the ones who left."

"Um. They sneaked Miss Everest out, then. And sneaked in the new one." He explained about Everest's message.

"Señor! What a strange story this is!"

Jack told him also about his anonymous caller. "Would you stick around here a little longer, in case he comes back—whoever he is?"

"Of course, señor."

*"Gracias."* Jack went on up to his room.

Before he had opened the door so much as an inch, he knew someone was waiting. It was a feeling he had right in the gut.

149

He knew, too, that it wasn't Vern.

He reached for the light switch. But the lights were on. He swung the door wide. His bed was neatly turned down; and there was no one in the room. His suitcase, interestingly, stood in front of the closet instead of inside where he had left it.

A tall, bulky figure stepped in from the darkness of the balcony.

"Good evening." There was a revolver in Arthur Wheelock's hand.

"Sorry to have missed you at the house today." He seemed to have dropped the Texas accent, along with his gee-whiz friendliness.

"So I see." Jack stood motionless except to spread his hands, showing them empty. "I'd just as soon you'd missed me this time, too."

"I inquired earlier and they told me you weren't checking out today. Though that'll have to be changed." He glanced over at the desk, where the Everest article lay in plain sight; it had been inside the Manila envelope, which he'd left in a drawer when he'd gone to see Erin off. "I've been goin' over your article, there, and Jamie's changes." The accent was creeping back; maybe he hadn't known he'd let it go, there, in the stress of the moment, showing a piece of some other identity. "We were afraid he was gonna' try slippin' some kind of message into it."

Thank God the message and all the worksheets had been left in Erin's room. And Jack felt a quick surge of pleasure because they *were* ahead of the enemy in one respect—none of Wheelock's bunch knew Erin Bruce was included in the new scheme of things.

"I've made a few changes in the changes, just in case. And now I'd like you to send it off to your magazine editor, with a nice li'l note sayin' okay to print it. Right now." He motioned him over in the direction of the desk.

"We'll mail it from the hotel office," he said while Jack wrote a quick note to Tom on a sheet of hotel stationery. Wheelock nodded approval. "Seal it up."

He slid the article, with the note, back into the envelope, addressed it to Krug at the office and wrote *Air Mail* under the corner where the stamps would go.

"I'll go with you while you check out. You explain to the desk clerk that I've come from this photographer friend of yours, so's to take you back to where he's at."

Jack turned on him, almost forgetting the gun. "Vernon Fix? Where is he?"

"Why, he decided to go up in the mountains. To take pictures of the mountain sheep."

It almost had the ring of truth. It was the kind of thing Vern might have done. Except that if he had, Arthur Wheelock wouldn't have known a thing about it. He'd been in the States when Vern had disappeared without trace, and that had been days ago.

"We're lightin' out for his base camp this evenin'. A long ways, so we'll do part of it tonight. Your stuff's all packed." He nodded at Jack's suitcase. "And my name's Johnson, in case you feel any call to mention it."

"How'd you know I was looking for Vern?"

"Well, I knew he was here. And I figured you'd like to see him."

"Not at gunpoint, I wouldn't."

"You haven't got much choice. And listen—don't try anythin' fancy. Don't think you can make some kind of a break for it, while we're checkin' you out and all. I'd fire this thing, for one. For another, I didn't come here alone. And still another—then you'd never know what's become of your friend the photographer."

Reluctantly, Jack picked up his bag. "Is he alive?"

"That's what you're gonna find out. Isn't it?"

As they came down the steps at the end of the building, Miguel was leaning against his car. Jack prayed he would make no sign; better if Wheelock didn't know he had an ally.

Miguel came to attention, and started around the front bumper. Jack frowned; faintly shook his head. Sensing something wrong, the boy stopped abruptly, and dropped to his haunches, appearing to search for some object in the dust. He picked up something, wiped it on his pants

151

and after a quick glance, pocketed it. A pebble, probably; here one didn't find even bottle caps lying around.

"Boy!" Arthur Wheelock said sharply.

"*Si, señor?*"

"Are you Mr. Seavering's driver?"

A quick glance at Jack, and a small shrug. "*Si, señor.*" And a torrent of words in Spanish.

"Well, never mind—whatever that was." And to Jack, "You won't be needing him now, of course. Better pay him off."

"Miguel, I will not need you again."

Faced with a situation in which he did not know what was expected of him, Miguel had wisely taken refuge in his mother tongue and a look of blank incomprehension; Jack followed his lead, speaking slowly as to one who understands little English. "This gentleman has come from the friend I've been trying to find. From Señor Fix? You understand?"

Brilliant smile. "Señor Feex. *Buenas noches, señor.*" Miguel beamed at Wheelock.

"No, this is not Señor Fix. He comes from Señor Fix, and will take me to him, he says. So I do not need a car and driver myself any longer." He pulled out his wallet. "How much do I owe you?"

Again a flood of Spanish; obviously his driver was figuring up the sum. He even used his fingers to count on. At last he announced the amount, in pesos, and Jack had to convert it to dollars.

He wondered whether that included the extras—all the investigating Miguel had done. Even if it did, it wasn't enough. He counted off bills and gave him half again the price he had named, though loyalty was something you couldn't pay for, certainly, neither in dollars nor in pesos.

"Thank you, Miguel. You've done a good job."

"*Muchas gracias, señor. ¡Buena suerte!*"

"You can be sure that price was highway robbery," Wheelock said as they walked on—exactly as though they were friends.

"Look who's talking!" Jack said dryly. "By the way—do

I ever get my Olivetti back? But he received no answer—only a stony look.

At Wheelock's direction, he put his bag in the back seat of a white Ford with Mexican plates that was parked near the hotel entrance. They went in and he settled his bill; explained carefully, to the politely listening desk clerk, about the photograher friend he was joining, and arranged for stamps to be procured in time for the Everest article to be placed in the mail that would go on the morning plane.

"Isn't it late to be starting out for the mountains?" the Mexican asked—solicitously, not trying to push his opinions on a guest, but desirous of being helpful. "If your friend, Mr.—" he looked inquiringly at Wheelock—

"Johnson," said Wheelock.

"Mr. Johnson would like, we have a room for him. You could start at first light."

"Thanks, but no. Great-looking place here—" Wheelock glanced around at it—"but I've got to get back. We're only going tonight as far as my camper, parked up north of here a ways. Borrowed his friend's car to come down."

Was it Vern's car? Jack wondered as they got in, with himself in the driver's seat, naturally, and Wheelock next to him, the revolver leveled across his lap.

No sign of Miguel, nor of his blue Chevy. Had his driver guessed what had happened? Or did he care, now that he'd been paid, and handsomely at that.

They drove out of the hotel compound, with its carefully nurtured palm trees. As directed, Jack turned left onto the highway.

"Do you really have Vern up in the mountains someplace?"

"Ooohhhhh—I wouldn't say he quite made it that far." The playfulness of the answer made Jack think of a cat with a live mouse, and the suggestion of an effort cut short, an action interrupted, had a grimly lethal sound. No use asking questions. Wheelock would enjoy too much giving him the answers, which he was sure would be valueless.

He drove on—several miles to the small town, which

153

nestled on a curve of beach below a dark mountain that rose above the sea.

On through the town and up the coast.

Past a gate with the neatly lettered sign, *Posada de Baja,* affixed across the top—the fishing camp where Vern had stayed. In the distance he saw a line of small, low buildings that looked like individual cottages, visible against the glare of illumination beyond, where lights were strung for some outdoor activity—eating or entertainment.

Soon after passing the camp, he noticed a pair of headlights in the rear-view mirror. The sight was infinitesimally comforting; someone else, at least, was on this road tonight. Miguel? Surely, having been briefed as he had on the Everest plot, he would have smelled a rat when his employer so unceremoniously took off with a stranger? One who stayed so oddly a little behind him, at the left shoulder. Surely he'd guessed at the gun held at his ribs?

But if Miguel was following, Jack only hoped Wheelock did not suspect it. The headlights were far back; he mightn't have noticed yet. But soon he would—sitting as he was with his attention on his captive, his head turned to watch every move on the man next to him; the lights were surely not far out of his field of vision.

"Why did you tell the hotel clerk you had a camper parked somewhere? You haven't."

"Best way to shut him up. Red herring, besides. Let 'em look for a guy named Johnson, in a camper. *If* they look."

"I gather I'm going to be missing."

"Oh, no. You've gone to join your photographer buddy."

"Who's missing. Whoever escorted him out of the Posada de Baja didn't arrange for him to pay his bill first. So he's missing."

"Skipped, that's all. Anybody understads *that* trick."

Surely Miguel would have been struck by the similarity of Jack's departure to the disappearance of his friend . . . Though even if it were not Miguel behind them, but some stranger, it was better—

He became aware of amusement in the face of the man beside him.

"Can't keep from looking, can you—at the rear-view mirror." Again no Texas accent. "If you think it's anyone who's going to come to your aid when you try to get away, it's not. It's Dan Bayles, in our truck. We had time to work out all the details of this maneuver while you were at cocktails and dinner."

"I'm sure you did." But the news was a blow.

Miguel was probably still in Cabo San Lucas, in whatever beer parlor the fishing-boat captains frequented—living up his pay in the grandest fashion possible.

Consuela lay on her mattress, staring up into the darkness under the thatch. Had she been right not to tell Miguel, the boy from La Paz, what she knew about the man with the camera? The man's car had been parked for days in the shed with the horses and the truck. Covered up with something. Until tonight. It was just before Miguel had come again that two of them had come down from the hacienda and had driven away the truck *and* the car. So now there was nothing to show that it had ever been here. And Señor Donan had been so terrifying when he had said what would happen if she told anyone about the man who had taken pictures of him and Señorita Everest riding on the beach. Or about the car which had mysteriously appeared in the shed the next morning—it was there when she got up. But the man she had not seen again, after he drove away when he finished taking the pictures.

The fact that the car was here but the man had never appeared anymore was what made Consuela afraid to tell anyone what she knew.

And what did she know, really? Fortunately Rosalia and Emilio had not seen the man, or what had happened.

There was no reason she should have told Miguel, and perhaps made much trouble for them all. Miguel was only a boy from La Paz, about whom she knew nothing.

# 10

THEY DROVE FOR A LONG TIME. WITH THE TRUCK behind them.

No use trying to escape at this stage of the game. If he succeeded in wrecking the car or somehow overpowering Wheelock, Dan Bayles would be on him before he could get away.

Wait and see.

Though he couldn't see much. A blur of desert, in the moonlight, and at a distance, mountains.

At last Wheelock told him to pull over and wait, on the shoulder of the road. In a moment or two a pickup truck had drawn up beside them, and it was indeed Bayles who stuck his head out the window.

"What now?" Dan yelled.

Wheelock tilted his head to one side, the better to see into the truck cab, and called across, "We'd better wait here for a little light. Soon's the sky starts to turn, we'll be able to see what we're doing. Don't want to get the truck stuck someplace you can't get it out of."

"Right." Bayles parked just ahead of them, got out. He stood by Jack's window and spoke across him. "He givin' you any trouble?"

"Not a bit."

They waited. And waited. Art Wheelock got out and stretched, while Bayles kept an eye and his gun on the prisoner.

"Should be someplace along here pretty soon, to turn off," Jack heard Wheelock, behind the car, say to his guard. "What did Tim tell you the turnoff looked like?"

Tim. It would have to have been Tim Donan who spirited Vern away, that night last week. Because Tim had still been here, then; he and his wife, looking after the real Helene White.

"Didn't say what it looked like. Seems like this ought to be almost far enough, though."

A hope stirred, somewhere in Jack's mind, as he listened to this exchange. Did they really have Vern out here somewhere still? Alive?

Or had he simply been dumped in the desert. For some time, as they'd sat here, one of Dwight Percy's references to the Baja Peninsula had been in the forefront of his mind: the bit about people getting lost in these wastelands; running out of gas, or water; dying of thirst.

A lightening of the sky. The mountains ahead and to their right were closer than they'd seemed. He wasn't sure just when it was that they had begun to detach themselves from the darkness to the east and reveal bit by bit the stark and rugged flanks and escarpments. Nothing reassuring about them from where he sat.

Wheelock got in beside him, and Bayles into the truck, and they started off again, this time with the truck in the lead.

They went off at a good clip, then slowed, after a couple of miles. Judging by the conversation the other two had had, Jack assumed Bayles must be looking for some kind of turnoff.

It was light enough now to pale their headlights. Ahead, the truck stopped, and they pulled up behind it. Dan had gotten out and crossed in front of his vehicle, stepped over the shoulder where it looked as if a truck went off into the scrub growth.

He came back, shaking his head. "Just a gully," he shouted, got back in, and they were on their way again. Twice more he slowed, only to pick up speed again, and then at last his right-turn signal flashed on, and they saw it—a dirt road heading off between giant cactus.

They turned into it, after the truck. Going toward the mountains.

It was fast growing lighter, so that they could see the character of the ground. The scrub growth was thinning

157

out, the earth becoming increasingly barren. They kept going. Jack kept track, on the speedometer, of the distance traveled from the highway. Five miles. Eight. The road—hardly more than a trail—was navigable, but only barely.

"Let this car get hung up, or stuck in a hole, and you've *had* it," Wheelock said once, when they lost traction in a dust-filled rut. There was wildlife, here on the desert floor. Small lizards skittered across their path with a furtive, indecent quickness of movement. Twice he saw snakes. Rattlers, he thought.

The truck stopped, then after a minute went on. The trail divided here, and Bayles had had to make a decision. He had gone left.

And then the car did get stuck. The right rear wheel slipped off a smooth piece of stone and into sand. He tried to pull out frontwards, then backwards, and ended hung up crosswise of the track—if you could call it that anymore.

"Okay, get out," were his orders.

Bayles had stopped and come back. Stood, watching.

Wheelock took the keys out of the ignition, went around to the trunk and opened it; inspected what was within, then motioned Jack to have a look.

A sleeping bag. A suitcase—Vern's, he recognized it, and anyway his initials were on it. Two camera cases. He recognized those, too. Wheelock picked up one of the cases, opened it to look at the camera. Vern's favorite, the Nikon with the zoom lens. It could have been the zoom, no doubt, that had gotten him in trouble—he didn't need to be close to get a good, clear view with it; like a telescope.

He felt sick. He hadn't really believed, he guessed, till now, that something had happened to Vern.

"You doubted that it was your friend's car?" Wheelock looked thoughtfully at the second camera, then took the Nikon and slung it around his neck by the strap.

A man who just couldn't resist, apparently, nice things that belonged to someone else.

He closed the trunk. "Get in the truck. In the back."

Jack swung up at the rear of the pickup, and Art Wheelock got in behind him. Kept the revolver on him. There was a safe distance between them; impossible to jump the man. Dan Bayles started up again, and they bounced along over the desert.

By now there didn't even seem to be a track, or path. They were driving over apparently virgin earth. Not too difficult—this thing was four-wheel drive. Though care must be taken or it, too, could get stuck. He tried to take bearings so that he could find his way back. He wasn't sure he'd be able to follow the tire tracks; they could disappear in dry dust, fill in again. And on some of the stony terrain they would leave no trace at all.

Just as Art Wheelock had promised last night, they were headed for the mountains—coming closer and closer, now, to the nearest one. How far had they come since leaving Vern's car? he wondered. Five miles? It was hard to gauge distances out here, the light was deceptive. The other mountains disappeared, gradually, eclipsed by the one nearest them, and as they approached its arid lower slope, its top, too, receded from view, hidden by an escarpment halfway up the side.

"Far enough, Dan. Stop anytime," Wheelock called out. The truck rolled to a halt, the engine was cut, and Dan got out, a hunting rifle in one hand.

"Okay. Come on." Wheelock dropped to the ground behind the truck and motioned Jack to come.

The three of them started out.

"Just climb," Wheelock said, and Jack went first.

The lower slope was easy. There wasn't exactly a path, but the scrub grew in patches, with barren areas leading one from another. At first the little lizards, starting up with their odd, sudden movement almost under his feet, caused an involuntary tendency to recoil, but he soon got used to them.

The going became harder and his breath grew shorter, with the effort of proceeding so rapidly upward.

The other two had exchanged weapons. It had been Dan's revolver Art had held on him. They were staying close behind, Wheelock with the rifle crooked in his arm,

Bayles taking the upgrade easily, his gun in its holster; but Jack didn't doubt he could draw it fast enough.

Not even a little chance to outdistance them.

They climbed for perhaps half an hour. Hard on the feet —he wore loafers, and he could feel the rock surface and stones right through the soles. Though the air was dry, he was sweating enough that his shirt had grown damp, and the lightweight slacks felt heavy and hot.

"To the right," Wheelock directed.

Soon enough he saw what was to the right of them. Some kind of cleft in the side of the mountain; he remembered noticing it from below. He reached the edge, and stopped. Whether an upheaval of the earth's crust had caused the steep drop, or the declivity had been created by water, at some past time, coursing down these slopes, he had no idea. In any case, there was a straight drop of about seventy-five feet to the floor of a rock-strewn chasm.

"On, Seavering—that way." As Jack moved upward along the edge of the cliff, Wheelock came to the verge and looked over.

"Keep moving along the edge."

They proceeded in single file along the rim. Was this what had happened to Vern? Pushed over to crack his head open below, and left to feed the vultures? Because Vern sure as hell wasn't around to drive his car, wear the clothes in his suitcase, use his beloved cameras, anymore, was he?

Carefully turning his head, he kept track of the two of them out of the corner of one eye—Bayles right behind, now, Wheelock trailing in third place.

He caught a movement—Wheelock signaling Bayles with one arm—and was aware at once of Bayles—stealthily and fast—closing the gap between himself and his forward-plodding prisoner.

He whirled, and threw himself at Bayles. But Bayles was ready—he had the quick reflexes of a fighter. They grappled, and Jack was sent staggering backwards, almost to the edge, where he would have trod on empty air. The knowledge forced him to step forward—and right into a waiting punch to the jaw.

He wasn't used to this kind of thing; he'd never boxed or wrestled in his life. His chief reaction to the pain of the blow was one of absolute rage, but something told him it was useless to hit back. He feinted, as though to hit Bayles with his right fist, then instead tackled him; he *had* played a little high-school football.

Dan went down on top of him, and they rolled together in the dust. He found both his arms pinioned. He was trying, teeth bared, to break the hold on his right arm when he looked up and saw Art Wheelock with a rock in his hand. Only two or three feet away.

There was a terrific blow on his head, and he saw stars.

He felt sick, nauseated with the pain. Then he was aware of the ground slipping away from beneath him. His fingers scrabbled on receding earth, on stones, and abruptly he was falling free. Nothing to hold to.

Over the edge.

He landed hard; the breath knocked out of him. There was an excruciating pain in his left wrist, but there was no time to wonder what had happened to it—and compared to how his head felt, it was nothing.

He forced his eyes to open. Above, to his right, was the wall of the cleft. He had fallen only partway down it. To his left the ground dropped away—a long, smooth expanse of what looked like powder, or fine sand. A dull orange color. A long way, still, to the bottom, but the look of the slope made him wonder whether he couldn't slide right down it. No one peering over the edge, above, but they would be, any second—expecting to see him lying below.

It hurt to move, but he took the plunge—right down the almost vertical face on the seat of his pants. Soft clay-dust, the surface, not bad at first. But as he gained momentum, the fall was a telescoped nightmare—very fast, and painful. He lost control, near the bottom, and rolled over and over, sideways, till he jolted to a sudden halt.

Not thought, but instinct, told him to fall limp, at the end, and stay there. When he stopped rolling, in a horribly uncomfortable position with a sharp rock sticking into his back, he moved not a muscle.

And soon was rewarded by some shouted commentary from above.

"No, he hasn't moved. Can you see him from there?" Wheelock.

"Not too well." The second voice from another direction, farther to the left. "I'll try from a little lower."

He opened one eye a slit, but all he could see was a wall of the cleft.

Time went by and nothing happened.

Bayles called out again, a little closer. "I can see him good from here. Hasn't moved." He must have worked his way a little distance down the wall.

"I can see him *real* well." Wheelock again, from the top of the rim. "Got this zoom lens on the camera." Oh, God! With that thing, Wheelock might as well be leaning right over him, watching for the slightest flutter of an eyelash. He concentrated on breathing as shallowly as possible—within seconds feeling as if he were going to black out.

"Looks like you got him with that rock. Lotta blood on his head. Or maybe he hit it when he fell." How close was Dan? . . .

Now that he thought of it, he could feel the blood congealing on his scalp. Though maybe that was the power of suggestion.

"Any way to get down there, Dan?"

"No. Break my leg if I tried," he called. "Listen, he's dead. A fall like that?"

"Hey!" Wheelock, with a note of excitement. "Don't much want to go down there myself. See what's keepin' him company?"

"Buzzards. Yeah. Oh, they're everywhere." So they'd come for him already—the great soaring, swooping black birds.

"No, not them. Snake. I just found it with the lens. Great big rattler sittin' right next to 'im."

He'd thought he was as badly off as it was possible to be; evidently he hadn't realized the possibilities.

So he'd die of fright.

"If he wasn't dead, that thing'd get him if he even twitched."

"Oh, yeah, I see it now—coiled up?"

Why didn't they at least tell him where it was? How close?

He had probably startled the snake when he fell, and it had immediately coiled, ready to strike. He remembered, now, a funny dry sound as he came to rest—he'd thought it was the rattle of pebbles accompaning his fall . . . Which way—to the left, hadn't it been?

It was watching him, no doubt, waiting for him to do something.

Well, it would have to wait a long time. Art Wheelock could train the zoom lens on him as long as he liked; he'd see no more movement than if rigor mortis had set in. The knowledge that two armed men were watching him so attentively was bad enough, but it was the rattler that would keep him motionless—if need be, for twenty years.


Myra was sitting over her fourth or fifth cup of coffee when Helene White came into the kitchen. It was the coffee, she was sure, that made Myra's nerves so bad, so that she was jumpy and mean; and it was boredom that drove her to pour cup after cup—*something* to do all day, at least drink coffee. And boredom, too, made her jumpy and mean.

Helene gave her a look of pure hatred. "I'm going riding now," she said—a statement made superfluous by the fact that she had on her boots and breeches; but she preferred treating Myra as if she were colossally stupid.

"Yeah. Tim's gone out a'ready." The lavishly mascaraed eyes rested on her without interest, without even animosity.

"I thought you couldn't wait to get back here so you could have your hair done." The dark streak in the part was still there, and the bleached ends were dry and strawlike, a mess after the months of swimming and sun in Baja, and the amateur hairdressing, since Myra'd had to bleach it and wash and set it herself while they were in residence

163

at the hacienda. She'd complained about it the whole time.

"Oh, I got to get permission," she said sourly. "When Tim can spare me a car and some time, I guess I'll finally get to go to Western Spring. Big deal." Myra was thirty-five, and fast losing her looks. Theoretically, she was happy to be getting such good pay; but she hadn't the imagination to visualize a future in which she could go out and spend it. She wanted to spend it now.

Helene went out the door and through the service court. High above the ranch a plane glinted in the early morning sun. She looked up at it. A small plane, but not Jamie's; she'd thought for a second it could be Reg coming back, but it wasn't—the pilot was going on over.

Why had they taken Jamie down to Baja? And brought her up here? It was a boon, at least, to have a change of scene—she'd been long enough at Cabo San Lucas. And here she had Tasha. Neither of the horses Tim had picked up for them in Baja, at her insistance, had been much good. Plugs. But it had gotten her out of the house, at least, and she'd loved riding along the beach, no matter on what kind of mount. And it had made things more difficult for Tim, having to keep her well away from Consuela and the children, so that she couldn't communicate with them in any way.

They'd been told, she gathered, that she was a danger-ous lunatic, as a result of a blow on the head she'd re-ceived in the accident; and that her poor brother had sent her down there in hopes of a cure.

Not that there was anything Consuela could have done, anyway—or Rosalia, or Emilio. If they'd even tried, and Tim had found out, they would have had Jamie killed. Or so they said. And she wouldn't put anything past Art Wheelock—anything at all.

Same deal here at the ranch, now. Tim wouldn't even let her talk to the stableboys. He brought her horse, him-self, to the service-court entrance. Dangerous lunatic again? Likely to set fire to the stables? She supposed so. She wondered what the ranch hands and stable personnel had been told about her during the past year and more, while she'd been gone. In an asylum somewhere? Or kept in the house in a strait-jacket?

Surprising she hadn't gone round the bend. All this time spent exclusively with Tim and his wife. She had almost put an end to the whole thing when they'd crossed the border, this time. She had been tempted, certainly: throw herself on the protection of some amazed customs inspector. But it wouldn't have worked. Tim, already through customs ahead of Myra and their charge, would have melted away into the throng of travelers—and vengeance would have been taken on Jamie..

Or would it? How could you know?

She didn't even speak, as Tim rode up leading Tasha. Nor did he. His big face, with the small, slitted eyes and small mouth, was quite expressionless.

She mounted quickly, before he could get off his horse to give her a leg up. She hated Tim; she didn't want him touching her, not even through the leather of her boot. And she feared him—she thought he was at heart a killer. He'd taken real pleasure in his threat the other day, when she'd first gotten to go out again on Tasha. "Try to get away from me, Helene, and I'll shoot your little horse dead." She believed he would welcome the opportunity.

On Tasha she was no longer entirely alone. There was a living, thinking presence inside the beautifully shaped white head. Tasha and she loved one another.

They moved off, now, along the bridle path, past the barn, heading toward Coyote Gulch—Tasha, like a Michelangelo horse, all graceful curves and flowing mane and tail, leading the way, and Tim's big roan following, his rider tall in the saddle because, though his legs were only average in size, his body was long. Long and thick.

With his gun in its holster, of course.


"Wait a little longer, Dan," came another call from above. "To make sure. Keep your eye on 'im."

"Yeah."

Time dragged by. A shadow flitted quickly over his closed eyelids—one of the vultures passing over, checking?

He remembered some story he'd read about a deadly poisonous snake crawling into a man's sleeping bag. But that had been for the body warmth. No warmth needed here, the rock was hot in the morning sun. The snake would do nothing, he thought, unless he moved. Was it sitting now staring at him, testing the air with its forked tongue?

The stone pressing into his back was becoming unbearable. His wrist hurt horribly, and he'd like to get it in a more comfortable position. But he daren't. The damn rattler waiting, and Wheelock.

He wondered how much longer he could stand this without moving.

He concentrated on Linna, to fill the time. Must get out of here, for her sake. And there was Everest, of course. Funny how he'd been almost obsessed, it seemed, with extracting James Everest from the predicament he was in—and now what mattered most was getting Linna out.

Maybe something would happen to Everest, and just Linna would make it. No. Oh, no. He wouldn't want to have to get Linna that way. He only wanted her if she chose him over Jamie.

So forget it. She's made her choice—long ago. Before she ever met you.

Without thinking, he moved.

Instantly froze again.

But nothing had happened. Had *it* gone? Had *they* gone?

He opened both eyes, slitted. Within his range of vision, nothing stirred. And then a buzzard sailed over. He was aware, suddenly, of movement behind him, and was seized for a moment by pure terror as he thought of the rattlesnake. Slowly, slowly he pivoted his head, and saw that another buzzard stood not far off, ensconced on a rock, flexing his wings. No snake. At least he didn't see it, not yet.

Inch by inch he examined the ground around him, then slowly moved his head this way, then that, till he had studied every bit of terrain visible. He levered himself up gradually, on his good hand, till he was sitting. Saw no snake. It must have gone.

So, he thought, had the others. He squinted upwards at a spur of land that sloped out from the rim above—the place Dan Bayles had probably watched him from. No one there now.

Directly above him was a bulge of rock in the side of the cleft's wall; it must have been there that he'd landed, instead of falling free the whole distance. Only fifteen feet or so from the top, and barely large enough to arrest his fall. Below it he could see the marks he had left in the smooth orange clay-dust as he'd slid down; and the bottom stretch of almost sheer slope—hard, rocky, bone-shattering—made him shudder as he remembered rolling over it, falling out of control. He was a mass, now, of bruises, scrapes and knocks.

He tried moving the fingers of his left hand, and at least they all worked. Reached over to feel his wrist, and as he did so, he heard it. A dry rattle, just to his left.

This time he identified the sound instantly—in time to freeze with his hand in midair. Knowing where the noise had come from, he saw it at once, coiled in a hollow with a jumble of stones, its dirty-patterned scales so cunningly camouflaged against its background that his eyes had previously passed over it without detecting its presence. Its head was lifted, and its little tail, as well, with the lumpy rattles.

It was perhaps eight feet away.

How thick it was, and heavy-looking.

Did it recognize his raised hand as a threat? Slowly, slowly, he began to lower his arm, so gradually that no motion was visible. Behind him, a faint flopping sound. The buzzard on the rock; he paid no attention to it. But the snake shifted its coils a bit. Readying itself for a strike? or a retreat?

After several hours, it seemed, his fingers touched rock; he had finished lowering his hand to the ground. He sat motionless in the hot, hot sun. His companion was flicking its tongue in and out, tasting the bright, dry air.

How long, he wondered, might it wait there, so beautifully organized to confront the danger he represented? They could be here together for weeks . . .

Suddenly the vulture behind him launched itself into the air and took off over his head with a great flapping of wings. For a split second his eyes left the vision of swift and certain death within whose reach he sat, as trapped and helpless as any rabbit; and when he lowered his eyes again to the dirty, subtle pattern of scales, he couldn't believe, for a moment, what he saw, and then he knew the ordeal was over. The heavy body was strung out, moving off, with the strange undulating motion that belongs to creatures that have neither feet nor fins. It was going away.

If she was there, he'd missed her. No sign of a girl out riding, as he'd flown over the Everest ranch. Too early?

Or *(if* she was there) didn't they let her go riding, these days? According to those letters Jack had told him about, they did. The letters Linna had received.

*If* . . . He and Jack Seavering had been so sure. It was certain that last week she had been at Cabo San Lucas. It was a good guess that last year she had been in New York. It would appear, anyhow, that they might have been moving Helene from one of Jamie's places to another, for safekeeping; but not to the New York apartment anymore, because Dwight Percy had told Jack the building was kaput.

At least it had seemed logical, when they'd laid out their campaign, that she'd be here. But she could be anywhere. In a Mexican village . . . Anywhere at all . . .

Erin flew on to the north. Hovering over the Everest place would be the worst thing he could do; alert them that something was going on. He'd come back, in a little while, fly over again going south.

Damn it, she always went riding early. He knew, he'd ridden with her any number of times. It had been a quarter of eight, Texas time, when he'd flown over. Where was she?

It'd gone fine, till now. Everything. (Though if she wasn't here, what good did that do!)

He'd picked up the telescope-sighted rifle in El Paso

168

last night—a Winchester Model 70. Also a handgun, an automatic, German. And ammunition for both. It had not been difficult—as most things were not difficult for Erin Bruce. People did flipflops for him, anytime he needed or wanted something; they felt privileged to be asked to do some favor for a famous movie star. Some of the brightness rubbed off on them. Most of the people he met were like that. Notably not Helene, of course. Oh, no!

He flew west, now. Over the Pecos River—a name and place so familiar to decades of Western fans, but seldom seen actually, on the screen, since most of those movies were shot in California.

Surely this whole thing wasn't a wild-goose chase? And the F.B.I. were doing *something,* presumably, since he'd called them about Jamie's message. Making inquiries?

It was time to head back. As he banked the Beechcraft to the right, he felt a little thrill pass over him, like the scary exhilaration at the top of a roller coaster. Was that from the thought of Helene, with her princess-like look, or was it because of the imminent danger?

This time . . . This time he'd see her . . .

It was farther than he'd thought, from the mountain to the primitive track they'd followed. Unless he had come the wrong way? But he didn't think so. He was sure he remembered that tall cactus, like a man thumbing a ride; and the scatter of stones over there, to the left; and the far hilltop he'd fixed in his mind, to the right, seemed to be still in the correct position.

One good thing, anyway—he didn't have Wheelock and Bayles to worry about anymore. Not till later. When he had come out, on the mountain, at the bottom end of the long cleft, he had seen at once that the truck was gone.

If only, he thought, they've left the key to Vern's car . . . It had been in the lock of the trunk, last he'd seen of it.

The buzzards still trailed him—inspired, probably, by the scent of blood. The back of his head was all gummy with it, as Bayles had remarked. Dabbing at it with his handkerchief had only been useless and painful. He needed water to clean it up. Plus aspirin, quadruple strength, for the headache.

His wrist still hurt—he didn't know whether he'd broken a bone or if it was merely sprained. He'd bound it up with the blood-daubed handkerchief, and that helped a little.

It was broiling out here. Away from the shore, with its pleasant breezes, the land was an inferno.

He wondered how Erin was doing. Even if they'd guessed right, as to where Helene was, would there be any way to get at her?

He looked at his watch. And was amazed to discover how much time had passed. Nearly eleven o'clock. How much longer was it going to take him to get back, by whatever means he could contrive, to Cabo San Lucas? It had been a long drive to wherever he was, even without this additional part across the wastelands.

As he trudged on through the sparse scrub, he thought he saw in the distance something, at last, that had not grown out of the desert. Something man-made and shiny. The car? . . . Half-hidden by a clump of cactus.

He drew nearer, and saw the tracks of the truck, where it had detoured around the stricken vehicle, picking the ground carefully so as not to become stranded.

For the last few yards he could hardly stand the suspense. Would they have left the key in it . . . ?

Whether they had or not was immaterial, he saw when he reached the car, which sat derelict and forlorn, with two wheels hanging in space where the ground dropped away from under it. He said, "Damn! Damn them!"

A large splotch, darker than the surrounding earth, spread under the front end of the Ford. They had drained the radiator before going on.

He had no idea how far he had come, since leaving Vern's stranded car. A long way. Long way still to go.

This *was* a kind of road. Did anyone ever use it? Silver prospectors, going into the mountains? He'd heard there used to be silver mines, but they'd been abandoned years ago, Miguel had told him. Well, did anybody live up in the mountains now?

Someone, just anyone, coming along this track on a donkey. How wonderful that would be.

Because this *was* a road. It really was. It even had ruts. How could it have ruts if it wasn't traveled on?

But there was no one in sight, either before or behind.

He was parched. Had been for hours. He didn't even notice anymore that his wrist throbbed, and his head—too many other things felt worse. Like the soles of his feet, and he still had to walk on them. Blisters on his heels. Raw blisters.

He didn't even mind the buzzards anymore. Something else living, at least, besides himself. And the quick little lizards. Hadn't seen another snake, thank God.

Two planes had gone over—one going south, one going north. Nowhere near him, they were close to the coastline . . . Erin would get back and wonder what had become of him. Early afternoon, Erin had said . . .

He put the one foot in front of the other, the other in front of that one, no longer even looking up. He would make it to the paved road.

He became gradually aware of a sound. It was the sound of an engine, at some distance. He must finally be getting close to the highway? He hadn't supposed he could move any faster than his current snail's pace, but now he broke into a shambling trot that was torture to his blisters.

Rapidly the noise grew nearer and louder, and all at once he caught sight of what was making the sound; it came over a little rise. The truck. It was back. They were returning to check, to make sure he hadn't survived that fall and the snake and the long hike.

Crouching low, he took off to the right through the desert growth. The nearest refuge, a dip in the earth, was rather too close to the track, but there was nowhere else to hide, and he flattened himself to the ground, just over the edge of the declivity, and hoped that the fretwork of little leafless branches, standing no more than a foot high, would camouflage him. Hastily he removed his shirt, fumbling, using only the one good hand; the color of skin

171

fitted much less obviously into the scene than did an expanse of bright blue cotton. He stuffed the shirt under his chest.

With his cheek against the warm dirt Jack peered sideways at the spot where the truck would again come into his range of vision.

The buzzards. The damn buzzards. They'd give him away. He'd forgotten them until one swept soundlessly over his head; but there it was, he might as well have sent up a flare.

The truck labored into view, grinding along not as fast as he'd thought, in second gear. Not twenty feet way. He noticed how the dark green paint had faded in the strong Baja sun; in places the metal was almost bare. In fact, he realized suddenly, this was not the same truck.

An ancient Mexican was at the wheel, his eyes wide, his eyebrows raised as if in surprise that his vehicle was making it at all, a slight grin, of concentration maybe, on the lips of his unshaven face.

Jack lurched to his feet and hobbled toward the road, track, trail, whatever, that he'd so hastily left. No need to wave him down, the driver stopped.

"*Buenos días*," he had begun when he looked into the cab and his mouth almost fell open as he saw Miguel, seated beside the old man.

Miguel. At this particular moment the best friend he had ever had!

"Señor Seavering!" Miguel slid down from the truck cab on his side and came around to help Jack navigate, and in a couple of minutes they were all together on the seat.

"Miguel!" Jack shook his hand.

"I am sorry, señor, that it has taken so long to reach you! It was necessary to secure a truck, because when I saw where they were going, I knew my Chevrolet would get stuck, without four-wheel drive. This is Jesus, Señor Seavering—"

Jack beamed at the old man.

"Jesus is a relative of the family at whose house I have been staying, in Cabo San Lucas. This is his truck. He had

172

a job to do with it this morning, first, before we could come to look for you."

"You followed us last night?"

"Yes. After what had happened to your friend, leaving also in the middle of the night . . . I stayed out of sight behind you, driving with the lights of the car turned off. It was lucky I was so far behind, señor, because that was how I saw the truck which had been parked with its lights off, waiting. It followed your car when you turned on the highway, coming out of the hotel."

And last night he'd written off Miguel, figuring he was out having a great good time.

First, they retrieved the things frm Vern's car—not a very long trek when you weren't on foot.

"But you do not know what happened to Señor Feex?" Miguel asked as they finished loading everything into the back of the truck.

"No, but I can imagine." He related to Miguel, on the trip back along the track, his experiences of the morning. Miguel, in turn, gave the story in Spanish to Jesus, who was voluble in his response. "Ve-ry bad," he said of the snake, apparently the only words in English he knew to fit the case. He puffed out his cheeks, made himself seemingly larger by throwing out his arms, and collapsed on the steering wheel in a graphic depiction of death by snake venom. Fortunately they could not go off the road, as the track and surrounding ground here were all on a level.

Safely, they reached the paved road.

"How did you know where they took me? It was dawn when we left the highway, light enough to see along the road, and there was no one in sight."

"'I stayed far, *far* behind, señor. From far away I saw them turn off, and I watched which way they went, but I did not follow. I knew I must find a jeep or truck."

He tried to thank Miguel—without much luck. It would seem that any Mexican driver would do the same for his client—a matter of professional ethics.

* * *

There was no news, all day, of Erin Bruce. Or, more specifically, he did not come.

Jack re-registered at the hotel, with no comments about the "Mr. Johnson" with whom he had last night departed; he did not want the local police getting into the middle of the very touchy Everest situation. He took a long, hot shower in his old room, and when he came out ready to collapse into bed, found an Ace bandage lying on top of the spread. Either Miguel had found it for him or the hotel clerk, not quite believing his disclaimers of real injury, had sent it up.

Much appreciated.

He fell asleep at once, and when he woke it was dark.

"My God," he said under his breath, looking out at the last purple afterglow in the sky. "Where's Erin?"

Rubbing his eyes with his good hand, and limping, as all his sore spots and bruises and outraged tendons clamored for attention, he hobbled out onto the balcony. Below, the surf broke restlessly on the jumbled formation of rocks.

What had become of Erin and his mission? Wasn't she there? Or had he missed her and stayed over for another try tomorrow?

Or, he had found her, and they had gotten away. He visualized the plane of flaming wreck, its tall blond pilot riddled with bullets.

Damn this isolation, at the end of nowhere, where there was no possibility of news—any news! If there had been a shootout, or the plane had crashed, there was no way he would hear of it—not till he got back to the States.

# PART THREE

# 11

EARL CADY STEPPED DOWN OUT OF THE LAND Rover in front of the hangar.

"See yu later," he said, and Billy drove off, heading north on fence patrol.

He crossed the stubbly grass at the end of the ranch landing strip, heading for the little office where there was a hot plate and a coffeepot. His day started early; already it had been so long since breakfast he felt decaffeinated.

Plane going over. He watched it. Looked like the same one that'd come over yesterday about this time, passed over twice, coming and going. Some rancher must've got himself a new toy—because this part of the countryside sure wasn't on any flight path from anywhere to anywhere.

He went into the grubby little room, which smelled of dead flies and aviation fuel, and turned on the burner. Carried the coffeepot into the windowless little head and half-filled it with water from the washstand, brought it back and put it on to boil. Ladled some instant coffee in with a bent spoon.

He stared out the flyspecked window, out over the grasslands behind the ranch buildings. The girl was out there, riding her horse. He'd seen her go out awhile ago. Tim Donan keeping her company. She must be better, since they were letting her ride again—she'd been shut up in the house ever since he'd come to work here. Not right in the head, Mr. Wheelock had told him. But now they were letting her out—certainly with someone to look after her, though.

Tim Donan. Him he could shove right up his own—

Not that he cared if Tim was in charge of Miss Everest. But he acted like he instead of Billy was boss of the whole guard detail. Used to be, so he'd made clear.

"So where've you been in the meantime?" Earl had asked him. Seeing as Donan sure hadn't been at the ranch on the payroll, since Earl had been employed here.

"That's not your business. And take my advice, Cady— questions like that can get you into trouble."

Causing him to wonder all the more.

Because it was a strange outfit, this. He knew from his own experience. Not only Mr. Everest never went any-place, but Dan and Reg, and Mr. Wheelock, too, seemed all the time to expect that somebody might try to break in here. Why? When it was so well guarded.

What was there to break in for? Not a bunch of cows or the horses, certainly.

And it wasn't just fear somebody might kidnap Mr. Everest, either, because he wasn't even here now—first time he'd left the place since Earl came—and security was tighter than ever.

Plane was coming back—that little plane.

Coffee was ready, he stirred it up and poured some into a blue cup he'd washed last time he'd used it. Walked outside with it to see just what that plane was up to, if anything.

Take that crazy spy and holdup job he'd done a couple weeks ago. When those reporters had been here. Mr. Wheelock had found out one of them was staying on in Western Spring, day after the big interview.

"Search his room. He's tryin' to write an article on Mr. Everest that he don't want done. You find any notes on it, partic'larly anything scribbled on little pieces of paper, bring 'em to me."

And when he hadn't found anything, "Maybe it's on him. There's some kind of a note that's been passed to him —that's the information he's plannin' to use. So look for any kind of thing like that; I want it."

He still wondered what was in the note. He hadn't found it, not even when he'd personally searched the guy.

Must be grounds for blackmail of some kind, such a flap about it. Maybe worth a fortune?

The plane was coming back. Flying low. Flying right over the broad, close-cropped pastureland behind the ranch house, where Miss Everest and Tim Donan were riding.

The pilot was looking for something? No, he wasn't; he'd found it. He was waggling his wings. Must be someone who knew the girl.

Hey, this would never do . . . And there came Donan, with Miss Everest in tow. Heading back fast toward the house. The plane had banked to the right, coming around. Coming in lower, looked like it—

God! He whirled, dropping his cup to the ground, the coffee spilling and soaking into the dirt, and headed back into the office. Plane looked like it might try to come in for a landing.

He switched on the radio transmitter. "Billy! Hey, Billy! You hear me?"

"Yeah, listen, there's—"

"Plane's comin' in to land. Get back here!" Without waiting for an answer, he grabbed the rifle from its place on the wall, and was out the door. Yes, there comes the plane! He positioned himself at the end of the runway. Tried to wave off the pilot. Surely he didn't really want to land here; he was making some kind of a mistake.

The plane came in, touched down, braked to a stop.

Earl trotted across, looked up as a blond young fellow opened the door and glanced about. Did a double take— kid almost looked like the actor in that movie he'd seen the other night, *The Leningrad Affair.*

"You can't land here," he called, standing next to the wing tip with the rifle, held at waist level, aimed at his visitor's chest. "This is private property."

"Sorry. My radio's busted. I couldn't make contact with the control tower at Midland, so I couldn't get permission to land. Can I use your phone, or—"

"You can't land here; boss's—"

Lightly the tall young man jumped down. "But I *have* landed here." He ignored the rifle; walked right toward

179

Earl, relaxed and easy, just as if Earl had told him he was welcome.

The safety was off. He could have pulled the trigger. Why didn't he? Because he'd never shot anybody before?

He started to back off, but it was too late. The fellow reached out and before Earl knew what had happened, he'd knocked the barrel to the side and punched him in the jaw. He went staggering back, dropped the rifle, landed sitting on the ground. And by then the damned pilot had picked up the Remington and had it trained on him.

"Now into the building there."

No arguing. Earl got up. Slowly.

"Come on! Hurry it up!" But Earl took his time. Faked a limp and gimped along toward the door of the hangar office. This sky bandit wouldn't know that Billy was on his way back in the Land Rover. If he could delay—

"Quick! Move!"

With the feel of the barrel against his spine, Earl moved.


It did not go as he had hoped.

An improvement, though, on yesterday, when he hadn't even caught a glimpse of her.

His landing at the airstrip was successful—at first—in luring her guard away, leaving Helene quite alone. Beyond her the land rose in a series of hills, but where she and her horse were now, the ground was level enough— he was sure he could land. He'd flown carefully over it to have a good look.

He waited—having tied up his slack-jawed captive and locked him in the hangar's little bathroom—while he watched the man on the brownish horse cover the ground between them like James Arness on his way to save the rancher's daughter. Till it was time to taxi the plane back to the other end of the runway for takeoff. He got in. Started the engines. As he turned the plane on the runway, he looked out his window and saw man and horse falter; slow. Then in a wide arc they headed back toward Helene.

Hell and damn! The guard had just realized that he'd fallen for a diversionary tactic; that a handy little plane like Erin's could come down right on the grazing land and pluck Helene Everest off of it.

If he hurried . . . He taxied to the other end of the strip. Turned into the wind. Just in time—a Land Rover appeared, to the left of the plane, coming at a fast clip over the semi-arid grassland.

He took off just as the vehicle slammed to a stop at the edge of the runway.

He'd never reach her now before the horseman did . . . Unless . . .

He banked and came over the place that she had been, to see what she was doing.

The Arab was going flat out, away from Helene's guard —headed for the hills.

Hills! God . . . But there was no other way for her to go.

He flew on ahead. Hunted over the rocky, uneven crests of the hummocks beneath him. Couldn't land in any of the valleys, they were too steep and narrow—and with the hills waiting, all around, to smack a plane in the nose if it should fail to climb sharply enough.

There seemed to be one possibility. A sort of plateau-like hill, smoother than any of the others. The top of it seemed not too far removed from level. Short, though, for a landing. He flew over it twice, and decided it would have to do; he'd make it, or he'd pile up.

He headed back to find out how she was doing.

Her horse was picking its way slowly up one of the hillsides. Poor footing, no doubt; the man was gaining on her.

Twice he came back to check on her progress. He circled first over her, then over the landing spot he'd chosen, so she'd know in what direction to go. Surely she understood what he was trying to do—Helene was a girl who was always two jumps ahead of you . . .

Time, finally, to make a try for the landing. When she came over the last hill, then, he'd be waiting. And also, then, he could cover her with the rifle.

He didn't know how tense he was over the landing until he'd completed it. He grinned in relief. He'd barely, barely had enough room to come down. Inches, only to spare. And the ground nerve-rackingly uneven, but he and the plane together had made it. A very bumpy landing. He turned the plane around and took it back to where he'd touched down; ready to take off again.

Holding the rifle, he jumped onto the grass of the hilltop. Settled himself to wait.

She would have a choice, he saw, when she came over the summit of the hill opposite. She could go down the steep side of it, and up this one—also steep—or she could go far over to the left, where the shoulder of the one hill touched the other, linking the two; and cross by means of the gap.

He saw her, coming over the top of the hill.

She waved. Like someone on a summer holiday.

How far would the man be behind her? She, too, saw the choice of routes. Chose the one by way of the link between the hills—by no means as grueling a climb as the route directly down and up. But she would have to stay on the other hill for a considerable distance.

The suspense was agonizing, as Erin watched her, not knowing at what moment the man on the brown horse would come over the brow of the hill in pursuit.

She traversed the slope in what seemed almost slow motion. Well, he supposed the ground was uneven; and it was on a slant. She couldn't gallop a horse on it. But if her guard caught up—

He looked across through the telescopic sight of the rifle. Um. Pretty good.

And there came the man.

He at once turned his horse to parallel her course, along the top of the slope. He was on better ground, because he moved more rapidly than Helene seemed able to. The distance between them was fast lessening.

If Erin didn't stop him, she wouldn't make it. He lifted the rifle. Looked through the sight. Shoot his mount from under him? He put the cross hairs on the brown shoulder. No; half-measures wouldn't do. If the man was armed, he could still stop Helene from where he was now, horse or no horse. And he would be armed, for sure. From what Jack Seavering had said about this gun-happy bunch . . . Weapon on the far side, he couldn't see it from here.

He moved the cross hairs up the man's plaid chest. Was he going to kill a man? Really? He'd gone through these motions before, any number of times. The big difference was the blank cartridges, and the stuntmen who'd done the falling off the horses. Could he—

He squeezed the trigger.

God, he'd missed! Must have, because horse and rider continued unchecked. He ejected the shell and looked across.

An answer was not long in coming. The man had drawn a revolver and fired it downhill. There was a spurt of dust not far behind Helene and her horse, and the sound of the gun's firing came across the small valley to Erin.

She had almost reached the connecting bit of land between the two hills, but her pursuer was closer than ever. Erin tried to remember what all he should allow for, in aiming—motion of his target, and gravity, certainly, at this distance. He aimed a little above and slightly ahead of the patch of plaid. Squeezed.

Missed.

Damn!

And the man was firing again, now, at Helene, who had come almost to a standstill as she tried to make her way across a jagged outcrop of rock.

In a fury, Erin shot again, though not with care—with anger and the conviction that this time he knew exactly where the bastard would be when his bullet reached the other hill.

Got him.

The guard had reined in, and sat slouched over in the saddle. As Erin watched, he dismounted. On the wrong side, at that—probably because the horse offered him cover. He turned the animal around, staying on its other side, and began to retrace his route. Hit, apparently, but not too seriously. He stopped and picked up something.

His gun. He'd dropped it.

Helene had made it, now, over the rock outcrop.

Erin grinned. He had put her bodyguard out of business; even if he were still capable of firing, she was now out of range of the revolver. Across the way, the dismounted horseman opted for the protection of a group of boulders.

Erin fired one more shot across, for the hell of it, and then replaced the rifle in the cockpit.

Helene came fast, now, up the shoulder of the hill. It was no time at all before she was leaning down to give him her hand and ask, "Is Jamie all right?"

"I think so. We had to get you first."

"Oh!" She was dismayed. "He's still being held?" She slid down from the saddle and stood looking up at him. The deep-set hazel eyes held the same marvelous attraction for him as always.

"He won't let us make a move till we have you safe."

"But, Erin!" She grasped his arm. "They'll kill him if I get away!"

He looked over his shoulder—across to where his recent adversary had taken refuge. Not in sight, though the horse was. His eyes swept the hillside, and the narrow valley below. Coming around the base of the other hill was the Land Rover he'd seen near the airstrip.

"Darling, we've no time." He pointed, and she looked. "Oh . . ."

"Jamie next. It's all worked out. He's in Cabo San Lucas; they won't know there that I have you. Not till we've got him free."

Her smile was dazzling.

"Get that horse out of here," he ordered.

"Tasha." She wound the reins around the saddlehorn. Kissed the white muzzle just above the black nostrils. Pointed her away from the takeoff area, and smacked her on the rump. "*Gid*dap!"

The mare took off at a gallop.

Erin swung up into the plane, reached down for Helene. Barely in time. The Land Rover had stopped on the slope below, and its driver got out. He had a rifle, Erin saw. And he meant to use it.

No use worrying about that. He concentrated on the takeoff. Bad enough without someone shooting at you; when he'd barely had room to land, and the ground was not exactly as smooth as, say, a billiard table. He gunned the motors, extended the flaps, and they went tearing along the stretch of grass.

Ran out of runway, and beside him he heard Helene suck in her breath.

"Nothing to it," he assured her, as the hillside below them fell away. "Just like the carrier takeoffs in World War Two. Run out of deck and you're airborne." He'd relied on it.

For the second time this week, Dwight had made it in to his office for a few hours' work. No messing with the train; Mrs. Groves had driven him into New York. Monday, and again today—Wednesday.

He felt O.K. this morning, still. Oh, some pains from the incisions, but he was used to those.

No word yet. Nothing since Sunday, when Jack Seavering had called from Tucson. His nerves were fraying, by now, from the worry.

Two of them, against the combine; Jack, and the photographer friend he had told Dwight about, from their little magazine. And Dwight thought again that Jamie had indeed picked the right man to help him; warning Seavering that he could be walking into a trap hadn't slowed him down an iota. As he'd known it would not.

With a prodigious effort, he wrenched his mind from its squirrelcage contemplation of the Jamie Everest situation and applied it to an appraisal of the manuscript before him on the desk. A first novel of real promise; another Faulkner, or—

He glanced up to find his secretary standing in front of him.

"Mr. Percy—" Her myopic eyes, behind the outsize steel-rimmed glasses, looked perplexed. (Miss Saddler tried to follow all the younger fashion trends, but they never did much for her.)

"Yes, Gwen?"

"There's a reporter here to see you. From the *Times*."

Dwight shook his head emphatically. "I can't talk to—"

"He says a report's just come in from Texas that Helene Everest was rescued this morning from Mr. Everest's ranch, where she'd been held by kidnappers."

"From Hardy?" He stared at her.

"Yes. Rescued by plane. The pilot was someone named . . . Aaron Blumberg? He contacted the police about it, but now they can't find either him or Helene Everest . . ."

"Aaron Blumberg . . ." What was familiar, now, about that name?

"The man from the *Times* wants to know if it's a hoax?"

Not Aaron Blumberg. Erin Bruce . . . And Jack Seavering had pulled it off! Half of it, anyway.

"Mr. Percy—?"

"You can tell the reporter, Gwen, that it's no hoax. But I can't talk with him—tell him I've been taken ill."


Dan Bayles answered the ring at the door in the front wall.

"Yes?" He looked through the little grill in the wood.

"Well, open up! I'm not going to just stand here. Let me in!"

Dan surveyed the jowly, tanned face with the dark brown circles under the eyes and wondered where he had seen it before.

Martin Case frowned; impatient; playing his part and enjoying it—having been an actor as well as a director, all his life. "Don't tell me you don't know who I am!" Stark incredulity. "I'm Martin Case."

Oh. Very famous movie director, always played a small part himself in every movie he made—usually part of some bad guy, a real stinker.

"I'm sorry, Mr. Case. Recognize you, of course. But Mr. Everest isn't seeing anyone."

"He'll see me! Old friends."

"Not today; sorry, but he can't see you today."

"The hell he can't! Listen, he promised me when I got ready to make a new version of that oldie of his, *After the*

*Night,* I could use this house for the filming. This house right here that you're not letting me into. I've got a crew here, ready to go to work—"

"Just a minute, Mr. Case. I'll check." This was clearly out of his department. Mr. Wheelock better deal with it himself.

But Mr. Wheelock—backed up by Reg—did not have much luck, either, with the problem.

Four or five of those Hollywood people out there, milling around. One with a camera—most unnerving; the fellow even crawled up onto some high rocks on the other side of the driveway to get shots of the house. They'd come in some kind of a truck, Art saw, with a couple of Mexicans and a load of equipment.

"I'm speakin' as a friend of Jamie's, Mr. Case—flew down here with 'im the other day for some fishin'." The joviality sounded strained. "But he's got goin' on a part of his book, y'understand, and he don't want any interruptions. Won't even speak t'*me,* I'll tell yu. Won't want to see any friends, new or old, right now. Not till he's finished this writin' stint."

"I understand perfectly. We're not going to disturb Jamie—wouldn't think of it." Art let out a relieved breath. "But we *are* coming in. If Jamie's busy writing, he's shut up in his workroom. Isn't he?"

Art could only nod. "But—"

"And with his powers of concentration, he wouldn't know it even if we staged a battle scene here—opened fire with cannon, brought in a battering ram; he wouldn't even hear it. Would he, now?" Martin Case had never, as a matter of fact, met Jamie Everest. But Erin had briefed him on the great man's habits and crotchets; the only thing capable of disturbing him when at work was a ringing phone.

"I haven't authority to let you in, Mr. Case. Couldn't risk it."

"He'll never know we're here. Listen, he'll be furious if you—"

"I can't help it. I haven't the authority—"

187

"It's imperative that we get in, you see. Today. We've a shooting schedule. And my cameraman—" he indicated the young bearded fellow with a camera, who was now taking pictures from the top of a tall palm tree, though how he'd gotten up there Art couldn't imagine. "My cameraman has to look everything over, see how much room we have to get around in, room for his equipment and all, study the light . . ." Martin Case smiled. Ingratiating. The character up the palm was no more a cameraman than he was a member of the Mafia; he was Yvonne's hairdresser.

"And Miss Cartel." Case took Yvonne by the shoulders and presented her full-face to Wheelock on the other side of the grill in the door. Up close so that he'd have a good view of her fabulous violet-colored eyes, her sunny, silken hair, her pouting lips; not too close, so that he was exposed also to her cleavage. "It is essential that Miss Cartel get inside the house so that we can see how the interiors are. The colors must be exactly right for her, you see. We'll probably have to paint all the rooms—except of course Jamie's study, workroom, or whatever, and the kitchen and servants' quarters. We'll of course restore everything to its original color when we're through—unless Jamie likes the changes better."

Yvonne Cartel smiled beautifully at Art Wheelock, then made a delightful little moue. Yvonne had never in her life had a room repainted to go with her coloring; she had had exactly two parts, to date, both one-shots in T.V. situation comedies. But she was in a position now to hope for better things.

"You recognized Miss Cartel, of course," Martin Case prompted Wheelock.

"Oh, yes. A pleasure to meet you, Miss Cartel."

"She barely missed an Oscar nomination this year."

"Make it next time, I'm sure." Art became aware of someone breathing down his neck, and stepped aside to give Reg a view of Miss Cartel's lips and cleavage, the latter seeming almost to have been propped up, so that the two orbs were right under her chin.

"Reg, here, works for Jamie." Art peeked from one side

188

so that he could see Case. "Reg, explain to him why we can't let them in."

"No way, Mr. Case. It'd mean my job."

They came in from the sea, the three of them: Jack, Erin, and Helene.

Erin had tried—unsuccessfully—to leave Helene in Western Spring, where he'd landed at the tiny municipal airport to call the police and the F.B.I. For one thing, she didn't have a Mexican tourist card. For another, he'd wanted to keep her out of danger.

"You need me. I know the ground so well."

He couldn't deny that she did.

"Dump me here and I'll have you arrested before you can get clearance to take off. Rape? Or what would you fancy?"

And so they'd come down at El Paso to get a tourist card for her.

He'd tried, too, to leave her at the hotel.

"No way. You need me."

"You're going to yell rape again, I suppose?"

"Oh, robbery will do."

So here she was.

Jack found it amazing that two people could so resemble each other in appearance—Helene and her double— and be so different. Where the impostor was stiff and dour, Jamie's sister was gracious and vivacious—and as Linna had told him, willful. And there was a look of class about her that the other woman could not have imitated in a million years.

The three of them sat together, clutching their equipment, in the cabin of the fishing boat Jack had hired, the water churning in its wake, and the noise of the motor loud in their ears. They hoped Jamie's guards would not notice their odd timing. Although the boats invariably went out early in the morning, returning late in the day, it was now afternoon. They were going the wrong way, toward the fishing grounds.

The captain—a hawk-beaked, light-skinned Mexican

who could not understand why they did not go fishing ("Such a waste of the opportunity, *caballeros!*")—stayed well inshore, as Helene had instructed him.

"Getting close," she said to Erin. "Our harbor is on the other side of the headland." And a few minutes later Jamie's cruiser, riding at anchor in the little cove, came into view.

With no slackening of speed, their boat continued on course. Jack scanned the rocks and terraces, across the cove. A climb of a hundred and fifty feet, he'd guess, from sea level to the top. "I don't see anyone around up there." He consulted Erin. "Do you?"

"Not yet."

"They wouldn't bother to watch the water side," Helene said. "No one's ever thought of climbing it except me, and I didn't get far."

The only parts of the house that overlooked the cove were Jamie's writing tower, his second-floor bedroom suite, under it the kitchen and seldom-used dining room, and the side windows of the living room. The little man Eli, in the kitchen, would be the most likely to spot them.

"They seem to use the central courtyard most of the time—don't they, Helene?" Jack said.

"Yes, everyone always has. That's why we'll probably be in trouble when we reach the top. If anyone's near the pool, they'll be able to look down at the lower terrace and they'll see us."

It was the retaining wall of the dining terrace that they'd have to scale. Which was why they'd put off the attempt till siesta time, when hopefully no one would be about. They'd waited till after four.

"We'll hope anyway that Martin's keeping everyone busy at the front." It had been Erin who had organized the diversionary maneuver.

Helene got up from her place beside him and left the shelter of the cabin, to crouch at the side of the boat, looking inappropriately carefree in her improvised suit— the bottom half borrowed from Yvonne Cartel, the top half (Yvonne's wouldn't have fit her ever) consisting of a

190

bandanna she'd scrounged somewhere. ("I can hardly go in my breeches and boots, now, can I!" she'd pointed out.)

They passed Jamie's boat and drew close in now.

"Okay—it's time!" Helene took a long, shallow dive toward shore.

Without waiting for her to surface, Erin carefully shoved overboard the foam-rubber mattress Miguel had found for them, and followed it in. Jack dropped their ladder over, slipped into the water and recovered it. He cast a glance anxiously shoreward and up. No sign of anyone—nor could there be, for here they were in the lee of the promontory and out of sight of the house.

As he started for shore with the ladder, he looked across at Erin. The rifle and the automatic, wrapped in towels, encased—each—in a double layer of plastic bags and lashed on top of the mattress, appeared to have survived the plunge.

Helene touched bottom first. "Watch out for sea urchins!" she warned as Erin, then Jack, came up beside her. She had mentioned them before—very painful if you stepped on one, its poison would cripple you.

And watch not to be dashed against the rocks, Jack noted to himself as the long swells broke ahead of them and to either side.

His wrist was better today, but still he was not looking forward to having to use it, pulling himself up the cliff face above them. From here it looked even more formidable than from a distance.

They arrived safely at a jumble of rocks, above which there was no way up the slick, wet incline. They progressed from one slimy boulder to another, bracing themselves each time a wave broke, threatening to knock them over or suck them back with it into the foaming pools between the chunks of stone.

Helene went first, Erin next, between them dragging the mattress—a nuisance, with the ropes that were tied around it getting repeatedly snagged. Jack followed with the ladder—all eight cumbersome feet of it—trying to manage with his good hand. Small crabs scuttled on the wet stone surfaces, as sudden in their movements as yesterday's lizards; and looking down the crevices at the sandy bottom, he several times saw one of the sea urchins —black, spiny, looking like small naval mines.

They passed out of reach of the surf, and onto pebbly sand. Helene unwound a long end of one of the ropes tied around the mattress. Carrying it with her, she crossed the sand and began to climb, in a fissure twisting obliquely upward. It was barely large enough to give her purchase, with hands and feet, and she made slow progress of it, slipping once or twice, saving herself with her handhold on the rock.

Erin went up behind her. Though some of the toeholds looked too insubstantial to support his greater weight, he managed well, climbing rapidly and surely in his dripping tennis shoes. The two of them reached a ledge, and motioned for Jack to start the mattress up. As they pulled at the other end of the rope, he guided it from below—a soggy dead weight, heavier by a ton with the water it had soaked up. Finally they had it. The ladder went up the same way, and then they lowered the rope end for him.

He knotted it around his waist, then barefooted, tendersoled, trying to save his bad hand, he started his climb. It wasn't really far to where the other two waited; it just seemed far. They kept the rope taut, but although it prevented him from falling, he still had to make his own way up.

Made it at last, and stood panting with Erin. Water from their shorts and shirts dribbled onto the stone. From here they could see their fishing boat, anchored now around the next headland, from where the captain would watch for their descent. And if they did not come down again, of course . . .

Upward again, and this time they used the ladder for a stretch on which there was no handhold. They found a rockshelf to set it on, and Erin tossed up the loose end of rope to belay it around a projection above them.

"Looks highly unprofessional," Jack complained as he went up it.

"No, it's great," said Helene. "I was never able to make it past here."

"Easy with pitons," Erin suggested.

"Well, who takes pitons with them when they go swimming?"

They were making good progress when without warning the rifle broke loose from its moorings on top of the mattress. It went slithering down the cliff face, as all three of them watched it, fascinated, appalled. It caromed off a jutting piece of rock and plunged into the water.

"At least they couldn't hear it fall, over the sound of the surf," Erin said cheeringly.

"The automatic okay?" Jack asked.

"Yes, still secure."

They interrupted the climb for a conference. "When we get to the wall at the top," Erin told Helene, "you stay, and Jack and I go on."

"I'm coming with you!"

"You are not! You are to stay out of sight, out of the action completely. I don't want you underfoot. When we come back, Linna will be first over the wall, and you're to help her down the ladder."

Helene smiled nicely. "What if you don't come back? Then I'll have to come and salvage the survivors."

"That won't be necessary!"

Jack watched impatiently as Erin kissed her—altogether too much like the movies. No wonder he'd been so easy to recruit; he couldn't leave the girl alone.

"Christ, do we have to hang around for that kind of stuff?"

"Come on." Erin led the way on up.

It had been this morning that Jamie had told her.

Yesterday he had clung all day, she knew, to the hope that somehow Jack Seavering would be back; would bring the police, the F.B.I., and would rescue them.

Because he *had* concealed a message, in code, amongst his comments on the article. And Jack would, he assured her, have figured it out.

"It will take time, though. They'll have to hunt first for

Helene. Once the Mexican police are alerted to look for her—well, we've got to be optimistic."

But today, after Reg had unlocked the door to Linna's suite and she'd come out for breakfast, served in the shade of one of the loggias, by the pool, she knew as soon as she saw Jamie sitting alone there that something was very wrong.

"What is it?" she asked, as she unfolded her napkin. Jamie looked strained, his grey eyes haunted.

He shook his head, and she saw that Eli had come up beside her, quite soundlessly, and awaited her breakfast order.

"Just the melon, Eli." It was already before her on a green pottery plate. "And some coffee."

He filled her cup from the silver pot and padded away.

"What's wrong?" she said.

"Reg told me last night—after I left you. Jack Seavering won't be back."

"Why not?" She dreaded asking, her mind coiling away from what might have happened.

"He's dead."

Jack Seavering dead. She'd never even thought to worry about him; only about Jamie. The sun shone, in the courtyard beside her; a small grey bird lighted on the bougainvillaea trailing from a balcony rail opposite. Life went right on. It didn't seem possible that anything so final as death had—

"How?" *My preference is still the vintage wine,* she'd said. What a cutting, graceless thing—

If only she could call back the words!

"Art and Dan took him into the mountains. Shoved him over a cliff."

Dry-eyed, she stared at Jamie. It must be true, she supposed . . . She tried to visualize Jack Seavering lying broken and smashed, never to move again, on the floor of some desert canyon, so far from where he belonged. *My preference is still the vintage wine . . .*

She could see Jamie's thought so clearly in his face: he might just as well, himself, have done this to Jack. She reached out and took his hand. Because he needed her to.

194

Well, that had been this morning. As of this afternoon she knew that Jamie, still, was essentially the walking wounded. There was no longer any hope of rescue—not for her, nor Jamie, nor Helene. But the heaviest part of the burden that weighed so crushingly upon him was the realization that his attempt to reach freedom had dragged others to their death.

"Sue Ann. Jack must have talked to her, that's why she suddenly, after all this time, became a threat and got herself killed. Then a photographer from *Perspective*, name of Vernon Fix. Reg told me he was caught taking pictures near the house, so they took him out and abandoned him in the desert, miles from anywhere. Likable old guy, I remember him from the interview back at Hardy. Now, Jack." He didn't add her name to the list, but she knew, from the way he looked at her, that he privately included it.

Shocked as Linna had been, when she first came, at Jamie's light, sarcastic manner with his captors, she was even more shocked now when the badinage stopped. At lunch Jamie scarcely spoke. It was she who took up the needling.

"Unmurder, Inc.," she said, to no one in particular. "All those people dead? And not a shot fired. Accident specialists." She was rewarded by Art's throwing a suspicious, critical look at Reg. If their crimes were being talked about behind his back, Art knew which one of his co-conspirators would have done the talking.

"What are you saving for me," she asked, directly of Wheelock. "A scorpion?"

Jamie shook his head warningly at her, and Lucille Garvan said, "Nifty. Almost as good as an asp."

So now after the usual late Mexican lunch, Dan had locked them into Jamie's private suite. And it was Reg, today, who took the chore of watching, from under the loggia on the other side of the swimming pool, to make sure they didn't climb down from the balcony into the central patio—for whatever purpose they could conceivably have in mind in doing so.

He and Linna could have been locked up separately; could have been given trays at every meal; but that wasn't how things had been before, and they weren't now. His jailers had tried always to make life as agreeable for him as possible—since they wanted to keep him happily writing.

They had, also enjoyed the captive-captor game, he knew. Things would have been terribly dull for all of them if they hadn't entertained themselves with this whole set-up.

Damn their hides.

Now, he and Linna sat on the couch under the window of his sitting room, away from the eyes of Reg Curtiss. They'd been talking, still about their hopes of getting out of here. At least Linna had. "But, Jamie! Dwight Percy knows something is wrong. So does Jack's boss at the magazine. They'll do something; one of them will, or both, when Jack and Vernon Fix just never . . . when they don't come back. It's not the same as it was before, when no one outside the conspiracy knew anything about it."

He didn't tell her what was going to happen. Before any rescuers from the United States could get through the international red tape, the two of them would be liquidated—Helene, too, of course, wherever she was—and his companions of the last year would scatter, settling, whether they liked it or not, for whatever was already in their bulging bank accounts.

He should not have told her about Jack Seavering's death; and the other, the photographer. He should have let her go on hoping, for what time was left, that soon they'd be gotten out.

He wondered what had happened between her and Seavering. Something had, he could tell by the way she spoke of him.

His arm was about her shoulders. Dearest Linna! If only she hadn't gotten involved in all this.

Suddenly he heard shouting.

He looked out the window behind them. There was only his boat lying there in the cove. No one in it. Nothing else to be seen.

196

"What—" said Linna, and got up and crossed the room to the balcony, to look out into the courtyard.

He followed, and they stood just within the doors.

It was Dan Bayles now, guarding them below, instead of Reg.

He could have sworn someone was calling his name. Bellowing, rather, the stentorian voice floating through the dry, still air over the living room's tile roof, from the direction of the front wall.

"Jaa-mie . . . Jaaa-miiiiie!"

He did not recognize the voice.

Linna's hand was on his wrist—something warning in the urgent pressure of her fingers. "Seaward," was all she said, very low, and his eyes turned toward the ocean, sparkling blue beyond the dining terrace.

For a moment he didn't believe it. Someone was coming over the wall down there at the top of the cliff; the wall—three feet high on this side, but seven feet on the other side—with all that broken glass imbedded in the top, rows of it, like shark's teeth. Something had been thrown across it, covering the sharp points. And the man couldn't be ten feet tall, but he nevertheless was standing on the other side of the wall, where it crowned the drop-off, and where he wouldn't have supposed there'd be any kind of foothold. He was about to clamber onto the thing slung over the glass—a *mattress?*

It wasn't Jack Seavering; the momentary insane hope was snuffed out as he saw that the man was of a different build, his hair lighter. But then Jack, of course, was dead.

"Jaa-*miiiie!*" From the other direction, the voice again.

The man on the wall came over; dropped to the terrace, to the right of the dining pavilion. And if Jamie had had any doubt that rescue was at hand, it was laid to rest as he recognized Erin Bruce.

My God, the marines have landed! "Erin!" he said softly to Linna. His eyes slid back to Dan. His stomach muscles tightened as the figure in the shadow of the arches across the way stood up and sauntered out to the pool.

Erin was not within Dan's range of vision; not yet. He had crossed the lower terrace and couched, now, behind

197

the retaining wall next to the wide steps by which one mounted to the courtyard level. But if Dan should turn his head, he would have a prime view of anyone coming up the steps. The mattress, Jamie hoped, was not visible from the center of the courtyard because the dining pavilion was in the way—or so it appeared from this angle.

He stepped onto the balcony. He must pinpoint Dan's whereabouts for Erin, and at the same time keep their guard occupied. "What's all that shouting out at the front wall?" he called.

Dan came around the end of the pool. For a few steps he faced seaward, and must have been looking right over Erin Bruce's head. If he saw any portion of the mattress, it didn't register with him, because he seemed to notice nothing amiss.

"Oh, the shouting?" He now stood—to Jamie's relief— with his back to the open end of the courtyard. He tilted his face upward to look at the two of them on the balcony. He was wearing his gun, of course; Jamie had in fact never seen him without it. It was strapped on over his black shorts. "That movie producer, Martin Case, wants in to see you. That's all." He shrugged. He never smiled, even when he was pleased.

"Sounds like he won't take no for an answer!" Jamie grinned down at him. Out of the corner of his eye he could see a second man climbing over the wall. And Erin, now, reached the top of the steps; glided quickly behind the right-hand stone figure, of the two that guarded the patio; waited, studying the lay of the land.

"Why don't you let him in?" Jamie suggested. Behind Dan, Erin made his approach—barehanded, crouching like an Indian, his tennis-shoed feet silent on the tile paving. "Lucille can charm him a bit. Show him around—" Linna, at Jamie's side, put her hand in his, tightly clutching his fingers.

"Oh, sure," said Dan. "Why not let him in."

"Won't he think it's peculiar if you don't?" Linna asked him. "*No* one refuses a man like Martin Case."

"Art Wheelock can. He's—" But Dan was never to finish the sentence, because an arm was thrown around him from behind, pressing against his windpipe, cutting off his breath, at the same time that his revolver was plucked from his holster and its muzzle jammed into his ribs.

The scene below him was like a dream to Jamie—the dream of rescue he'd envisioned so many times that now he could hardly believe it. There, even, was the dead Jack Seavering, amazingly in one piece, holding an automatic on Dan Bayles while Erin, laying Dan's gun on a lounge chair, stuffed a gag in Bayle's mouth, fastened it in place, and uncoiling a length of rope from about his waist, commenced tying his furious captive's hands behind his back.

But it was real. Rescue had come. "Let's go," he said to Linna. Wheelock or one of the others might appear at any moment; there was no time to be lost. He put one long leg, then the other, over the wrought-iron railing of the balcony, stooped, let himself down, and dropped.

"Have you found Helene," he said anxiously to Jack. Asking the impossible, he knew.

"Yes. She's waiting for us."

Waiting for them! Yet already it seemed as if the long captivity had never happened. *That* was the dream, not this. Exuberant, he braced himself to catch Linna, who was letting herself down, hanging onto the bottom of the railing. She let go and dropped into his arms.

Erin again held the revolver on Dan. "Where can we lock him up?"

Jamie nodded toward the storage closet where the pool equipment was kept—a door beneath the loggia.

"Key?" queried Erin.

Jamie reached into the pocket of his guard's shorts and extracted a bunch of keys strung on a piece of cord. He smiled into his late keeper's face. "What a pleasure, Dan."

Jack, with the automatic, stood watch at the closet door with Linna while the others tied Dan's feet and secured him to a pipe. He pressed her hand, holding onto it with his left one so that the two of them would move as one when they broke for the wall.

199

"You're to stick with me," he instructed her. "Jamie goes with Erin. When we get to the wall, I'll help you onto it. We've put a mattress across. But be careful not to fall off the other side. A long drop, believe me! Helene will help you down—"

"Helene?" she said in surprise.

"Helene. It's a six- or seven-foot wall on that side, and we have a ladder against it. Okay?"

"Marvelous."

"There's barely room to brace the ladder against a rock, there; very little space to step off—except into thin air. Lose your balance and you'd go over into the water or onto the rocks below."

She was leaning against his shoulder, looking out with him across the courtyard toward the living room, the direction from which Wheelock and Reg would probably come. "They told us you were dead," she said.

For just a second he turned his head, to look into the phenomenal blue eyes; wondering how she'd taken the news. "A little premature with their announcement, I guess."

"Okay." Erin was behind them. "Finished."

"All clear out here."

They edged into the open, as the door was closed behind them and Jamie locked it. No one in sight.

Linna and Jack went first, the others close behind—past the corner of the pool, across the square red tiles toward the steps. The shouting, out front, seemed to have stopped. The only sound nearby was that of their hurrying feet, the only movement besides their own, in the courtyard, was the dappled motion of the water in the pool.

They reached the stone steps. Started down. Reached the bottom. Raced frantically across the lower level of stone paving, around the dining pergola, toward the wall, where the mattress still hung, lopsidedly, caught on the spears of glass.

Helene (against orders!) waited in the shelter of a scrubby palm tree, frowning, anxious eyes on her brother.

An exclamation from Erin: "You weren't supposed—"

But they had reached the wall.

"You first," Jack said to Linna, aware of Jamie, behind him, catching up his sister in a hug. "No, Helene had better go—she knows how the ladder is propped. Helene—" As he turned to her, the revolver report almost burst his eardrum.

Erin had fired. Jack looked back, through the pergola framework and the vines hanging over the dining table, past the flight of steps toward the house. He could see no one. "Go on," he urged Helene. They must get the two girls over the wall.

Before she could move, a shot was fired from above, plonking into the wall not two feet away.

"We have you covered." Art Wheelock's voice. And now Jack located the rifle barrel protruding from the arch at his end of the right-hand loggia. Art was behind a column.

Another shot, from off at the left; looked as if it came from a window near the base of the tower. Bullet had hit the mattress.

"Don't move," said Wheelock, "except to drop your guns. Or we'll have two dead Everests. I can pick 'em both off from here."

"Yes, he can." Erin cast a despairing look around at their little group. He tossed Dan Bayles's revolver to the stone paving at his feet. "We'll have to watch for a chance to surprise them, that's all."

Jack followed suit and dropped the automatic.

Martin Case was worried about the gunfire. Not good. Not at all.

But he'd had no instructions to do anything beyond creating a disturbance. Except, of course, if none of them came out again he was to report it to the Mexican police.

He'd better wait, though, a little. So he watched Yvonne posing, in one outlandish position after another, for Henry, who kept clicking away even though he'd long since used up his film..

What was going on inside? No one even posted at the door to keep an eye on them any longer; must all have

201

their hands full. Though there were no more shots. He wondered whether that was good or bad.

He crossed again to the heavy door and peered in through the little grill. A flower garden, and a lot of steps, going up to a wide front door which stood open. No one around. No, there came—oh, he was relieved to see it was Helene Everest, coming quickly down the steps toward him in a striped terry beach robe and a beach hat.

"Martin," she said as she came within speaking range, and saw his face framed in the opening.

"Hi," he said.

"I just wanted to tell you my brother's *furious!* It was a practical joke, you know, all that about Jamie being held prisoner. Erin and I thought it up. Well, the famous author's very mad—especially over our rigging up the fake rescue! Doesn't think it's funny at all . . ." She was nervous, he could tell; very upset.

"Went over like a lead balloon, eh?"

"Exactly." She achieved a little smile. He couldn't see her eyes because of the oversize dark glasses.

"Sorry," he sympathized. "It did sound a little far-out, didn't it?" He was able to laugh, now, at the wild story Erin had told him. "So when do I get in to see Jamie? Now that the funny games are over?"

"Tomorrow."

"Tomorrow?"

"Yes. Much better than today."

"If you say so."

"See you—" She turned away.

"Yes, he said to her back as she started up the steps to the house. "Anyhow it was fun while it lasted."

His look of amusement was gone as he signaled his little coterie to get into the truck. "Okay, Miguel, tell Jesus we're leaving."

The old Mexican started the engine, Miguel got in beside him, and the rest all piled into the back. The truck rolled down the incline.

"What happened, Marty?" Yvonne leaned against his clasped knees as they sat together in the truck bed, and

202

the others—Henry, Edward, and Bus, who was Martin's nephew, huddled close to hear over the whining gears.

"It didn't work. They got caught."

"But if Helene was able to come down and talk to you—" Lovingly, without thinking at all about it, she fingered her huge diamond.

"That wasn't Helene. It was her double."

"You're sure?" She caught only a glimpse of the girl through the grill, but she could have sworn—

"Darling, I never mistake a voice." He prided himself on never forgetting the particular qualities of any voice he had ever heard—the larynx, after all, was the most important thing an actor had. "The planes of her face, too —all wrong."

"God," she said. "That firing . . ."

"Do you think they're dead?" Henry asked in a hushed tone of Edward, who was Martin's secretary.

"They wouldn't shoot to kill—would they? Not on purpose—" Edward devoutly hoped nothing had happened to Erin Bruce, whom he much admired.

Bus looked inquiringly at his uncle—that great man from whom, as far as he was concerned, all blessings flowed. "What do we do now?"

"Now we go and try to convince the Mexican authorities that this whole thing isn't some kind of practical joke." And what sober, serious Mexican official was going to believe this crazy story?

The truck jolted on downhill, past the cove with the boat, out of sight of the house. Past the car shed and the little thatched-roof house with its fence of twigs. On out to the highway.


"They left, I gather," Art Wheelock said as Lucille came out through the center arch from the living room to join them by the pool. They had all heard the revving up of the truck engine and the complaining of the gears— now fading in the downhill distance.

"Yes, they left."

"Did he believe you?"

"He seemed to."

They stood by the swimming pool, the five captives lined up on one side. Reg and Art on the other, their weapons at the ready. Behind Art, at the living-room end of the pool, Erin's automatic and Dan's revolver lay on a table. Quite out of reach for any of the luckless five.

"Okay, Jamie, what did they do with Dan?" Art had tried, already, to find out from the other two men, and had gotten no answer.

Jamie Everest's lips curved downward at the corners in the odd smile so characteristic of him. "Why, they dumped him over; that sheer drop—you know the one." The place at the corner of his writing tower, the one with a clear drop to the ocean, where no security wall was needed.

Art looked taken aback; turned his head toward the spot indicated, tightening his grip involuntarily on the rifle, as it occurred to him that if Dan were truly gone, his side was one fewer in number. "Go see," he said to Lucille. He needed Dan.

The line of captives stood motionless while Lucille Garvan walked past them and out to the tower which rose at the end of the three-sided court, beside the steps to the lower terrace.

Like a firing squad, Jack thought, looking across the water: the two of them there with their guns, the five lined up here.

They saw her crane her neck, searching, as she stood a little back from the rocky edge, holding onto a window ledge of the tower. A buzzard, on motionless wings, glided past her, out over the surf below, lending to Jamie's fabrication a gratuitous credibility.

As they watched Lucille, a sound came from another direction: the musical clang of the bell that hung by the door in the front wall.

"Hell." Art threw a glance across at Reg. "What is this, trick or treat day?"

"Eli'll get it."

Lucille turned, at the far edge of the courtyard, and shook her head. She started back toward them and paused at the outer end of the pool. "I didn't see anything. Though how you could tell, with the undertow . . ."

A faint thumping noise accompanied her words.

"What's that?" Reg asked sharply.

Lucille's stony face lighted in a clever smile. "I imagine it's Dan."

"Of course it's Dan! Go let 'im out!" Art jerked his head in the direction of the storeroom. "Oh, here, Lucille —he'll be needing this." He stepped back a pace to pick up Dan's revolver; held it out.

She came around the pool, the heels of her sandals clacking on the tiles. As she took the heavy weapon from him, Eli appeared, stepping out of the shadowed living room into the sunlight of the patio.

"A caller," he said to Art Wheelock. "Mr. Percy?"

Art did not take his eyes off Erin Bruce, at whom his rifle pointed. "Percy? He said *Percy?*"

"Yes. Say he Mr. Everest's editor."

Wheelock shifted his attention for just a moment to Jack Seavering. "Another one of your tricks? . . . Reg!"

"Yeah."

"Can't be Percy. Man's too sick t'leave home. Go see who it is."

"What'll you do with this bunch while I'm gone?" His contempt for Art as a gunman couldn't have been more clear.

"Eli'll take over for you. Get going, Lucille—what're you waitin for?" He reached for the automatic. "Here, Eli. Take this. Keep it trained on our guests. Any of 'em starts to do anything, you shoot." He moved out to where Reg had stood and Eli took his place.

Without a backward glance, Reg strode into the house.

Lucille went the long way around the pool, past the diving board, passing close only to Helene, at the far corner nearest the storage closet. The others, standing motionless, watched her progress: Erin, next to Helene; Jack; then Linna beside Jamie.

With Dan's release the odds against them would lengthen. Not that their chances amounted to much now.

Lucille tried the closet door. "They've locked it!"

205

Art's face twisted in annoyance. "Well, there must be a key."

"Reg has a set of keys." She stepped nearer the end of the pool. "Though one of *them's* got it—" She scrutinized one face after another, in hopes the culprit would betray himself.

And she was careless. Helene moved so suddenly there was no time to draw back. Before Lucille realized the danger, she was shoved off the edge and into the water, the gun flying from her hand and sinking, out of reach, to the bottom.

The geyser caused by her impact had not yet hit the poolside when Erin cut the water with a dive toward Art Wheelock. That left Eli for Jack, and he took off fast, hoping to make it around the shallow end of the pool to where the wizened little character was trying uncertainly to cover them all.

The report rang out—loud in the partially enclosed space. Eli hadn't fired—so Jack knew it had been a shot from the rifle. No time, as he reached the corner of the pool, to see whether anyone was hit, he must reach—

He was struck as though by the blow of a giant fist; thought there must have been a second report, he didn't really hear it. Without knowing how he had gotten there, he was lying by the pool's edge and his face hurt where it had struck the tiles.

From some other place, it seemed, he surveyed the scene in the sun-washed patio with its shadowed arcades; withdrawn, suddenly, from the action.

No sound, other than the surf far below, the lapping of the water in the pool, and the dull throb of the filter pump.

Blood soaked his half-dried shirt; he noticed it with surprise.

He looked vaguely around. Erin had reached the other side of the pool, near Wheelock, where he hung onto the two uprights of the ladder, immobilized by his own automatic; Eli had decided what best to do with it. Wheelock looked coldly down the barrel of the rifle at Jack.

Where were the others? He could see only Lucille,

grasping the diving board, pulling herself up out of the water as he watched, to slither onto dry land.

Jamie held Linna in front of him, sheltered by the loggia's wide stucco column. Safe for the moment, anyway. As was Helene, behind the next pillar.

He peered out through the cascade of bougainvillaea festooning the archway. Felt, rather than heard, Linna's muffled exclamation. Jack Seavering was down. Blood soaked his shirt, ran onto the tiles by the pool.

Jamie's hands tightened on the skin of Linna's shoulders, and he was aware of her face, turned toward him for a moment—blanched, the color drained from it so that the little sprinkling of freckles stood out. Then she had broken from him, running, heedless of the danger, into the open.

"Linna!" he called. Saw his horror mirrored in Seavering's face as he, too, realized what she was doing.

Her frightened eyes and pale lips, framing an entreaty, turned fleetingly to Jamie over her shoulder. He did not catch the words.

Linna, dear God! Leaving the sanctuary of the loggia, he hurried to place himself between her and the rifle in Art Wheelock's hands.

He reached them; bent over the two forms huddled there on the tiles. No room to shield either of them; she knelt where the reporter had fallen, right at the edge of the pool. Jack lay on his side, facing Wheelock, and thank goodness at least his eyes were still open, he wasn't dead. Linna, with her arms around him, was trying to get him on his feet.

"Here." Jamie pushed her back, reach down and put an arm under Seavering's shoulder. "Can you make it, Jack?" Got him to a sitting position. Three of them helping now—Helene had joined them.

"Line up, all of you!" Art's voice cracked out. "Jamie, get back or I'll shoot. I *mean* it!"

And he knew Art would. Now he would, for the grand scheme was finished, the days of the goose that laid the golden eggs were done. "Come on." With Linna and Helene, he hoisted their casualty to his feet, wondering each second when the shot would come. At this range Art Wheelock would not miss.

The report was louder than he had expected. It filled the whole spacious courtyard with deafening, nerve-shattering sound. But he felt nothing.

Involuntarily he looked across at the man who had fired; and in amazement saw Art's rifle fall from his bloodied hand and clatter to the ground. Only then did he realize that the shot had come not from in front of them, but from behind.

He turned, looked sideways over Jack Seavering's head. Walking slowly out into the courtyard was Dwight. It was he who had fired. Impossible, but there he was, plodding forward like an old buffalo. Leveled in his hand was a revolver. That could only be Reg's, Jamie realized. And what had become of Reg? It seemed hours ago that he had gone off to deal with—yes, with Dwight.

As if he'd been doing this sort of thing all his life, his editor stopped and, taking a solid stance, raised the revolver just a bit, and fired again.

Fascinated, Jamie watched Art Wheelock crumple.

Before the man had even hit the ground, Erin, pulling himself upward out of the pool by means of the ladder, in one lunge flung himself on Eli and tore the automatic from his grasp.

Holding the gun on the little man, he carefully surveyed the body that lay almost at his feet. Then he knelt and felt Art's pulse.

Jamie maneuvered Jack Seavering to one of the lounges and eased him into it.

"Dead," Erin called to them. He stood up and inclined his head respectfully toward Dwight. "Shot through the temple."

With a tiny, quizzical smile, Dwight laid his weapon on the nearest table and lowered himself into a chair. "Didn't suppose I was that good a shot." He sighed, with a look at Jack, beside him. "Sorry I wasn't able to make it sooner."

"Dwight! Dwight, are you okay?" Jamie came around to lay a hand on his shoulder.

"Fine. A little tired!" He leaned forward to see past Jamie. "You going to survive?" he said gently to the *Perspective* reporter.

"No doubt of it." But Seavering looked ghastly, his face strained, his skin grey. He managed a grin for Dwight and then his eyes again sought Linna's. She was bending over him, pressing on the wound in his side with a bit of cloth she'd torn from his shirt.

"Hey, you!" Erin called. Lucille was trying to fade unobtrusively away in the middle distance. "Come back here." She came, and he lined her up beside Eli. "Where's the red-headed fellow?" He glanced questioningly at Dwight.

"Reg?" He grinned under the full white handlebar mustache. "I locked him in a cupboard. Like the spider to the fly, he said to me, 'Come in.' Don't know what he expected to do with me—what with all this going on up here. I surprised him and took his gun."

The faint thudding of Dan's feet against the wall began again from behind the door under the balcony.

"What in the devil is that?" Dwight cocked an ear toward the sound.

"The closets are full, I guess. That's the chief guard." Erin's eyed his two prisoners with distaste. "The police should come any time—Martin Case was to send them if things went wrong."

"Worriedly, Jamie bent over Jack. His eyes were closed. "How is he?" he asked Linna.

"I don't know." Her voice was none too steady. "We should get him to a doctor." Her eyes dropped to the red-stained cloth beneath her fingers.

"Feels fine," Jack said.

"You don't even know. You've been stunned." She reproved him as a worried mother might a child.

Helene leaned over Jack, touched his arm. "I'll go for a doctor."

"Oh, please, Helene!" Linna looked up gratefully.

"Take my taxi," Dwight told her. "It's waiting out front

—if the driver hasn't panicked and gone after the gun-fire."

"How did you get here?" Jamie asked.

"Got a flight out of Kennedy this morning, for San Diego; barely! Crossed to Tijuana and chartered a plane. Landed at the hotel—I didn't know whether anyone was even here, by this time."

Jamie picked up the revolver Dwight had laid aside. He should see to Reg. "You're really all right?" he asked, pausing beside his old and dear friend.

"Better than you'd think."

Well, he hoped so. He went with Helene into the house. Put an arm around her as they crossed the living room. "How did they find you?"

"Logic, I guess. I was at home in Hardy. Oh, Jamie, it's so good to see you!"

They reached the entry hall, with the great cupboard whose carved wooden doors covered most of one wall.

"Reg?"

A muffled shout of outrage from behind a door on the left.

"Go on, Helene. I hope you can find a doctor some-where . . ." And as she went out into the front garden—still in her bathing suit—and down the steps, he called after her, "Leave the gate open! All the way!"

A barrage of knocking broke out in the cupboard.

The ornament lock would not withstand the assault for long. Jamie turned the key and Reg pushed open the door and stepped down, flexing his shoulders to relieve the cramp. There was a massive, swollen bruise, as big as an egg, on the right side of his forehead.

"Bet you wouldn't pull that trigger," Reg said, gauging him.

"Don't be too sure—after what you've put me through!" Jamie motioned to him and Reg obediently passed ahead of him into the living room and across it. As cocky as ever, he sauntered through the central arch and out under the loggia to join the others.

"Smart-ass, aren't you?" he said to Dwight.

His eyes took in Lucille and Eli, standing together

under Erin's watchful gaze, then lighted on the body sprawled beyond them.

"Who liquidated our friend the accountant?"

"Dwight did," said Jamie.

"Why, you old bastard!" Reg seated himself on the table near Dwight. His bright brown eyes studied the editor. "So *that's* why you dragged your poor old carcass all the way cross-country, in your condition. To kill Art Wheelock."

Dwight had stiffened, like a dog whose known enemy has come within range. "If that's what it was going to take to save Jamie Everest—yes."

"And not a moment too soon," said Erin. "Or we'd all have had it."

"But that's not what I meant—was it, Dwight?" Reg persisted.

Dwight didn't look well; Jamie couldn't help noticing, even while he kept the revolver on Reg. All this had been so much more than a man in his state of health should have attempted . . .

"You had to kill Art," Reg said. "So he'd never talk."

Dwight's brows drew downward in a quick frown. "Jamie, I don't know what kind of pitch your pilot's trying to make here, but surely we don't want to listen to him shoot off his mouth?'"

"Let's lock him up till the police come," Erin suggested. "Along with these two."

Reg looked at Jamie and smiled. "Put Dwight Percy in with us, then, where he belongs. The silent partner."

For the second time today, Jamie felt as if he were in a dream. He heard Dwight say, with contempt and a touch of amusement, "The man's crazy! *Partner!*" He snorted. "Whose partner, I'd like to know—"

"Reg," Jamie said sharply. "The time for being funny has passed."

"Not a joke, boss." Reg's face wore a novel look of sincerity. And in spite of himself Jamie remembered wondering how Dwight could have overcome Curtiss, who was as wily and wary as a red fox. Still—

"Dwight's been calling the tune, I think, for the rest of

211

us," Reg went on. "I wasn't supposed to know—only Art knew that."

Dwight struggled to his feet. "That's outrageous! You're trying to say I was part of this—this monstrous *plot?*"

Jamie looked at his dearest friend, his friend of twenty-six years, the man who had dragged himself, old and ill, across a continent to be of help to him. "Dwight's a wealthy man, Reg. He wouldn't need—"

"Ever know a man with money who didn't want *more* money? He needed it for his paintings—isn't that so, Dwight?"

Dwight's face twisted a little to one side. "I don't know how you think I could have taken part in this! Let alone why . . ." His fingers fumbled at the buttons of his shirt. "You think I was *faking* my heart condition? Look!" He bared his chest and there they were—the long marks of the incisions, still an angry red, not old enough to have turned yet to white scars.

"Very touching exhibit," Reg said, unmoved. "The scheme was laid out *before* all that."

Dwight's face had turned dark, almost purple, Jamie saw as his editor turned to him and in one quick motion reached out and took the revolver from him.

He repositioned the gun in his own large hand, held it firmly on Reg. "There'll be no more of this!" His voice shook. "No more!"

"Threaten me if you like," Reg said. "Shoot me, even—in cold blood in front of all these witnesses. But I have the proof here."

"Money for my paintings, you say! Bargains I've picked up over the years at auctions! Five thousand dollars, ten thousand, for some—"

Quite unexpectedly Jack Seavering spoke. "And the El Greco? And the Goya?"

Reg was slowly extracting something from the back pocket of his slacks. A folded envelope, it looked like. "Here," he said.

"He has an *El Greco?*" echoed Erin. "And a Goya?"

Dwight did not fire. The gun was sagging in his hand. He turned a little toward Jamie, his eyes bugging out, a look in them of terror and incredulity. "Jamie—" he whispered; tried, with the left hand, to grasp Jamie's arm, and fell heavily, horribly, to the tile paving.

Reg lost no time. Dropping the envelope, he took off.

Erin fired a shot. "Let him go," said Jamie. He bent over Dwight.

He was still breathing, but his face twisted grotesquely to the right. He tried to speak, but all that emerged was garbled sound.

# 12

LINNA SAT ON THE EDGE OF JACK'S BED, IN ONE of the guest rooms, pressing with a hand towel on the two holes—in his side and in his back. She tried not to think of where the bullets might lie.

Two Mexican policemen in brown uniforms came and questioned them. One was lanky, young, and mustached, the other pear-shaped, grizzled, and also mustached, and both of them were very polite. Jack couldn't say much, he kept falling asleep.

Helene came, with the doctor—a round, dumpy little man with a fringe of grey hair around a bald spot like a tonsure. And they were in luck, he was an American surgeon who'd been vacationing at the hotel.

Linna relinquished her place at the bedside, and Helene moved a lamp closer so that Dr. McNulty could see.

"Half an inch higher, or lower, or further to the right, and you'd have been a dead man," he said complacently to his patient. "The bullet grazed a rib, came out at the back."

"Oh, I thought there were *two!*" Linna said, weak with relief.

"You've lost some blood, and your side's going to be damn sore. Luckily I'd never think of coming to a Godforsaken place like Baja without a few essentials like antitetanus serum. I'll just clean this up and we'll give you a shot. What did you do to your wrist?"

When he had finished and Helene took him off to attend Dwight Percy, Jack fell asleep again. And Linna watched him, in the quiet room lit now by only a single table lamp, with its shade of pierced tin.

How ironic that she'd waited four years and come all this distance to find that Jamie had been right the first time about their love affair. She saw it now as she never could before: for her, a case of hero worship, escalated into a tempestuous romance. She'd been flattened, enraptured, she'd seen herself as part of the Everest legend. It had been an ego trip. And for Jamie? She didn't know . . .

Her eyes went over Jack Seavering's bruised and sunburned face, with the bloody scrape on one cheek. The gash in his scalp didn't show, with his head on the pillow, but she knew it was there. And the injured wrist . . . He certainly needed looking after.

If she hadn't met him, she'd never have discovered that love had another dimension—one she had never known about.

Though how she could ever tell Jamie . . .

Late—after midnight—Jamie came to see how Jack was.

"He's asleep," he said.

He drew her over to the door, put both hands on her shoulders. She wondered what was wrong, his expression was so grave. "Now that the excitement's all over, shall we get it straight, Linna?" He spoke softly, so as not to disturb Jack. "It will never work out—you and me. You see that now, don't you?"

She must, it seemed, be as transparent as a pane of glass.

"Oh, Jamie—" She hated to make an end of things—as one hates to leave home, to leave school for the last time, to grow older.

"We're different generations, Linna. We live in different worlds . . . Yesterday that didn't matter; what we were to each other then was the last sweet draught of the cup —no more. What we said, or felt, or looked was no promise to one another."

"Jamie—"

"Today there's a future again, and yours is not meant to include an eccentric middle-aged recluse with nothing but ink in his veins. Understood?"

He'd included everything, hadn't he? Even the things she'd said and tried to make herself believe.

She touched his cheek with her fingers. He was very dear to her; he always would be. "I love you very much," she said—now that he wouldn't take her up on it.

"I know."

But she'd always been out of her depth with Jamie; that was one of the realities she had tried not to think about. Perhaps that was what he meant by "different worlds" . . .

They sat at a table in the courtyard in the morning sun —across the pool from the policeman guarding the door to Dwight Percy's room. Jack had finished his juice, which Rosalia, the shy, round-faced Mexican maid, had brought him, and now Jamie solicitously poured his coffee. He felt ghastly. He hurt inside and out, and the pain of the bullet wound still throbbed like a second heartbeat.

"Dwight's under arrest, I gather."

"Yes. For killing Art Wheelock. At least I was able, last night, to prevent their carting him off to jail. Because of his condition."

"How is he?"

"No change." Jamie looked older today, with lines etched into his face that yesterday hadn't been there. "The doctor said he had a massive stroke. Whole right side's paralyzed, and his speech affected. He's had arteriosclerosis, you know; which can as readily cause a stroke as a heart attack."

"I'm sure. What have they done with the rest of your crew?"

"They're being held in the town—Dan, Lucille and Eli, anyway; till someone, here or in the States, decides what to do about them. Not Reg, though. In the middle of all the excitement he took off in my plane. No telling where he is by now."

Already the violent scenes of the afternoon before seemed to Jack like something he'd watched at a movie; they couldn't have happened in this tranquil, cloistered place. . . .

"The ones at Hardy will have gotten away too, I suppose," he said, trying not to wonder where Linna was this morning, or think of the tender tableau she'd made with Everest at the door of his room last night, during one of his conscious periods. "No question of Erin sticking around to see that they were nailed—he had to get back here."

"He says the F.B.I. were making inquiries, the last he knew. Perhaps they were able to pick them up. There would only have been about four of them at Hardy that were in on the plot—Tim Donan and his wife, and a couple of strong-arm troubleshooters who work for Art. How much even those two knew about things, I wouldn't be sure. You see, it's been so damned easy for this bunch! Except for Dan, they've used my own security people; under Reg, they've gone on doing exactly what they've done for years—keeping everyone out and guarding my property—with no idea, probably, that I'd had a mutiny within the walls."

Rosalia returned with the rest of Jack's breakfast—barely in time, he suspected, to forestall his keeling over. He felt so lightheaded.

"Oddly," said Jamie as Jack inspected the *tostadas* in a little basket, and the thick steak, under a cover, that would help replace the red corpuscles that had drained out of him yesterday, "I don't much care whether Reg is caught. He did what he could, all along, to make my captivity bearable. I still believe he'd never have harmed me physically, and I think he loathed Art Wheelock nearly as much as I came to."

"I guess we'll never know what that 'proof' was he had—"

"No, I have it."

"You have it?"

"You've a right to see it, I think. It concerns you." He took from his shirt pocket—reluctantly, Jack thought—a folded envelope. Extracted what it contained, and spread it on the tablecloth.

It was not exactly a letter; it was a message. No return address, only the date, April twenty-fifth. It was not addressed to anyone, nor signed, and it was printed in large, careful block letters.

HE KNOWS THE WHOLE THING, EXCEPT FOR THE SUBSTITUTION—WHICH HE SUSPECTS. HE HAS YOU TIED IN WITH IT AS WELL. NO PROOF, BUT HE'S BOUND TO GO ON DIGGING.

SEE THAT THIS TIME HE DOESN'T COME BACK.

PERHAPS HE DOES NOT DRIVE WELL?

Or fall over a cliff well, either, thought Jack.

Jamie laid the envelope, then, on top of the message. It was addressed in the same block letters to Arthur Wheelock at his office, and labeled PERSONAL.

And it was postmarked New Canaan, Conn., April 25, 4:15 P.M.

"You recognize the printing, I suppose?" Jack asked.

"It's like enough," he said sadly. "He's tried, there, to disguise it, but it has the same look as the comments he puts in my margins."

"April twenty-fifth. Wednesday of last week. That was the day I had lunch with Percy at his house and told him everything I knew."

Jamie shook his head. "I keep asking myself, why? Not just the money. I wonder if it wasn't, finally, a sense of outrage he had at the inequities of life. We both worked on my books, but what he's made out of them was a pittance compared to my income. He's only on salary, you see, and it's no astronomical sum. He's joked for years about my 'Midas touch'—maybe he mentioned it so often out of bitterness."

Jamie stared out the open end of the courtyard at the ocean, shimmering blue in the sun. Jack thought he didn't even see it.

"There must have been some terrible lack in his life that would explain how he could come to do such a thing . . ."

"You sound as if you hardly even blame him."

Jamie shrugged. "What good does blame do? Neatly placing the blame somewhere never remedied anything."

True, but how many people ever realized that . . . ?

218

Jack wondered where Linna was. "What will you do now?" he asked.

Everest sighed. "I don't know. I'm afraid freedom has come a little late. It's been all those years, you see. I made my own prison, when I shut myself away after my wife's death. In twenty-four years James White, that bruised young man with so many emotions, has atrophied. Only the Everest legend is left."

The grey eyes, with a look of emptiness in them, gazed steadily at Jack. "You have liberated a straw man, my friend."

He grinned. "You exaggerate—"

"No. Do you suppose Dwight could have turned on me, committed me, actually, to slavery, if he felt that I had any more humanity than some damned robot, or computer, which could produce books?

"And Linna . . ." He frowned. "Be sure to take Linna with you when you go—she's yours." There was a glint of animosity in his eyes, the stiffness of wounded pride in the set of his face.

"I'll ask her."

Feeling a thousand years old and dizzy besides, Jack made his way down the steps of the front garden, adamantly refusing help from Erin.

"Forgot to tell you—Martin and the group sent get-well wishes."

"That's nice." He was leaving as he had come, in bare feet, but wearing a shirt of Jamie's, since his was a ruin. Taking with him Vern's camera with the zoom lens.

"Here." Jamie had pressed it on him. "This is your friend's. The police didn't impound it, so you might as well take it along."

"I guess I might as well. In case he turns up." Vern had no family, since Gladys's death—no chick or child of any kind. Jack supposed he was as logical a person as any to be his heir.

He thought of Vern's bones picked clean by the buzzards, somewhere out on the desert or in a cleft of the mountains. And shuddered.

"You're sure Linna left . . ." he said to Erin as he wove his way carefully toward the open doorway in the thick wall with its trimming of broken glass at the top.

"Well, she certainly commandeered my taxi when I got here from the hotel. Emilio had to go up for her luggage, but—"

With a lift of the heart he saw, as they passed through the doorway, that she had not as yet gone. She stood with Helene by the taxi while a small boy, the one they'd seen watering the palms the first day they'd come, loaded her two cases into the car.

He eased his aching carcass across the hand-laid stone paving and put his arm around her.

"Nice of you to wait for me." He was glad to be able to lean on her a little. Close up in the clear sunlight, she looked more delicate than he'd supposed. Surprising. He'd thought of her as lithe, strong, stubborn—never delicate.

"How do you feel?"

"Like an old flat tire," he told her, "with a patch on it." He crawled into the back seat and closed his eyes until she finished talking to Helene and got in.

"I'll be over to check on you at the hotel," Erin told him.

"Yes—thanks." He raised leaden eyelids in time to nod good-by to Helene and Erin and the small boy.

"You were really going to leave without me," he said accusingly as they jolted away.

"As if you'd never done that to *me!* I was sure, anyway, if you wanted to you'd catch up."

"In my condition?"

"Physical condition doesn't seem to be much of a deterrent, I've noticed, when you've decided to do something."

They had almost reached the highway when their driver had to slow for a car coming toward them. Jack recognized it as Miguel's.

As they came abreast, on the dirt drive, Miguel drew up and hailed him out the window. "Señor Seavering!"

"Miguel! *Buenos días!*"

"Mission accomplished, Señor Seavering—"

"Yes indeed. We whomped 'em."

Miguel's passenger, some moth-eaten old Mexican in a wide-brimmed hat and faded serape, was getting out of the Chevy on the far side. He shambled around the front of the car toward them just as Jack's eyes started to close again—looked as though the poor old fellow was spastic or—

His eyes flew open and he stared straight up into the gargoyle features of Vernon Fix, who was leaning in the window.

"You look terrible," Vern said. "I never *saw* anybody look so terrible!" He opened the door. "Come on. Miguel will take us all to the hotel. Fella', you should be in bed!"

"This is Linna Emries," he remembered to say.

The two of them bundled him into Miguel's car, and they turned around and followed the taxi back toward the hotel.

"You went underground?" Jack asked. "Is that why we couldn't find you?"

"Hardly. Wish I had. I wore my clothes to tatters before I finally stumbled into civilization. Civilization? A village in the mountains. Been there a week waiting for transportation: Uncle José with his string of burros . . ."

"Yes indeed, Miguel," Jack said, holding onto Linna's hand. "Mission accomplished!"

"I heard from the police that you'd been shot to death yesterday," Vern suggested.

Jack shook his head. "Nine lives."

# Epilogue

THE STRAW MAN—AS HE NOW THOUGHT OF HIM-self—went up the tower stairs again and into his writing room.

He'd be leaving soon, to accompany Dwight on the flight to the hospital at La Paz; the authorities had finally given consent for him to be moved to a place where he could get proper treatment.

Under guard, of course. Erin would fly them up.

Like a patient after surgery, Jamie felt terrible, but knew he would get better.

It had been when Jack was shot that he'd known he couldn't keep her; the way things were had been all too evident . . . He hadn't even found it hard to tell her. It was now, when it was over, that it was hard. But eventually he would get better.

He'd talked to Dwight just now. Though God knew Dwight couldn't answer him. He'd stood there looking down at the grotesquely twisted lips, the staring eyes, and had said, "I'll be going with you, Dwight. I'll stay with you till you're better." Did that sound like a promise, he wondered—or a threat? What would it be like to lie help-lessly day after day with the person you'd maliciously in-jured always at your side?

He wondered which had predominated, in his own mind, when he'd made the decision to stick with his editor— Christian duty, or a subtle form of revenge? And left Dwight to wonder, possibly, the same thing.

Who of us truly understands his own motives?

Dwight's, for instance—

Pure and simple envy. Overwhelming greed. Hatred.

223

Surely he must have grown to hate Jamie, to be able to do this thing to him?

He would never know.

He began to cheer up, as he leaned on the sill and looked out from the tower window. A whale spouting, to the southwest. A good omen?

He would do something new, after Dwight was better —as much better as he was likely to get. Go teach writing at a university? Maybe. Something that would involve him again with people.

Words began, somewhere in his head, like a message coming in on teletype. Something for the book he'd been working on. It was something he'd learned only today, and it would go on the last page—which he would not reach for a long time. He was still in the first third of the book.

He turned to his work table and picked up a pen and began, with the old, familiar excitement, to write—before the wording should escape him.